D0978575

The Elusive Pimpernel

Baroness Orczy

Dover Publications, Inc.
Mineola, New York

Bibliographical Note

This Dover edition, first published in 2007, is an unabridged republication of a standard edition of the work originally published by Dodd, Mead and Company, New York, in 1908.

Library of Congress Cataloging-in-Publication Data

Orczy, Emmuska Orczy, Baroness, 1865–1947.
    The elusive pimpernel / Baroness Orczy.
        p. cm.
    Originally published: New York : Dodd, Mead and Co., 1908.
    ISBN 0-486-45464-9 (pbk.)
    1. Blakeney, Percy, Sir (Fictitious character)—Fiction. 2. Nobility—Great Britain—Fiction. 3. France—History—Revolution, 1789–1799—Fiction. I. Historical fiction. II. Adventure stories.

PR6029.R25 E4 2007
823/.912 22

2006052786

Manufactured in the United States of America
Dover Publications, Inc., 31 East 2nd Street, Mineola, N.Y. 11501

CONTENTS

The Elusive Pimpernel

CHAPTER I

There was not even a reaction.

On! ever on! in that wild, surging torrent; sowing the wind of anarchy, of terrorism, of lust of blood and hate, and reaping a hurricane of destruction and of horror.

On! ever on! France, with Paris and all her children still rushes blindly, madly on; defies the powerful coalition,—Austria, England, Spain, Prussia, all joined together to stem the flow of carnage,—defies the Universe and defies God!

Paris this September, 1793!—or shall we call it Vendemiaire, Year I. of the Republic?—call it what we will! Paris! a city of bloodshed, of humanity in its lowest, most degraded aspect. France herself a gigantic self-devouring monster, her fairest cities destroyed, Lyons razed to the ground, Toulon, Marseilles, masses of blackened ruins, her bravest sons turned to lustful brutes or to abject cowards seeking safety at the cost of any humiliation.

That is thy reward, oh mighty, holy Revolution! apotheosis of equality and fraternity! grand rival of decadent Christianity.

Five weeks now since Marat, the bloodthirsty Friend of the People, succumbed beneath the sheath-knife of a virgin patriot, a month since his murderess walked proudly, even enthusiastically, to the guillotine! There has been no reaction—only a great sigh! . . . Not of content or satisfied lust, but a sigh such as the man-eating tiger might heave after his first taste of long-coveted blood.

A sigh for more!

1

A king on the scaffold; a queen degraded and abased, await-
ing death, which lingers on the threshold of her infamous
prison; eight hundred scions of ancient houses that have made
the history of France; brave generals, Custine, Blanchelande,
Houchard, Beauharnais; worthy patriots, noble-hearted women,
misguided enthusiasts, all by the score and by the hundred, up
the few wooden steps which lead to the guillotine.

An achievement of a truth!

And still that sigh for more!

But for the moment,—a few seconds only,—Paris looked
round her mighty self, and thought things over!

The man-eating tiger for the space of a sigh licked his powerful jaws and pondered!

Something new!—something wonderful!

We have had a new Constitution, a new Justice, new Laws, a
new Almanack!

What next?

Why, obviously!—How comes it that great, intellectual, aes-
thetic Paris never thought of such a wonderful thing before?

A new religion!

Christianity is old and obsolete, priests are aristocrats,
wealthy oppressors of the People, the Church but another form
of wanton tyranny.

Let us by all means have a new religion.

Already something has been done to destroy the old! To destroy! always to destroy! Churches have been ransacked, altars
spoliated, tombs desecrated, priests and curates murdered; but
that is not enough.

There must be a new religion; and to attain that there must
be a new God.

"Man is a born idol-worshipper."

Very well then! let the People have a new religion and a new
God.

Stay!—Not a God this time!—for God means Majesty, Power,
Kingship! everything in fact which the mighty hand of the people of France has struggled and fought to destroy.

Not a God, but a goddess.

A goddess! an idol! a toy! since even the man-eating tiger must play sometimes.

Paris wanted a new religion, and a new toy, and grave men, ardent patriots, mad enthusiasts, sat in the Assembly of the Convention and seriously discussed the means of providing her with both these things which she asked for.

Chaumette, I think it was, who first solved the difficulty:— Procureur Chaumette, head of the Paris Municipality, he who had ordered that the cart which bore the dethroned queen to the squalid prison of the Conciergerie should be led slowly past her own late palace of the Tuileries, and should be stopped there just long enough for her to see and to feel in one grand mental vision all that she had been when she dwelt there, and all that she now was by the will of the People.

Chaumette, as you see, was refined, artistic;—the torture of the fallen Queen's heart meant more to him than a blow of the guillotine on her neck.

No wonder, therefore, that it was Procureur Chaumette who first discovered exactly what type of new religion Paris wanted just now.

"Let us have a Goddess of Reason," he said, "typified if you will by the most beautiful woman in Paris. Let us have a feast of the Goddess of Reason, let there be a pyre of all the gew-gaws which for centuries have been flaunted by overbearing priests before the eyes of starving multitudes, let the People rejoice and dance around that funeral pile, and above it all let the new Goddess tower smiling and triumphant. The Goddess of Reason! the only deity our new and regenerate France shall acknowledge throughout the centuries which are to come!"

Loud applause greeted the impassioned speech.

"A new goddess, by all means!" shouted the grave gentlemen of the National Assembly, "the Goddess of Reason!"

They were all eager that the People should have this toy; something to play with and to tease, round which to dance the mad Carmagnole and sing the ever-recurring "Ça ira."

Something to distract the minds of the populace from the

consequences of its own deeds, and the helplessness of its legis-
lators.

Procureur Chaumette enlarged upon his original idea; like a
true artist who sees the broad effect of a picture at a glance and
then fills in the minute details, he was already busy elaborating
his scheme.

"The goddess must be beautiful . . . not too young . . . Reason
can only go hand in hand with the riper age of second youth . . .
she must be decked out in classical draperies, severe yet sug-
gestive . . . she must be rouged and painted . . . for she is a mere
idol . . . easily to be appeased with incense, music and laughter."

He was getting deeply interested in his subject, seeking minu-
tiæ of detail, with which to render his theme more and more
attractive.

But patience was never the characteristic of the
Revolutionary Government of France. The National Assembly
soon tired of Chaumette's dithyrambic utterances. Up aloft on
the Mountain, Danton was yawning like a gigantic leopard.

Soon Henriot was on his feet. He had a far finer scheme than
that of the Procureur to place before his colleagues. A grand
National fête, semi-religious in character, but of the new religion which destroyed and desecrated and never knelt in worship.

Citizen Chaumette's Goddess of Reason by all means—
Henriot conceded that the idea was a good one—but the goddess merely as a figure-head: around her a procession of un-
frocked and apostate priests, typifying the destruction of ancient
hierarchy, mules carrying loads of sacred vessels, the spoils of
ten thousand churches of France, and ballet girls in bacchana-
lian robes, dancing the Carmagnole around the new deity.

Public Prosecutor Foucquier Tinville thought all these
schemes very tame. Why should the People of France be led to
think that the era of a new religion would mean an era of milk
and water, of pageants and of fireworks? Let every man, woman,
and child know that this was an era of blood, of blood and again
of blood.

"Oh!" he exclaimed in passionate accents, "would that all the traitors in France had but one head, that it might be cut off with one blow of the guillotine!"

He approved of the National fête, but he desired an apotheosis of the guillotine; he undertook to find ten thousand traitors to be beheaded on one grand and glorious day: ten thousand heads to adorn the Place de la Révolution on a great, never-to-be-forgotten evening, after the guillotine had accomplished this record work.

But Collot d'Herbois would also have his say. Collot lately hailed from the South, with a reputation for ferocity unparalleled throughout the whole of this horrible decade. He would not be outdone by Tinville's bloodthirsty schemes.

He was the inventor of the "Noyades," which had been so successful at Lyons and Marseilles. "Why not give the inhabitants of Paris one of these exhilarating spectacles?" he asked with a coarse, brutal laugh.

Then he explained his invention, of which he was inordinately proud. Some two or three hundred traitors, men, women, and children, tied securely together with ropes in great, human bundles and thrown upon a barge in the middle of the river: the barge with a hole in her bottom! not too large! only sufficient to cause her to sink slowly, very slowly, in sight of the crowd of delighted spectators.

The cries of the women and children, and even of the men, as they felt the waters rising and gradually enveloping them, as they felt themselves powerless even for a fruitless struggle, had proved most exhilarating, so Citizen Collot declared, to the hearts of the true patriots of Lyons.

Thus the discussion continued.

This was the era when every man had but one desire, that of outdoing others in ferocity and brutality, and but one care, that of saving his own head by threatening that of his neighbour.

The great duel between the Titanic leaders of these turbulent parties, the conflict between hot-headed Danton on the one side and cold-blooded Robespierre on the other, had only just begun; the great, all-devouring monsters had dug their claws into one another, but the issue of the combat was still at stake.

Neither of these two giants had taken part in these deliberations anent the new religion and the new goddess. Danton gave signs now and then of the greatest impatience, and muttered something about a new form of tyranny, a new kind of oppression.

On the left, Robespierre in immaculate sea-green coat and carefully gauffered linen was quietly polishing the nails of his right hand against the palm of his left.

But nothing escaped him of what was going on. His ferocious egoism, his unbounded ambition was even now calculating what advantages to himself might accrue from this idea of the new religion and of the National fête, what personal aggrandisement he could derive therefrom.

The matter outwardly seemed trivial enough, but already his keen and calculating mind had seen various side issues which might tend to place him—Robespierre—on a yet higher and more unassailable pinnacle.

Surrounded by those who hated him, those who envied and those who feared him, he ruled over them all by the strength of his own cold-blooded savagery, by the resistless power of his merciless cruelty.

He cared about nobody but himself, about nothing but his own exaltation: every action of his career, since he gave up his small practice in a quiet provincial town in order to throw himself into the wild vortex of revolutionary politics, every word he ever uttered had but one aim—Himself.

He saw his colleagues and comrades of the old Jacobin Clubs ruthlessly destroyed around him: friends he had none, and all left him indifferent; and now he had hundreds of enemies in every assembly and club in Paris, and these too one by one were being swept up in that wild whirlpool which they themselves had created.

Impassive, serene, always ready with a calm answer, when passion raged most hotly around him, Robespierre, the most ambitious, most self-seeking demagogue of his time, had acquired the reputation of being incorruptible and self-less, an enthusiastic servant of the Republic.

The sea-green Incorruptible!

And thus whilst others talked and argued, waxed hot over schemes for processions and pageantry, or loudly denounced the whole matter as the work of a traitor, he, of the sea-green coat, sat quietly polishing his nails.

But he had already weighed all these discussions in the balance of his mind, placed them in the crucible of his ambition, and turned them into something that would benefit him and strengthen his position.

Aye! the feast should be brilliant enough! gay or horrible, mad or fearful, but through it all the People of France must be made to feel that there was a guiding hand which ruled the destinies of all, a head which framed the new laws, which consolidated the new religion and established its new goddess: the Goddess of Reason.

Robespierre, her prophet!

CHAPTER II

A Retrospect

The room was close and dark, filled with the smoke from a defective chimney.

A tiny boudoir, once the dainty sanctum of imperious Marie Antoinette; a faint and ghostly odour, like unto the perfume of spectres seemed still to cling to the stained walls and to the torn Gobelin tapestries.

Everywhere lay the impress of a heavy and destroying hand: that of the great and glorious Revolution.

In the mud-soiled corners of the room a few chairs, with brocaded cushions rudely torn, leant broken and desolate against the walls. A small footstool, once gilt-legged and satin-covered, had been overturned and roughly kicked to one side, and there it lay on its back, like some little animal that had been hurt, stretching its broken limbs upwards, pathetic to behold.

From the delicately wrought Buhl table the silver inlay had been harshly stripped out of its bed of shell.

Across the Lunette painted by Boucher and representing a chaste Diana surrounded by a bevy of nymphs, an uncouth hand had scribbled in charcoal the device of the Revolution: *Liberté, Egalité, Fraternité ou la Mort,* whilst—as if to give a crowning point to the work of destruction and to emphasize its motto, someone had decorated the portrait of Marie Antoinette with a scarlet cap, and drawn a red and ominous line across her neck.

And at the table two men were sitting in close and eager conclave.

Between them a solitary tallow candle, unsnuffed and weirdly flickering, threw fantastic shadows upon the walls, and illumined with fitful and uncertain light the faces of the two men.

How different were these in character!

One, high cheek-boned, with coarse, sensuous lips, and hair elaborately and carefully powdered; the other pale and thin-lipped, with the keen eyes of a ferret and a high intellectual forehead, from which the sleek brown hair was smoothly brushed away.

The first of these men was Robespierre, the ruthless and incorruptible demagogue; the other was Citizen Chauvelin, ex-ambassador of the Revolutionary Government at the English Court.

The hour was late, and the noises from the great, seething city preparing for sleep came to this remote little apartment in the now deserted Palace of the Tuileries, merely as a faint and distant echo.

It was two days after the Fructidor Riots. Paul Déroulède and the woman Juliette Marny, both condemned to death, had been literally spirited away out of the cart which was conveying them from the Hall of Justice to the Luxembourg Prison, and news had just been received by the Committee of Public Safety that at Lyons, the Abbé du Mesnil, with the ci-devant Chevalier d'Egremont and the latter's wife and family, had effected a miraculous and wholly incomprehensible escape from the Northern Prison.

But this was not all. When Arras fell into the hands of the Revolutionary army, and a regular cordon was formed round the town, so that not a single royalist traitor might escape, some three score women and children, twelve priests, the old aristocrats Chermeuil, Delleville and Galipaux and many others, managed to pass the barriers and were never recaptured.

Raids were made on the suspected houses: in Paris chiefly where the escaped prisoners might have found refuge, or better still where their helpers and rescuers might still be lurking. Foucquier Tinville, Public Prosecutor, led and conducted these raids, assisted by that bloodthirsty vampire, Merlin. They heard

of a house in the Rue de l'Ancienne Comédie where an Englishman was said to have lodged for two days.

They demanded admittance, and were taken to the rooms
where the Englishman had stayed. These were bare and squalid,
like hundreds of other rooms in the poorer quarters of Paris.
The landlady, toothless and grimy, had not yet tidied up the one
where the Englishman had slept: in fact she did not know he
had left for good.

He had paid for his room, a week in advance, and came and
went as he liked, she explained to Citizen Tinville. She never
bothered about him, as he never took a meal in the house, and
he was only there two days. She did not know her lodger was
English until the day he left. She thought he was a Frenchman
from the South, as he certainly had a peculiar accent when he
spoke.

"It was the day of the riots," she continued; "he would go out,
and I told him I did not think that the streets would be safe for
a foreigner like him: for he always wore such very fine clothes,
and I made sure that the starving men and women of Paris
would strip them off his back when their tempers were roused.
But he only laughed. He gave me a bit of paper and told me that
if he did not return I might conclude that he had been killed,
and if the Committee of Public Safety asked me questions about
him, I was just to show the bit of paper and there would be no
further trouble."

She had talked volubly, more than a little terrified at Merlin's
scowls, and the attitude of Citizen Tinville, who was known to
be very severe if anyone committed any blunders.

But the Citizeness—her name was Brogard and her husband's brother kept an inn in the neighbourhood of Calais—
the Citizeness Brogard had a clear conscience. She held a li-
cense from the Committee of Public Safety for letting apartments, and she had always given due notice to the Committee
of the arrival and departure of her lodgers. The only thing was
that if any lodger paid her more than ordinarily well for the
accommodation and he so desired it, she would send in the
notice conveniently late, and conveniently vaguely worded as

to the description, status and nationality of her more liberal patrons.

This had occurred in the case of her recent English visitor.

But she did not explain it quite like that to Citizen Foucquier Tinville or to Citizen Merlin.

However, she was rather frightened, and produced the scrap of paper which the Englishman had left with her, together with the assurance that when she showed it there would be no further trouble.

Tinville took it roughly out of her hand, but would not glance at it. He crushed it into a ball and then Merlin snatched it from him with a coarse laugh, smoothed out the creases on his knee and studied it for a moment.

There were two lines of what looked like poetry, written in a language which Merlin did not understand. English, no doubt.

But what was perfectly clear, and easily comprehended by any one, was the little drawing in the corner, done in red ink and representing a small star-shaped flower.

Then Tinville and Merlin both cursed loudly and volubly, and bidding their men follow them, turned away from the house in the Rue de l'Ancienne Comédie and left its toothless landlady on her own doorstep still volubly protesting her patriotism and her desire to serve the government of the Republic.

Tinville and Merlin, however, took the scrap of paper to Citizen Robespierre, who smiled grimly as he in his turn crushed the offensive little document in the palm of his well-washed hands.

Robespierre did not swear. He never wasted either words or oaths, but he slipped the bit of paper inside the double lid of his silver snuff box and then he sent a special messenger to Citizen Chauvelin in the Rue Corneille, bidding him come that same evening after ten o'clock to room No. 16 in the ci-devant Palace of the Tuileries.

It was now half-past ten, and Chauvelin and Robespierre sat opposite one another in the ex-boudoir of Queen Marie Antoinette, and between them on the table, just below the tallow-candle, was a much creased, exceedingly grimy bit of paper.

It had passed through several unclean hands before Citizen Robespierre's immaculately white fingers had smoothed it out and placed it before the eyes of ex-Ambassador Chauvelin.

The latter, however, was not looking at the paper, he was not even looking at the pale, cruel face before him. He had closed his eyes and for a moment had lost sight of the small dark room, of Robespierre's ruthless gaze, of the mud-stained walls and greasy floor. He was seeing, as in a bright and sudden vision, the brilliantly-lighted salons of the Foreign Office in London, with beautiful Marguerite Blakeney gliding queenlike on the arm of the Prince of Wales.

He heard the flutter of many fans, the frou-frou of silk dresses, and above all the din and sound of dance music, he heard an inane laugh and an affected voice repeating the dog-gerel rhyme that was even now written on that dirty piece of paper which Robespierre had placed before him:

> "We seek him here, and we seek him there,
> Those Frenchies seek him everywhere!
> Is he in heaven, is he in hell,
> That demmed elusive Pimpernel?"

It was a mere flash! One of memory's swiftly effaced pictures, when she shows us for the fraction of a second, indelible pictures from out our past. Chauvelin, in that same second, while his own eyes were closed and Robespierre's fixed upon him, also saw the lonely cliffs of Calais, heard the same voice singing: "God save the King!" the volley of musketry, the despairing cries of Marguerite Blakeney; and once again he felt the keen and bitter pang of complete humiliation and defeat.

CHAPTER III

Ex-Ambassador Chauvelin

Robespierre had quietly waited the while. He was in no hurry: being a night-bird of very pronounced tastes, he was quite ready to sit here until the small hours of the morning watching Citizen Chauvelin mentally writhing in the throes of recollections of the past few months.

There was nothing that delighted the sea-green Incorruptible quite so much as the aspect of a man struggling with a hopeless situation, and feeling a net of intrigue drawing gradually tighter and tighter around him.

Even now, when he saw Chauvelin's smooth forehead wrinkled into an anxious frown, and his thin hand nervously clutched upon the table, Robespierre heaved a pleasurable sigh, leaned back in his chair, and said with an amiable smile:

"You do agree with me, then, Citizen, that the situation has become intolerable?"

Then as Chauvelin did not reply, he continued, speaking more sharply:

"And how terribly galling it all is, when we could have had that man under the guillotine by now, if you had not blundered so terribly last year."

His voice had become hard and trenchant like that knife to which he was so ready to make constant allusion. But Chauvelin still remained silent. There was really nothing that he could say.

"Citizen Chauvelin, how you must hate that man!" exclaimed Robespierre at last.

Then only did Chauvelin break the silence which up to now he had appeared to have forced himself to keep.

"I do!" he said with unmistakable fervour.

"Then why do you not make an effort to retrieve the blunders of last year?" queried Robespierre blandly. "The Republic has been unusually patient and long-suffering with you, Citizen Chauvelin. She has taken your many services and well-known patriotism into consideration. But you know," he added significantly, "that she has no use for worthless tools."

Then as Chauvelin seemed to have relapsed into sullen silence, he continued with his original ill-omened blandness:

"Ma foi! Citizen Chauvelin, were I standing in your buckled shoes, I would not lose another hour in trying to avenge mine own humiliation!"

"Have I ever had a chance?" burst out Chauvelin with ill-suppressed vehemence. "What can I do single-handed? Since war has been declared I cannot go to England unless the Government will find some official reason for my doing so. There is much grumbling and wrath over here, and when that damned Scarlet Pimpernel League has been at work, when a score or so of valuable prizes have been snatched from under the very knife of the guillotine, then, there is much gnashing of teeth and useless cursings, but nothing serious or definite is done to smother those accursed English flies which come buzzing about our ears."

"Nay! you forget, Citizen Chauvelin," retorted Robespierre, "that we of the Committee of Public Safety are far more helpless than you. You know the language of these people, we don't. You know their manners and customs, their ways of thought, the methods they are likely to employ: we know none of these things. You have seen and spoken to men in England who are members of that damned League. You have seen the man who is its leader. We have not."

He leant forward on the table and looked more searchingly at the thin, pallid face before him.

"If you named that leader to me now, if you described him,

we could go to work more easily. You could name him, and you would, Citizen Chauvelin."

"I cannot," retorted Chauvelin doggedly.

"Ah! but I think you could. But there! I do not blame your silence. You would wish to reap the reward of your own victory, to be the instrument of your own revenge. Passions! I think it natural! But in the name of your own safety, Citizen, do not be too greedy with your secret. If the man is known to you, find him again, find him, lure him to France! We want him—the people want him! And if the people do not get what they want, they will turn on those who have withheld their prey."

"I understand, Citizen, that your own safety and that of your government is involved in this renewed attempt to capture the Scarlet Pimpernel," retorted Chauvelin drily.

"And your head, Citizen Chauvelin," concluded Robespierre.

"Nay! I know that well enough, and you may believe me, and you will, Citizen, when I say that I care but little about that. The question is, if I am to lure that man to France what will you and your government do to help me?"

"Everything," replied Robespierre, "provided you have a definite plan and a definite purpose.

"I have both. But I must go to England in, at least, a semi-official capacity. I can do nothing if I am to hide in disguise in out-of-the-way corners."

"That is easily done. There has been some talk with the British authorities anent the security and welfare of peaceful French subjects settled in England. After a good deal of correspondence they have suggested our sending a semi-official representative over there to look after the interests of our own people commercially and financially. We can easily send you over in that capacity if it would suit your purpose."

"Admirably. I have only need of a cloak. That one will do as well as another."

"Is that all?"

"Not quite. I have several plans in my head, and I must know that I am fully trusted. Above all, I must have power—decisive, absolute, illimitable power."

There was nothing of the weakling about this small, sable-clad man, who looked the redoubtable Jacobin leader straight in the face and brought a firm fist resolutely down upon the table before him. Robespierre paused a while ere he replied; he was eying the other man keenly, trying to read if behind that earnest, frowning brow there did not lurk some selfish, ulterior motive along with that demand for absolute power.

But Chauvelin did not flinch beneath that gaze which could make every cheek in France blanch with unnamed terror, and after that slight moment of hesitation Robespierre said quietly:

"You shall have the complete power of a military dictator in every town or borough of France which you may visit. The Revolutionary Government shall create you, before you start for England, Supreme Head of all the Sub-Committees of Public Safety. This will mean that in the name of the safety of the Republic every order given by you, of whatsoever nature it might be, must be obeyed implicitly under pain of an arraignment for treason."

Chauvelin sighed a quick, sharp sigh of intense satisfaction, which he did not even attempt to disguise before Robespierre.

"I shall want agents," he said, "or shall we say spies? and, of course, money."

"You shall have both. We keep a very efficient secret service in England and they do a great deal of good over there. There is much dissatisfaction in their Midland counties—you remember the Birmingham riots? They were chiefly the work of our own spies. Then you know Candeille, the actress? She has found her way among some of those circles in London who have what they call liberal tendencies. I believe they are called Whigs. Funny name, isn't it? It means perruque, I think. Candeille has given charity performances in aid of our Paris poor, in one or two of these Whig clubs, and incidentally she has been very useful to us."

"A woman is always useful in such cases. I shall seek out the Citizeness Candeille."

"And if she renders you useful assistance, I think I can offer her what should prove a tempting prize. Women are so vain!" he added, contemplating with rapt attention the enamel-like polish on his finger-nails. "There is a vacancy in the Maison Molière. Or—what might prove more attractive still—in connection with the proposed National fête, and the new religion for the people, we have not yet chosen a Goddess of Reason. That should appeal to any feminine mind. The impersonation of a goddess, with processions, pageants, and the rest. . . . Great importance and prominence given to one personality. . . . What say you, Citizen? If you really have need of a woman for the furtherance of your plans, you have that at your disposal which may enhance her zeal."

"I thank you, Citizen," rejoined Chauvelin calmly. "I always entertained a hope that some day the Revolutionary Government would call again on my services. I admit that I failed last year. The Englishman is resourceful. He has wits and he is very rich. He would not have succeeded, I think, but for his money— and corruption and bribery are rife in Paris and on our coasts. He slipped through my fingers at the very moment when I thought that I held him most securely. I do admit all that, but I am prepared to redeem my failure of last year, and . . . there is nothing more to discuss.—I am ready to start."

He looked round for his cloak and hat, and quietly readjusted the set of his neck-tie. But Robespierre detained him a while longer: that born mountebank, born torturer of the souls of men, had not gloated sufficiently yet on the agony of mind of this fellow-man.

Chauvelin had always been trusted and respected. His services in connection with the foreign affairs of the Revolutionary Government had been invaluable, both before and since the beginning of the European War. At one time he formed part of that merciless decemvirate which—with Robespierre at its head—meant to govern France by laws of bloodshed and of unparalleled ferocity.

But the sea-green Incorruptible had since tired of him, then had endeavoured to push him on one side, for Chauvelin was keen and clever, and, moreover, he possessed all those qualities of selfless patriotism which were so conspicuously lacking in Robespierre.

His failure in bringing that interfering Scarlet Pimpernel to justice and the guillotine had completed Chauvelin's downfall. Though not otherwise molested, he had been left to moulder in obscurity during this past year. He would soon enough have been completely forgotten.

Now he was not only to be given one more chance to regain public favour, but he had demanded powers which in consideration of the aim in view, Robespierre himself could not refuse to grant him. But the Incorruptible, ever envious and jealous, would not allow him to exult too soon.

With characteristic blandness he seemed to be entering into all Chauvelin's schemes, to be helping him in every way he could, for there was something at the back of his mind which he meant to say to the ex-ambassador, before the latter took his leave: something which would show him that he was but on trial once again, and which would demonstrate to him with perfect clearness that over him there hovered the all-powerful hand of a master.

"You have but to name the sum you want, Citizen Chauvelin," said the Incorruptible, with an encouraging smile, "the government will not stint you, and you shall not fail for lack of authority or for lack of funds."

"It is pleasant to hear that the government has such uncounted wealth," remarked Chauvelin with dry sarcasm.

"Oh! the last few weeks have been very profitable," retorted Robespierre; "we have confiscated money and jewels from emigrant royalists to the tune of several million francs. You remember the traitor Juliette Marny, who escape to England lately? Well! her mother's jewels and quite a good deal of gold were discovered by one of our most able spies to be under the care of a certain Abbé Foucquet, a calotin from Boulogne—devoted to the family, so it seems."

"Yes?" queried Chauvelin indifferently.

"Our men seized the jewels and gold, that is all. We don't know yet what we mean to do with the priest. The fisherfolk of Boulogne like him, and we can lay our hands on him at any time, if we want his old head for the guillotine. But the jewels were worth having. There's a historic necklace worth half a million at least."

"Could I have it?" asked Chauvelin.

Robespierre laughed and shrugged his shoulders.

"You said it belonged to the Marny family," continued the ex-ambassador. "Juliette Marny is in England. I might meet her. I cannot tell what may happen: but I feel that the historic necklace might prove useful. Just as you please," he added with renewed indifference. "It was a thought that flashed through my mind when you spoke—nothing more."

"And to show you how thoroughly the government trusts you, Citizen Chauvelin," replied Robespierre with perfect urbanity, "I will myself direct that the Marny necklace be placed unreservedly in your hands; and a sum of fifty thousand francs for your expenses in England. You see," he added blandly, "we give you no excuse for a second failure."

"I need none," retorted Chauvelin drily, as he finally rose from his seat, with a sigh of satisfaction that this interview was ended at last.

But Robespierre too had risen, and pushing his chair aside he took a step or two towards Chauvelin. He was a much taller man than the ex-ambassador. Spare and gaunt, he had a very upright bearing, and in the uncertain light of the candle he seemed to tower strangely and weirdly above the other man: the pale hue of his coat, his light-coloured hair, the whiteness of his linen, all helped to give to his appearance at that moment a curious spectral effect.

Chauvelin somehow felt an unpleasant shiver running down his spine as Robespierre, perfectly urbane and gentle in his manner, placed a long, bony hand upon his shoulder.

"Citizen Chauvelin," said the Incorruptible, with some degree of dignified solemnity, "meseems that we very quickly understood one another this evening. Your own conscience, no doubt, gave you a premonition of what the purport of my summons to you would be. You say that you always hoped the Revolutionary Government would give you one great chance to redeem your failure of last year. I, for one, always intended that you should have that chance, for I saw, perhaps, just a little deeper into your heart than my colleagues. I saw not only enthusiasm for the cause of the People of France, not only abhorrence for the enemy of your country, I saw a purely personal and deadly hate of an individual man—the unknown and mysterious Englishman who proved too clever for you last year. And because I believe that hatred will prove sharper and more far-seeing than selfless patriotism, therefore I urged the Committee of Public Safety to allow you to work out your own revenge, and thereby to serve your country more effectually than any other— perhaps more pure-minded patriot would do. You go to England well-provided with all that is necessary for the success of your plans, for the accomplishment of your own personal vengeance. The Revolutionary Government will help you with money, passports, safe conducts; it places its spies and agents at your disposal. It gives you practically unlimited power, wherever you may go. It will not enquire into your motives, nor yet your means, so long as these lead to success. But private vengeance or patriotism, whatever may actuate you, we here in France demand that you deliver into our hands the man who is known in two countries as the Scarlet Pimpernel! We want him alive if possible, or dead if it must be so, and we want as many of his henchmen as will follow him to the guillotine. Get them to France, and we'll know how to deal with them, and let the whole of Europe be damned."

He paused for a while, his hand still resting on Chauvelin's shoulder, his pale green eyes holding those of the other man as if in a trance. But Chauvelin neither stirred nor spoke. His triumph left him quite calm; his fertile brain was already busy with his plans. There was no room for fear in his heart, and it was without the slightest tremor that he waited for the conclusion of Robespierre's oration.

"Perhaps, Citizen Chauvelin," said the latter at last, "you have already guessed what there is left for me to say. But lest there should remain in your mind one faint glimmer of doubt or of hope, let me tell you this. The Revolutionary Government gives you this chance of redeeming your failure, but this one only; if you fail again, your outraged country will know neither pardon nor mercy. Whether you return to France or remain in England, whether you travel North, South, East or West, cross the Oceans, or traverse the Alps, the hand of an avenging People will be upon you. Your second failure will be punished by death, wherever you may be, either by the guillotine, if you are in France, or if you seek refuge elsewhere, then by the hand of an assassin.

"Look to it, Citizen Chauvelin! for there will be no escape this time, not even if the mightiest tyrant on earth tried to protect you, not even if you succeeded in building up an empire and placing yourself upon a throne."

His thin, strident voice echoed weirdly in the small, close boudoir. Chauvelin made no reply. There was nothing that he could say. All that Robespierre had put so emphatically before him, he had fully realised, even whilst he was forming his most daring plans.

It was an "either—or" this time, uttered to *him* now. He thought again of Marguerite Blakeney, and the terrible alternative he had put before *her* less than a year ago.

Well! he was prepared to take the risk. He would not fail again. He was going to England under more favourable conditions this time. He knew *who* the man was, whom he was bidden to lure to France and to death.

And he returned Robespierre's threatening gaze boldly and unflinchingly; then he prepared to go. He took up his hat and cloak, opened the door and peered for a moment into the dark corridor, wherein, in the far distance, the steps of a solitary sentinel could be faintly heard: he put on his hat, turned to look once more into the room where Robespierre stood quietly watching him, and went his way.

CHAPTER IV

The Richmond Gala

It was perhaps the most brilliant September ever known in England, where the last days of dying summer are nearly always golden and beautiful.

Strange that in this country, where that same season is so peculiarly radiant with a glory all its own, there should be no special expression in the language with which to accurately name it.

So we needs must call it "fin d'été": the ending of the summer; not the absolute end, nor yet the ultimate departure, but the tender lingering of a friend obliged to leave us anon, yet who fain would steal a day here and there, a week or so in which to stay with us: who would make that last pathetic farewell of his endure a little while longer still, and brings forth in gorgeous array for our final gaze all that he has which is most luxuriant, most desirable, most worthy of regret.

And in this year of grace 1793, departing summer had lavished the treasures of her palette upon woodland and river banks; had tinged the once crude green of larch and elm with a tender hue of gold, had brushed the oaks with tones of warm russet, and put patches of sienna and crimson on the beech.

In the gardens the roses were still in bloom, not the delicate blush or lemon ones of June, nor yet the pale Banksias and climbers, but the full-blooded red roses of late summer, and deep-coloured apricot ones, with crinkled outside leaves faintly kissed by the frosty dew. In sheltered spots the purple clematis still lingered, whilst the dahlias, brilliant of hue, seemed overbearing in their gorgeous insolence, flaunting their crudely coloured petals against sober backgrounds of mellow leaves, or the dull, mossy tones of ancient, encircling walls.

The Gala had always been held about the end of September. The weather, on the riverside, was most dependable then, and there was always sufficient sunshine as an excuse for bringing out Madam's last new muslin gown, or her pale-coloured quilted petticoat. Then the ground was dry and hard, good alike for walking and for setting up tents and booths. And of these there was of a truth a most goodly array this year: mountebanks and jugglers from every corner of the world, so it seemed, for there was a man with a face as black as my lord's tricorne, and another with such flat yellow cheeks as made one think of batter pudding, and spring aconite, of eggs and other very yellow things.

There was a tent wherein dogs—all sorts of dogs, big, little, black, white or tan—did things which no Christian with respect for his own backbone would have dared to perform, and another where a weird-faced old man made bean-stalks and walking sticks, coins of the realm and lace kerchiefs vanish into thin air.

And as it was nice and hot one could sit out upon the green and listen to the strains of the band, which discoursed sweet music, and watch the young people tread a measure on the sward.

The quality had not yet arrived: for humbler folk had partaken of very early dinner so as to get plenty of fun, and long hours of delight for the sixpenny toll demanded at the gates.

There was so much to see and so much to do: games of bowls on the green, and a beautiful Aunt Sally, there was a skittle alley, and two merry-go-rounds: there were performing monkeys and dancing bears, a woman so fat that three men with arms outstretched could not get round her, and a man so thin that he could put a lady's bracelet round his neck and her garter around his waist.

There were some funny little dwarfs with pinched faces and a knowing manner, and a giant come all the way from Russia—so 'twas said.

The mechanical toys too were a great attraction. You dropped a penny into a little slit in a box and a doll would begin to dance and play the fiddle: and there was the Magic Mill, where for another modest copper a row of tiny figures, wrinkled and old and dressed in the shabbiest of rags, marched in weary procession up a flight of steps into the Mill, only to emerge again the next moment at a further door of this wonderful building looking young and gay, dressed in gorgeous finery and tripping a dance measure as they descended some steps and were finally lost to view.

But what was most wonderful of all and collected the goodliest crowd of gazers and the largest amount of coins, was a miniature representation of what was going on in France even at this very moment.

And you could not help but be convinced of the truth of it all, so cleverly was it done. There was a background of houses and a very red-looking sky. "Too red!" some people said, but were immediately quashed by the dictum of the wise, that the sky represented a sunset, as anyone who looked could see. Then there were a number of little figures, no taller than your hand, but with little wooden faces and arms and legs, just beautifully made little dolls, and these were dressed in kirtles and breeches—all rags mostly—and little coats and wooden shoes. They were massed together in groups with their arms all turned upwards.

And in the centre of this little stage on an elevated platform there were miniature wooden posts close together, and with a long flat board at right angles at the foot of the posts, and all painted a bright red. At the further end of the board was a miniature basket, and between the two posts, at the top, was a miniature knife which ran up and down in a groove and was drawn by a miniature pulley. Folk who knew said that this was a model of a guillotine.

And lo and behold! when you dropped a penny into a slot just below the wooden stage, the crowd of little figures started waving their arms up and down, and another little doll would ascend the elevated platform and lie down on the red board at the foot of the wooden posts. Then a figure dressed in brilliant scarlet put out an arm presumably to touch the pulley, and the tiny knife would rattle down on to the poor little reclining doll's neck, and its head would roll off into the basket beyond.

Then there was a loud whirr of wheels, a buzz of internal mechanism, and all the little figures would stop dead with arms outstretched, whilst the beheaded doll rolled off the board and was lost to view, no doubt preparatory to going through the same gruesome pantomime again.

It was very thrilling, and very terrible: a certain air of hushed awe reigned in the booth where this mechanical wonder was displayed.

The booth itself stood in a secluded portion of the grounds, far from the toll gates, and the band stand and the noise of the merry-go-round, and there were great texts, written in red letters on a black ground, pinned all along the walls.

"Please spare a copper for the starving poor of Paris."

A lady, dressed in grey quilted petticoat and pretty grey and black striped paniers, could be seen walking in the booth from time to time, then disappearing through a partition beyond. She would emerge again presently carrying an embroidered reticule, and would wander round among the crowd, holding out the bag by its chain, and repeating in tones of somewhat monotonous appeal: "For the starving poor of Paris, if you please!"

She had fine, dark eyes, rather narrow and tending upwards at the outer corners, which gave her face a not altogether pleasant expression. Still, they *were* fine eyes, and when she went round soliciting alms, most of the men put a hand into their breeches pocket and dropped a coin into her embroidered reticule.

She said the word "poor" in rather a funny way, rolling the "r" at the end, and she also said "please" as if it were spelt with a long line of "e's," and so it was concluded that she was French and was begging for her poorer sisters. At stated intervals during the day, the mechanical toy was rolled into a corner, and the lady in grey stood up on a platform and sang queer little songs, the words of which nobody could understand.

"Il était une bèrgere et ron et petit pataplon. . . ."

But it all left an impression of sadness and of suppressed awe upon the minds and susceptibilities of the worthy Richmond yokels come with their wives or sweethearts to enjoy the fun of the fair, and gladly did everyone emerge out of that melancholy booth into the sunshine, the brightness and the noise.

"Lud! but she do give me the creeps," said Mistress Polly, the pretty barmaid from the Bell Inn, down by the river. "And I must say that I don't see why we English folk should send our hard-earned pennies to those murdering ruffians over the water. Bein' starving, so to speak, don't make a murderer a better man if he goes on murdering," she added with undisputable if ungrammatical logic. "Come, let's look at something more cheerful now."

And without waiting for anyone else's assent, she turned towards the more lively portion of the grounds, closely followed by a ruddy-faced, somewhat sheepish-looking youth, who very obviously was her attendant swain.

It was getting on for three o'clock now, and the quality were beginning to arrive. Lord Anthony Dewhurst was already there, chucking every pretty girl under the chin, to the annoyance of her beau. Ladies were arriving all the time, and the humbler feminine hearts were constantly set a-flutter at sight of rich brocaded gowns, and the new Charlottes, all crinkled velvet and soft marabout, which were so becoming to the pretty faces beneath.

There was incessant and loud talking and chattering, with here and there the shriller tones of a French voice being distinctly noticeable in the din. There were a good many French ladies and gentlemen present, easily recognisable, even in the distance, for their clothes were of more sober hue and of lesser richness than those of their English compeers.

But they were great lords and ladies, nevertheless, Dukes and Duchesses and Countesses, come to England for fear of being murdered by those devils in their own country. Richmond was full of them just now, as they were made right welcome both at the Palace and at the magnificent home of Sir Percy and Lady Blakeney.

Ah! here comes Sir Andrew Ffoulkes with his lady! so pretty

and dainty does she look, like a little china doll, in her new-fashioned short-waisted gown: her brown hair in soft waves above her smooth forehead, her great, hazel eyes fixed in unaffected admiration on the gallant husband by her side.

"No wonder she dotes on him!" sighed pretty Mistress Polly after she had bobbed her curtsey to my lady. "The brave deeds he did for love of her! Rescued her from those murderers over in France and brought her to England safe and sound, having fought no end of them single-handed, so I've heard it said. Have not you, Master Thomas Jezzard?"

And she looked defiantly at her meek-looking cavalier.

"Bah!" replied Master Thomas with quite unusual vehemence in response to the disparaging look in her brown eyes, "'Tis not he who did it all, as you well know, Mistress Polly. Sir Andrew Ffoulkes is a gallant gentleman, you may take your Bible oath on that, but he that fights the murdering frogeaters single-handed is he whom they call The Scarlet Pimpernel: the bravest gentleman in all the world."

Then, as at mention of the national hero, he thought that he detected in Mistress Polly's eyes an enthusiasm which he could not very well ascribe to his own individuality, he added with some pique:

"But they do say that this same Scarlet Pimpernel is mightily ill-favoured, and that's why no one ever sees him. They say he is fit to scare the crows away and that no Frenchy can look twice at his face, for it's so ugly, and so they let him get out of the country, rather than look at him again."

"Then they do say a mighty lot of nonsense," retorted Mistress Polly, with a shrug of her pretty shoulders, "and if that be so, then why don't you go over to France and join hands with the Scarlet Pimpernel? I'll warrant no Frenchman'll want to look twice at your face."

A chorus of laughter greeted this sally, for the two young people had in the meanwhile been joined by several of their friends, and now formed part of a merry group near the band, some sitting, others standing, but all bent on seeing as much as there was to see in Richmond Gala this day. There was Johnny Cullen, the grocer's apprentice from Twickenham, and Ursula Quekett, the baker's daughter, and several "young 'uns" from the neighbourhood, as well as some older folk.

And all of them enjoyed a joke when they heard one and thought Mistress Polly's retort mightily smart. But then Mistress Polly was possessed of two hundred pounds, all her own, left to her by her grandmother, and on the strength of this extensive fortune had acquired a reputation for beauty and wit not easily accorded to a wench that had been penniless.

But Mistress Polly was also very kind-hearted. She loved to tease Master Jezzard, who was an indefatigable hanger-on at her pretty skirts, and whose easy conquest had rendered her somewhat contemptuous, but at the look of perplexed annoyance and bewildered distress in the lad's face, her better nature soon got the upper hand. She realized that her remark had been unwarrantably spiteful, and, wishing to make atonement, she said with a touch of coquetry which quickly spread balm over the honest yokel's injured vanity:

"La! Master Jezzard, you do seem to make a body say some queer things. But there! you must own 'tis mighty funny about that Scarlet Pimpernel!" she added, appealing to the company in general, just as if Master Jezzard had been disputing the fact. "Why won't he let anyone see who he is? And those who know him won't tell. Now I have it for a fact from my lady's own maid Lucy, that the young lady as is stopping at Lady Blakeney's house has actually spoken to the man. She came over from France, come a fortnight to-morrow; she and the gentleman they call Mossoo Déroulède. They both saw the Scarlet Pimpernel and spoke to him. *He* brought them over from France. Then why won't they say?"

"Say what?" commented Johnny Cullen, the apprentice.

"Who this mysterious Scarlet Pimpernel is."

"Perhaps he isn't," said old Clutterbuck, who was clerk of the vestry at the church of St. John's the Evangelist.

"Yes!" he added sententiously, for he was fond of his own sayings and usually liked to repeat them before he had quite done with them, "that's it, you may be sure. Perhaps he isn't."

"What do you mean, Master Clutterbuck?" asked Ursula Quekett, for she knew the old man liked to explain his wise saws, and as she wanted to marry his son, she indulged him whenever she could. "What do you mean? He isn't what?"

"He isn't. That's all," explained Clutterbuck with vague solemnity.

Then seeing that he had gained the attention of the little party round him, he condescended to come to more logical phraseology.

"I mean, that perhaps we must not ask, 'who *is* this mysterious Scarlet Pimpernel?' but 'who *was* that poor and unfortunate gentleman?'"

"Then you think . . ." suggested Mistress Polly, who felt unaccountably low-spirited at this oratorical pronouncement.

"I have it for a fact," said Mr. Clutterbuck solemnly, "that he whom they call the Scarlet Pimpernel no longer exists now: that he was collared by the Frenchies, as far back as last fall, and in the language of the poets, has never been heard of no more."

Mr. Clutterbuck was very fond of quoting from the works of certain writers whose names he never mentioned, but who went by the poetical generality of "the poets." Whenever he made use of phrases which he was supposed to derive from these great and unnamed authors, he solemnly and mechanically raised his hat, as a tribute of respect to these giant minds.

"You think that The Scarlet Pimpernel is dead, Mr. Clutterbuck? That those horrible Frenchies murdered him? Surely you don't mean that?" sighed Mistress Polly ruefully.

Mr. Clutterbuck put his hand up to his hat, preparatory no doubt to making another appeal to the mysterious poets, but was interrupted in the very act of uttering great thoughts by a loud and prolonged laugh which came echoing from a distant corner of the grounds.

"Lud! but I'd know that laugh anywhere," said Mistress Quekett, whilst all eyes were turned in the direction whence the merry noise had come.

Half a head taller than any of his friends around him, his lazy blue eyes scanning from beneath their drooping lids the motley

throng around him, stood Sir Percy Blakeney, the centre of a
gaily-dressed little group which seemingly had just crossed the
toll-gate.

"A fine specimen of a man, for sure," remarked Johnnie
Cullen, the apprentice.

"Aye! you may take your Bible oath on that!" sighed Mistress
Polly, who was inclined to be sentimental.

"Speakin' as the poets," pronounced Mr. Clutterbuck sententiously, "inches don't make a man."

"Nor fine clothes neither," added Master Jezzard, who did not
approve of Mistress Polly's sentimental sigh.

"There's my lady!" gasped Miss Barbara suddenly, clutching
Master Clutterbuck's arm vigorously. "Lud! but she is beautiful
to-day!"

Beautiful indeed, and radiant with youth and happiness,
Marguerite Blakeney had just gone through the gates and was
walking along the sward towards the band stand. She was
dressed in clinging robes of shimmery green texture, the new-
fashioned high-waisted effect suiting her graceful figure to per-
fection. The large Charlotte, made of velvet to match the gown,
cast a deep shadow over the upper part of her face, and gave a
peculiar softness to the outline of her forehead and cheeks.

Long lace mittens covered her arms and hands and a scarf of
diaphanous material edged with dull gold hung loosely around
her shoulders.

Yes! she was beautiful! No captious chronicler has ever denied that! and no one who knew her before, and who saw her
again on this late summer's afternoon, could fail to mark the additional charm of her magnetic personality. There was a tenderness in her face as she turned her head to and fro, a joy of living
in her eyes that was quite irresistibly fascinating.

Just now she was talking animatedly with the young girl who
was walking beside her, and laughing merrily the while:

"Nay! we'll find your Paul, never fear! Lud! child, have you
forgotten he is in England now, and that there's no fear of his
being kidnapped here on the green in broad daylight."

The young girl gave a slight shudder and her child-like face became a shade paler than before. Marguerite took her hand and gave it a kindly pressure. Juliette Marny, but lately come to England, saved from under the very knife of the guillotine, by a timely and daring rescue, could scarcely believe as yet that she and the man she loved were really out of danger.

"There is Monsieur Déroulède," said Marguerite after a slight pause, giving the young girl time to recover herself and pointing to a group of men close by. "He is among friends, as you see."

They made such a pretty picture, these two women, as they stood together for a moment on the green with the brilliant September sun throwing golden reflections and luminous shadows on their slender forms. Marguerite, tall and queen-like in her rich gown, and costly jewels, wearing with glorious pride the invisible crown of happy wifehood: Juliette, slim and girlish, dressed all in white, with a soft, straw hat on her fair curls, and bearing on an otherwise young and child-like face, the hard imprint of the terrible sufferings she had undergone, of the deathly moral battle her tender soul had had to fight.

Soon a group of friends joined them. Paul Déroulède among these, also Sir Andrew and Lady Ffoulkes, and strolling slowly towards them, his hands buried in the pockets of his fine cloth breeches, his broad shoulders set to advantage in a coat of immaculate cut, priceless lace ruffles at neck and wrist, came the inimitable Sir Percy.

CHAPTER V

Sir Percy and His Lady

To all appearances he had not changed since those early days of matrimony, when his young wife dazzled London society by her wit and by her beauty, and he was one of the many satellites that helped to bring into bold relief the brilliance of her presence, of her sallies and of her smiles.

His friends alone, mayhap—and of these only an intimate few—had understood that beneath that self-same lazy manner, those shy and awkward ways, that half-inane, half-cynical laugh, there now lurked an undercurrent of tender and passionate happiness.

That Lady Blakeney was in love with her own husband, nobody could fail to see, and in the more frivolous cliques of fashionable London this extraordinary phenomenon had oft been eagerly discussed.

"A monstrous thing, of a truth, for a woman of fashion to adore her own husband!" was the universal pronouncement of the gaily-decked little world that centred around Carlton House and Ranelagh.

Not that Sir Percy Blakeney was unpopular with the fair sex. Far be it from the veracious chronicler's mind even to suggest such a thing. The ladies would have voted any gathering dull if Sir Percy's witty sallies did not ring from end to end of the dancing hall, if his new satin coat and 'broidered waistcoat did not call for comment or admiration.

But that was the frivolous set, to which Lady Blakeney had never belonged.

It was well known that she had always viewed her good-natured husband as the most willing and most natural butt for her caustic wit; she still was fond of aiming a shaft or two at him, and he was still equally ready to let the shaft glance harmlessly against the flawless shield of his own imperturbable good humour, but now, contrary to all precedent, to all usages and customs of London society, Marguerite seldom was seen at routs or at the opera without her husband; she accompanied him to all the races, and even one night—oh horror!—had danced the gavotte with him.

Society shuddered and wondered! tried to put Lady Blakeney's sudden infatuation down to foreign eccentricity, and finally consoled itself with the thought that after all this nonsense could not last, and that she was too clever a woman and he too perfect a gentleman to keep up this abnormal state of things for any length of time.

In the meanwhile, the ladies averred that this matrimonial love was a very one-sided affair. No one could assert that Sir Percy was anything but politely indifferent to his wife's obvious attentions. His lazy eyes never once lighted up when she entered a ball-room, and there were those who knew for a fact that her ladyship spent many lonely days in her beautiful home at Richmond whilst her lord and master absented himself with persistent if unchivalrous regularity.

His presence at the Gala had been a surprise to everyone, for all thought him still away, fishing in Scotland or shooting in Yorkshire, anywhere save close to the apron strings of his doting wife. He himself seemed conscious of the fact that he had not been expected at this end-of-summer fête, for as he strolled forward to meet his wife and Juliette Marny, and acknowledged with a bow here and a nod there the many greetings from subordinates and friends, there was quite an apologetic air about his good-looking face, and an obvious shyness in his smile.

But Marguerite gave a happy little laugh when she saw him coming towards her.

"Oh, Sir Percy!" she said gaily, "and pray have you seen the show? I vow 'tis the maddest, merriest throng I've seen for many a day. Nay! but for the sighs and shudders of my poor little Juliette, I should be enjoying one of the liveliest days of my life."

She patted Juliette's arm affectionately.

"Do not shame me before Sir Percy," murmured the young girl, casting shy glances at the elegant cavalier before her, vainly trying to find in the indolent, foppish personality of this society butterfly, some trace of the daring man of action, the bold adventurer who had snatched her and her lover from out the very tumbril that bore them both to death.

"I know I ought to be gay," she continued with an attempt at a smile, "I ought to forget everything, save what I owe to . . ."

Sir Percy's laugh broke in on her half-finished sentence.

"Lud! and to think of all that I ought not to forget!" he said loudly. "Tony here has been clamouring for iced punch this last half-hour, and I promised to find a booth wherein the noble liquid is properly dispensed. Within half an hour from now His Royal Highness will be here. I assure you, Mlle. Juliette, that from that time onwards I have to endure the qualms of the damned, for the heir to Great Britain's throne always contrives to be thirsty when I am satiated, which is Tantalus' torture magnified a thousandfold, or to be satiated when my parched palate most requires solace; in either case I am a most pitiable man."

"In either case you contrive to talk a deal of nonsense, Sir Percy," said Marguerite gaily.

"What else would your ladyship have me do this lazy, hot afternoon?"

"Come and view the booths with me," she said. "I am dying for a sight of the fat woman and the lean man, the pig-faced child, the dwarfs and the giants. There! Monsieur Déroulède," she added, turning to the young Frenchman who was standing close beside her, "take Mlle. Juliette to hear the clavecin players. I vow she is tired of my company."

The gaily-dressed group was breaking up. Juliette and Paul Déroulède were only too ready to stroll off arm-in-arm together, and Sir Andrew Ffoulkes was ever in attendance on his young wife.

For one moment Marguerite caught her husband's eye. No one was within earshot.

"Percy," she said.

"Yes, m'dear."

"When did you return?"

"Early this morning."

"You crossed over from Calais?"

"From Boulogne."

"Why did you not let me know sooner?"

"I could not, dear. I arrived at my lodgings in town, looking a disgusting object. . . . I could not appear before you until I had washed some of the French mud from off my person. Then His Royal Highness demanded my presence. He wanted news of the Duchesse de Verneuil, whom I had the honour of escorting over from France. By the time I had told him all that he wished to hear, there was no chance of finding you at home, and I thought I should see you here."

Marguerite said nothing for a moment, but her foot impatiently tapped the ground, and her fingers were fidgeting with the gold fringe of her scarf. The look of joy, of exquisite happiness, seemed to have suddenly vanished from her face; there was a deep furrow between her brows.

She sighed a short, sharp sigh, and cast a rapid upward glance at her husband.

He was looking down at her, smiling good-naturedly, a trifle sarcastically perhaps, and the frown on her face deepened.

"Percy," she said abruptly.

"Yes, m'dear."

"These anxieties are terrible to bear. You have been twice over to France within the last month, dealing with your life as lightly as if it did not now belong to me. When will you give up these mad adventures, and leave others to fight their own battles and to save their own lives as best they may?"

She had spoken with increased vehemence, although her voice was scarce raised above a whisper. Even in her sudden, passionate anger she was on her guard not to betray his secret. He did not reply immediately, but seemed to be studying the beautiful face on which heartbroken anxiety was now distinctly imprinted.

Then he turned and looked at the solitary booth in the distance, across the frontal of which a large placard had been recently affixed, bearing the words: "Come and see the true representation of the guillotine!"

In front of the booth a man dressed in ragged breeches, with Phrygian cap on his head, adorned with a tri-colour cockade, was vigorously beating a drum, shouting volubly the while:

"Come in and see, come in and see! the only realistic presentation of the original guillotine. Hundreds perish in Paris every day! Come and see! Come and see! the perfectly vivid performance of what goes on hourly in Paris at the present moment."

Marguerite had followed the direction of Sir Percy's eyes. She too was looking at the booth, she heard the man's monotonous, raucous cries. She gave a slight shudder and once more looked imploringly at her husband. His face—though outwardly as lazy and calm as before—had a strange set look about the mouth and firm jaw, and his slender hand, the hand of a dandy accustomed to handle cards and dice and to play lightly with the foils, was clutched tightly beneath the folds of the priceless Mechlin frills.

It was but a momentary stiffening of the whole powerful frame, an instant's flash of the ruling passion hidden within that very secretive soul. Then he once more turned towards her, the rigid lines of his face relaxed, he broke into a pleasant laugh, and with the most elaborate and most courtly bow he took her hand in his and raising her fingers to his lips, he gave the answer to her question:

"When your ladyship has ceased to be the most admired woman in Europe, namely, when I am in my grave."

CHAPTER VI

FOR THE POOR OF PARIS

There was no time to say more then. For the laughing, chatting groups of friends had once more closed up round Marguerite and her husband, and she, ever on the alert, gave neither look nor sign that any serious conversation had taken place between Sir Percy and herself.

Whatever she might feel or dread with regard to the foolhardy adventures in which he still persistently embarked, no member of the League ever guarded the secret of his chief more loyally than did Marguerite Blakeney.

Though her heart overflowed with a passionate pride in her husband, she was clever enough to conceal every emotion save that which Nature had insisted on imprinting in her face, her present radiant happiness and her irresistible love. And thus before the world she kept up that bantering way with him, which had characterized her earlier matrimonial life, that good-natured, easy contempt which he had so readily accepted in those days, and which their entourage would have missed and would have enquired after, if she had changed her manner towards him too suddenly.

In her heart she knew full well that within Percy Blakeney's soul she had a great and powerful rival: his wild, mad, passionate love of adventure. For it he would sacrifice everything, even his life; she dared not ask herself if he would sacrifice his love.

Twice in a few weeks he had been over to France: every time he went she could not know if she would ever see him again. She could not imagine how the French Committee of Public

Safety could so clumsily allow the hated Scarlet Pimpernel to slip through its fingers. But she never attempted either to warn him or to beg him not to go. When he brought Paul Déroulède and Juliette Marny over from France, her heart went out to the two young people in sheer gladness and pride because of *his* precious life, which *he* had risked for them.

She loved Juliette for the dangers Percy had passed, for the anxieties she herself had endured; only to-day, in the midst of this beautiful sunshine, this joy of the earth, of summer and of the sky, she had suddenly felt a mad, overpowering anxiety, a deadly hatred of the wild adventurous life, which took him so often away from her side. His pleasant, bantering reply pre-cluded her following up the subject, whilst the merry chatter of people round her warned her to keep her words and looks under control.

But she seemed now to feel the want of being alone, and, somehow, that distant booth with its flaring placard, and the crier in the Phrygian cap, exercised a weird fascination over her.

Instinctively she bent her steps thither, and equally instinc-tively the idle throng of her friends followed her. Sir Percy alone had halted in order to converse with Lord Hastings, who had just arrived.

"Surely, Lady Blakeney, you have no thought of patronising that gruesome spectacle?" said Lord Anthony Dewhurst, as Marguerite almost mechanically had paused within a few yards of the solitary booth.

"I don't know," she said, with enforced gaiety, "the place seems to attract me. And I need not look at the spectacle," she added significantly, as she pointed to a roughly-scribbled notice at the entrance of the tent: "In aid of the starving poor of Paris."

"There's a good-looking woman who sings, and a hideous me-chanical toy that moves," said one of the young men in the crowd. "It is very dark and close inside the tent. I was lured in there for my sins, and was in a mighty hurry to come out again."

"Then it must be my sins that are helping to lure me too at the present moment," said Marguerite lightly. "I pray you all to let me go in there. I want to hear the good-looking woman sing, even if I do not see the hideous toy on the move."

"May I escort you then, Lady Blakeney?" said Lord Tony.

"Nay! I would rather go in alone," she replied a trifle impatiently. "I beg of you not to heed my whim, and to await my return, there, where the music is at its merriest."

It had been bad manners to insist. Marguerite, with a little comprehensive nod to all her friends, left the young cavaliers still protesting and quickly passed beneath the roughly constructed doorway that gave access into the booth.

A man, dressed in theatrical rags and wearing the characteristic scarlet cap, stood immediately within the entrance, and ostentatiously rattled a money box at regular intervals.

"For the starving poor of Paris," he drawled out in nasal monotonous tones the moment he caught sight of Marguerite and of her rich gown. She dropped some gold into the box and then passed on.

The interior of the booth was dark and lonely-looking after the glare of the hot September sun and the noisy crowd that thronged the sward outside. Evidently a performance had just taken place on the elevated platform beyond, for a few yokels seemed to be lingering in a desultory manner as if preparatory to going out.

A few disjointed comments reached Marguerite's ears as she approached, and the small groups parted to allow her to pass. One or two women gaped in astonishment at her beautiful dress, whilst others bobbed a respectful curtsey.

The mechanical toy arrested her attention immediately. She did not find it as gruesome as she expected, only singularly grotesque, with all those wooden little figures in their quaint, arrested action.

She drew nearer to have a better look, and the yokels who had lingered behind, paused, wondering if she would make any remark.

"Her ladyship was born in France," murmured one of the men, close to her, "she would know if the thing really looks like that."

"She do seem interested," quoth another in a whisper.

"Lud love us all!" said a buxom wench, who was clinging to the arm of a nervous-looking youth, "I believe they're coming for more money."

On the elevated platform at the further end of the tent, a slim figure had just made its appearance, that of a young woman dressed in peculiarly sombre colours, and with a black lace hood thrown lightly over her head.

Marguerite thought that the face seemed familiar to her, and she also noticed that the woman carried a large embroidered reticule in her bemittened hand.

There was a general exodus the moment she appeared. The Richmond yokels did not like the look of that reticule. They felt that sufficient demand had already been made upon their scant purses, considering the meagreness of the entertainment, and they dreaded being lured to further extravagance.

When Marguerite turned away from the mechanical toy, the last of the little crowd had disappeared, and she was alone in the booth with the woman in the dark kirtle and black lace hood.

"For the poor of Paris, Madame," said the latter mechanically, holding out her reticule.

Marguerite was looking at her intently. The face certainly seemed familiar, recalling to her mind the far-off days in Paris, before she married. Some young actress no doubt driven out of France by that terrible turmoil which had caused so much sorrow and so much suffering. The face was pretty, the figure slim and elegant, and the look of obvious sadness in the dark, almond-shaped eyes was calculated to inspire sympathy and pity.

Yet, strangely enough, Lady Blakeney felt repelled and chilled by this sombrely-dressed young person: an instinct, which she could not have explained and which she felt had no justification, warned her that somehow or other, the sadness was not quite genuine, the appeal for the poor not quite heartfelt.

Nevertheless, she took out her purse, and dropping some few sovereigns into the capacious reticule, she said very kindly:

"I hope that you are satisfied with your day's work, Madame; I fear me our British country folk hold the strings of their purses somewhat tightly these times."

The woman sighed and shrugged her shoulders.

"Oh, Madame!" she said with a tone of great dejection, "one does what one can for one's starving countrymen, but it is very hard to elicit sympathy over here for them, poor dears!"

"You are a Frenchwoman, of course," rejoined Marguerite, who had noted that though the woman spoke English with a very pronounced foreign accent, she had nevertheless expressed herself with wonderful fluency and correctness.

"Just like Lady Blakeney herself," replied the other.

"You know who I am?

"Who could come to Richmond and not know Lady Blakeney by sight."

"But what made you come to Richmond on this philanthropic errand of yours?"

"I go where I think there is a chance of earning a little money for the cause which I have at heart," replied the Frenchwoman with the same gentle simplicity, the same tone of mournful dejection.

What she said was undoubtedly noble and selfless. Lady Blakeney felt in her heart that her keenest sympathy should have gone out to this young woman—pretty, dainty, hardly more than a girl—who seemed to be devoting her young life in a purely philanthropic and unselfish cause. And yet in spite of herself, Marguerite seemed unable to shake off that curious sense of mistrust which had assailed her from the first, nor that feeling of unreality and staginess with which the Frenchwoman's attitude had originally struck her.

Yet she tried to be kind and to be cordial, tried to hide that coldness in her manner which she felt was unjustified.

"It is all very praiseworthy on your part, Madame," she said somewhat lamely. "Madame . . . ?" she added interrogatively.

"My name is Candeille—Désirée Candeille," replied the Frenchwoman.

"Candeille?" exclaimed Marguerite with sudden alacrity, "Candeille . . . surely . . ."

"Yes . . . of the Variétés."

"Ah! then I know why your face from the first seemed familiar to me," said Marguerite, this time with unaffected cordiality. "I must have applauded you many a time in the olden days. I am an ex-colleague, you know. My name was St. Just before I married, and I was of the Maison Molière."

"I knew that," said Désirée Candeille, "and half hoped that you would remember me."

"Nay! who could forget Demoiselle Candeille, the most popular star in the theatrical firmament?"

"Oh! that was so long ago."

"Only four years."

"A fallen star is soon lost out of sight."

"Why fallen?"

"It was a choice for me between exile from France and the guillotine," rejoined Candeille simply.

"Surely not?" queried Marguerite with a touch of genuine sympathy. With characteristic impulsiveness, she had now cast aside her former misgivings: she had conquered her mistrust, at any rate had relegated it to the background of her mind. This woman was a colleague: she had suffered and was in distress; she had every claim, therefore, on a compatriot's help and friendship. She stretched out her hand and took Désirée Candeille's in her own; she forced herself to feel nothing but admiration for this young woman, whose whole attitude spoke of sorrows nobly borne, of misfortunes proudly endured.

"I don't know why I should sadden you with my story," rejoined Désirée Candeille after a slight pause, during which she seemed to be waging war against her own emotion. "It is not a very interesting one. Hundreds have suffered as I did. I had enemies in Paris. God knows how that happened. I had never harmed anyone, but someone must have hated me and must have wished me ill. Evil is so easily wrought in France these days. A denunciation—a perquisition—an accusation—then the flight from Paris . . . the forged passports . . . the disguise . . . the bribe . . . the hardships . . . the squalid hiding places. . . . Oh! I have gone through it all . . . tasted every kind of humiliation . . . endured every kind of insult. . . . Remember! that I was not a noble aristocrat . . . a Duchess or an impoverished Countess . . ."

she added with marked bitterness, "or perhaps the English cavaliers whom the popular voice has called the League of the
Scarlet Pimpernel would have taken some interest in me. I was
only a poor actress and had to find my way out of France alone,
or else perish on the guillotine."

"I am so sorry!" said Marguerite simply.

"Tell me how you got on, once you were in England," she continued after a while, seeing that Désirée Candeille seemed absorbed in thought.

"I had a few engagements at first," replied the Frenchwoman.
"I played at Sadler's Wells and with Mrs. Jordan at Covent
Garden, but the Aliens' Bill put an end to my chances of liveli-
hood. No manger cared to give me a part, and so . . ."

"And so?"

"Oh! I had a few jewels and I sold them. . . . A little money
and I live on that. . . . But when I played at Covent Garden I
contrived to send part of my salary over to some of the poorer
clubs of Paris. My heart aches for those that are starving. . . .
Poor wretches, they are misguided and misled by self-seeking
demagogues. . . . It hurts me to feel that I can do nothing more
to help them . . . and eases my self-respect if, by singing at public fairs, I can still send a few francs to those who are poorer than
myself."

She had spoken with ever-increasing passion and vehemence.
Marguerite, with eyes fixed into vacancy, seeing neither the
speaker nor her surroundings, seeing only visions of those same
poor wreckages of humanity, who had been goaded into thirst
for blood, when their shrunken bodies should have been clamouring for healthy food,—Marguerite thus absorbed, had totally
forgotten her earlier prejudices and now completely failed to
note all that was unreal, stagy, theatrical, in the oratorical decla-
mations of the ex-actress from the Variétés.

Pre-eminently true and loyal herself in spite of the many de-
ceptions and treacheries which she had witnessed in her life, she
never looked for falsehood or for cant in others. Even now she
only saw before her a woman who had been wrongfully persecuted, who had suffered and had forgiven those who had caused

her to suffer. She bitterly accused herself for her original mis-trust of this noble-hearted, unselfish woman, who was content to tramp around in an alien country, bartering her talents for a few coins, in order that some of those, who were the originators of her sorrows, might have bread to eat and a bed in which to sleep.

"Mademoiselle," she said warmly, "truly you shame me, who am also French-born, with the many sacrifices you so nobly make for those who should have first claim on my own sympa-thy. Believe me, if I have not done as much as duty demanded of me in the cause of my starving compatriots, it has not been for lack of good-will. Is there any way now," she added eagerly, "in which I can help you? Putting aside the question of money, wherein I pray you to command my assistance, what can I do to be of useful service to you?"

"You are very kind, Lady Blakeney . . ." said the other hesi-tatingly.

"Well? What is it? I see there is something in your mind. . . ."

"It is perhaps difficult to express . . . but people say I have a good voice . . . I sing some French ditties . . . they are a novelty in England, I think. . . . If I could sing them in fashionable sa-lons . . . I might perhaps . . ."

"Nay! you shall sing in fashionable salons," exclaimed Marguerite eagerly, "you shall become the fashion, and I'll swear the Prince of Wales himself shall bid you sing at Carlton House . . . and you shall name your own fee, Mademoiselle . . . and London society shall vie with the élite of Bath, as to which shall lure you to its most frequented routs. . . . There! there! you shall make a fortune for the Paris poor . . . and to prove to you that I mean every word I say, you shall begin your triumphant career in my own salon to-morrow night. His Royal Highness will be present. You shall sing your most engaging songs . . . and for your fee you must accept a hundred guineas, which you shall send to the poorest workman's club in Paris in the name of Sir Percy and Lady Blakeney."

"I thank your ladyship, but . . ."

"You'll not refuse?"

"I'll accept gladly . . . but . . . you will understand . . . I am not very old," said Candeille quaintly, "I . . . I am only an actress . . . but if a young actress is unprotected . . . then . . ."

"I understand," replied Marguerite gently, "that you are far too pretty to frequent the world all alone, and that you have a mother, a sister or a friend . . . which? . . . whom you would wish to escort you to-morrow. Is that it?"

"Nay," rejoined the actress, with marked bitterness, "I have neither mother, nor sister, but our Revolutionary Government, with tardy compassion for those it has so relentlessly driven out of France, has deputed a representative of theirs in England to look after the interests of French subjects over here!"

"Yes?"

"They have realised over in Paris that my life here has been devoted to the welfare of the poor people of France. The representative whom the government has sent to England is specially interested in me and in my work. He is a stand-by for me in case of trouble . . . in case of insults . . . A woman alone is oft subject to those, even at the hands of so-called gentlemen . . . and the official representative of my own country becomes in such cases my most natural protector."

"I understand."

"You will receive him?"

"Certainly."

"Then may I present him to your ladyship?"

"Whenever you like."

"Now, and it please you."

"Now?"

"Yes. Here he comes, at your ladyship's service."

Désirée Candeille's almond-shaped eyes were fixed upon a distant part of the tent, behind Lady Blakeney in the direction of the main entrance to the booth. There was a slight pause after she had spoken and then Marguerite slowly turned in order to see who this official representative of France was, whom at the young actress' request she had just agreed to receive in her house.

In the doorway of the tent, framed by its gaudy draperies, and with the streaming sunshine as a brilliant background behind him, stood the sable-clad figure of Chauvelin.

CHAPTER VII

Premonition

Marguerite neither moved nor spoke. She felt two pairs of eyes fixed upon her, and with all the strength of will at her command she forced the very blood in her veins not to quit her cheeks, forced her eyelids not to betray by a single quiver the icy pang of a deadly premonition which at sight of Chauvelin seemed to have chilled her entire soul.

There he stood before her, dressed in his usual sombre garments, a look almost of humility in those keen grey eyes of his, which a year ago on the cliffs of Calais had peered down at her with such relentless hate.

Strange that at this moment she should have felt an instinct of fear. What cause had she to throw more than a pitiful glance at the man who had tried so cruelly to wrong her, and who had so signally failed?

Having bowed very low and very respectfully, Chauvelin advanced towards her, with all the airs of a disgraced courtier craving audience from his queen.

As he approached she instinctively drew back.

"Would you prefer not to speak to me, Lady Blakeney?" he said humbly.

She could scarcely believe her ears, or trust her eyes. It seemed impossible that a man could have so changed in a few months. He even looked shorter than last year, more shrunken within himself. His hair, which he wore free from powder, was perceptibly tinged with grey.

"Shall I withdraw?" he added after a pause, seeing that
Marguerite made no movement to return his salutation.

"It would be best, perhaps," she replied coldly. "You and I,
Monsieur Chauvelin, have so little to say to one another."

"Very little indeed," he rejoined quietly; "the triumphant and
happy have ever very little to say to the humiliated and the de-
feated. But I had hoped that Lady Blakeney in the midst of her
victory would have spared one thought of pity and one of pardon."

"I did not know that you had need of either from me,
Monsieur."

"Pity perhaps not, but forgiveness certainly."

"You have that, if you so desire it."

"Since I failed, you might try to forget."

"That is beyond my power. But believe me, I have ceased to
think of the infinite wrong which you tried to do to me."

"But I failed," he insisted, "and I meant no harm to *you*."

"To those I care for, Monsieur Chauvelin."

"I had to serve my country as best I could. I meant no harm
to your brother. He is safe in England now. And the Scarlet
Pimpernel was nothing to you."

She tried to read his face, tried to discover in those in-
scrutable eyes of his, some hidden meaning to his words.
Instinct had warned her of course that this man could be nothing but an enemy, always and at all times. But he seemed so broken, so abject now, that contempt for his dejected attitude, and
for the defeat which had been inflicted on him, chased the last
remnant of fear from her heart.

"I did not even succeed in harming that enigmatical personage," continued Chauvelin with the same self-abasement. "Sir
Percy Blakeney, you remember, threw himself across my plans,
quite innocently of course. I failed where you succeeded. Luck
has deserted me. Our government offered me a humble post,
away from France. I look after the interests of French subjects
settled in England. My days of power are over. My failure is
complete. I do not complain, for I failed in a combat of wits . . .
but I failed . . . I failed . . . I failed . . . I am almost a fugitive and

I am quite disgraced. That is my present history, Lady Blakeney," he concluded, taking once more a step towards her, "and you will understand that it would be a solace if you extended your hand to me just once more, and let me feel that although you would never willingly look upon my face again, you have enough womanly tenderness in you to force your heart to forgiveness and mayhap to pity."

Marguerite hesitated. He held out his hand and her warm, impulsive nature prompted her to be kind. But instinct would not be gainsaid: a curious instinct to which she refused to respond. What had she to fear from this miserable and cringing little worm who had not even in him the pride of defeat? What harm could he do to her, or to those whom she loved? Her brother was in England! Her husband! Bah! not the enmity of the entire world could make her fear for *him!*

Nay! That instinct, which caused her to draw away from Chauvelin, as she would from a venomous asp, was certainly not fear. It was hate! She hated this man! Hated him for all that she had suffered because of him; for that terrible night on the cliffs of Calais! The peril to her husband who had become so infinitely dear! The humiliations and self-reproaches which he had endured.

Yes! it was hate! and hate was of all emotions the one she most despised.

Hate? Does one hate a slimy but harmless toad or a stinging fly? It seemed ridiculous, contemptible and pitiable to think of hate in connection with the melancholy figure of this discomfited intriguer, this fallen leader of revolutionary France.

He was holding out his hand to her. If she placed even the tips of her fingers upon it, she would be making the compact of mercy and forgiveness which he was asking of her. The woman Désirée Candeille roused within her the last lingering vestige of her slumbering wrath. False, theatrical and stagy—as Marguerite had originally suspected—she appeared to have been in league with Chauvelin to bring about this undesirable meeting.

Lady Blakeney turned from one to another, trying to conceal

her contempt beneath a mask of passionless indifference. Candeille was standing close by, looking obviously distressed and not a little puzzled. An instant's reflection was sufficient to convince Marguerite that the whilom actress of the Variétés Theatre was obviously ignorant of the events to which Chauvelin had been alluding: she was, therefore, of no serious consequence, a mere tool, mayhap, in the ex-ambassador's hands. At the present moment she looked like a silly child who does not understand the conversation of the "grown-ups."

Marguerite had promised her help and protection, had invited her to her house, and offered her a munificent gift in aid of a deserving cause. She was too proud to go back now on that promise, to rescind the contract because of an unexplainable fear. With regard to Chauvelin, the matter stood differently: she had made him no direct offer of hospitality: she had agreed to receive in her house the official chaperone of an unprotected girl, but she was not called upon to show cordiality to her own and her husband's most deadly enemy.

She was ready to dismiss him out of her life with a cursory word of pardon and a half-expressed promise of oblivion: on that understanding and that only she was ready to let her hand rest for the space of one second in his.

She had looked upon her fallen enemy, seen his discomfiture and his humiliation! Very well! Now let him pass out of her life, all the more easily, since the last vision of him would be one of such utter abjection as would even be unworthy of hate.

All these thoughts, feelings and struggles passed through her mind with great rapidity. Her hesitation had lasted less than five seconds: Chauvelin still wore the look of doubting entreaty with which he had first begged permission to take her hand in his. With an impulsive toss of the head, she had turned straight towards him, ready with the phrase with which she meant to dismiss him from her sight now and forever, when suddenly a well-known laugh broke in upon her ear, and a lazy, drawly voice said pleasantly:

"La! I vow the air is fit to poison you! Your Royal Highness, I entreat, let us turn our backs upon these gates of Inferno, where lost souls would feel more at home than doth your humble servant."

The next moment His Royal Highness the Prince of Wales had entered the tent, closely followed by Sir Percy Blakeney.

CHAPTER VIII

THE INVITATION

It was in truth a strange situation, this chance meeting between Percy Blakeney and ex-Ambassador Chauvelin.

Marguerite looked up at her husband. She saw him shrug his broad shoulders as he first caught sight of Chauvelin, and glance down in his usual lazy, good-humoured manner at the shrunken figure of the silent Frenchman. The words she meant to say never crossed her lips; she was waiting to hear what the two men would say to one another.

The instinct of the grande dame in her, the fashionable lady accustomed to the exigencies of society, just gave her sufficient presence of mind to make the requisite low curtsey before His Royal Highness. But the Prince, forgetting his accustomed gallantry, was also absorbed in the little scene before him. He, too, was looking from the sable-clad figure of Chauvelin to that of gorgeously arrayed Sir Percy. He, too, like Marguerite, was wondering what was passing behind the low, smooth forehead of that inimitable dandy, what behind the inscrutably good-humoured expression of those sleepy eyes.

Of the five persons thus present in the dark and stuffy booth, certainly Sir Percy Blakeney seemed the least perturbed. He had paused just long enough to allow Chauvelin to become fully conscious of a feeling of supreme irritation and annoyance, then he strolled up to the ex-ambassador, with hand outstretched and the most engaging of smiles.

"Ha!" he said, with his usual half-shy, half-pleasant-tempered smile, "my engaging friend from France! I hope, sir, that our demmed climate doth find you well and hearty to-day."

The cheerful voice seemed to ease the tension. Marguerite sighed a sigh of relief. After all, what was more natural than that Percy with his amazing fund of pleasant irresponsibility should thus greet the man who had once vowed to bring him to the guillotine? Chauvelin, himself, accustomed by now to the audacious coolness of his enemy, was scarcely taken by surprise. He bowed low to His Highness, who, vastly amused at Blakeney's sally, was inclined to be gracious to everyone, even though the personality of Chauvelin as a well-known leader of the regicide government was inherently distasteful to him. But the Prince saw in the wizened little figure before him an obvious butt for his friend Blakeney's impertinent shafts, and although historians have been unable to assert positively whether or no George Prince of Wales knew aught of Sir Percy's dual life, yet there is no doubt that he was always ready to enjoy a situation which brought about the discomfiture of any of the Scarlet Pimpernel's avowed enemies.

"I, too, have not met M. Chauvelin for many a long month," said His Royal Highness with an obvious show of irony. "And I mistake not, sir, you left my father's court somewhat abruptly last year."

"Nay, your Royal Highness," said Percy gaily, "my friend Monsieur . . . er . . . Chaubertin and I had serious business to discuss, which could only be dealt with in France. . . . Am I not right, Monsieur?"

"Quite right, Sir Percy," replied Chauvelin curtly.

"We had to discuss abominable soup in Calais, had we not?" continued Blakeney in the same tone of easy banter, "and wine that I vowed was vinegar. Monsieur . . . er . . . Chaubertin . . . no, no, I beg pardon . . . Chauvelin . . . Monsieur Chauvelin and I quite agreed upon that point. The only matter on which we were not quite at one was the question of snuff."

"Snuff?" laughed His Royal Highness, who seemed vastly amused.

"Yes, your Royal Highness . . . snuff . . . Monsieur Chauvelin here has—if I may be allowed to say so—so vitiated a taste in snuff that he prefers it with an admixture of pepper . . . Is that not so, Monsieur . . . er . . . Chaubertin?"

"Chauvelin, Sir Percy," remarked the ex-ambassador drily.

He was determined not to lose his temper and looked urbane and pleasant, whilst his impudent enemy was enjoying a joke at his expense. Marguerite the while had not taken her eyes off the keen, shrewd face. Whilst the three men talked, she seemed suddenly to have lost her sense of the reality of things. The present situation appeared to her strangely familiar, like a dream which she had dreamt oft times before.

Suddenly it became absolutely clear to her that the whole scene had been arranged and planned: the booth with its flaring placard, Demoiselle Candeille soliciting her patronage, her invitation to the young actress, Chauvelin's sudden appearance, all, all had been concocted and arranged, not here, not in England at all, but out there in Paris, in some dark gathering of blood-thirsty ruffians, who had invented a final trap for the destruction of the bold adventurer, who went by the name of the Scarlet Pimpernel.

And she also was only a puppet, enacting a part which had been written for her: she had acted just as *they* had anticipated, had spoken the very words they had meant her to say: and when she looked at Percy, he seemed supremely ignorant of it all, unconscious of this trap of the existence of which everyone here present was aware, save indeed himself. She would have fought against this weird feeling of obsession, of being a mechanical toy wound up to do certain things, but this she could not do; her will appeared paralysed, her tongue even refused her service.

As in a dream she heard His Royal Highness ask for the name of the young actress who was soliciting alms for the poor of Paris.

That also had been prearranged. His Royal Highness for the moment was also a puppet, made to dance, to speak and to act as Chauvelin and his colleagues over in France had decided that he should. Quite mechanically Marguerite introduced Demoiselle Candeille to the Prince's gracious notice.

"If your Highness will permit," she said, "Mademoiselle Candeille will give us some of her charming old French songs at my rout to-morrow."

"By all means! By all means!" said the Prince. "I used to know some in my childhood days. Charming and poetic. . . . I know. . . . I know. . . . We shall be delighted to hear Mademoiselle sing, eh, Blakeney?" he added good-humouredly, "and for your rout to-morrow will you not also invite M. Chauvelin?"

"Nay! but that goes without saying, your Royal Highness," responded Sir Percy, with hospitable alacrity and a most approved bow directed at his arch-enemy. "We shall expect M. Chauvelin. He and I have not met for so long, and he shall be made right welcome at Blakeney Manor."

CHAPTER IX

DEMOISELLE CANDEILLE

Her origin was of the humblest, for her mother—so it was said—had been kitchen-maid in the household of the Duc de Marny, but Désirée had received some kind of education, and though she began life as a dresser in one of the minor theatres of Paris, she became ultimately one of its most popular stars.

She was small and dark, dainty in her manner and ways, and with a graceful little figure, peculiarly supple and sinuous. Her humble origin certainly did not betray itself in her hands and feet, which were exquisite in shape and lilliputian in size.

Her hair was soft and glossy, always free from powder, and cunningly arranged so as to slightly overshadow the upper part of her face.

The chin was small and round, the mouth extraordinarily red, the neck slender and long. But she was not pretty: so said all the women. Her skin was rather coarse in texture and darkish in colour, her eyes were narrow and slightly turned upwards at the corners; no! she was distinctly not pretty.

Yet she pleased the men! Perhaps because she was so artlessly determined to please them. The women said that Demoiselle Candeille never left a man alone until she had succeeded in captivating his fancy if only for five minutes; an internal in a dance . . . the time to cross a muddy road.

But for five minutes she was determined to hold any man's complete attention, and to exact his admiration. And she nearly always succeeded.

56

Therefore the women hated her. The men were amused. It is extremely pleasant to have one's admiration compelled, one's attention so determinedly sought after.

And Candeille could be extremely amusing, and as Madelon in Molière's "Les Précieuses" was quite inimitable.

This, however, was in the olden days, just before Paris went quite mad, before the Reign of Terror had set in, and ci-devant Louis the King had been executed.

Candeille had taken it into her frolicsome little head that she would like to go to London. The idea was of course in the nature of an experiment. Those dull English people over the water knew so little of what good acting really meant. Tragedy? Well! passons! Their heavy, large-boned actresses might manage one or two big scenes where a commanding presence and a powerful voice would not come amiss, and where prominent teeth would pass unnoticed in the agony of a dramatic climax.

But Comedy!

Ah! ça non, par example! Demoiselle Candeille had seen several English gentlemen and ladies in those same olden days at the Tuileries, but she really could not imagine any of them enacting the piquant scenes of Molière or Beaumarchais.

Demoiselle Candeille thought of every English-born individual as having very large teeth. Now large teeth do not lend themselves to well-spoken comedy scenes, to smiles, or to double-entendre.

Her own teeth were exceptionally small and white, and very sharp, like those of a kitten.

Yes! Demoiselle Candeille thought it would be extremely interesting to go to London and to show to a nation of shopkeepers how daintily one can be amused in a theatre.

Permission to depart from Paris was easy to obtain. In fact the fair lady had never really found it difficult to obtain anything she very much wanted.

In this case she had plenty of friends in high places. Marat was still alive and a great lover of the theatre. Tallien was a personal admirer of hers, and Deputy Dupont would do anything she asked.

She wanted to act in London, at a theatre called Drury Lane. She wanted to play Molière in England in French, and had already spoken with several of her colleagues, who were ready to join her. They would give public representations in aid of the starving population of France; there were plenty of Socialistic clubs in London quite Jacobin and Revolutionary in tendency: their members would give her full support.

She would be serving her country and her countrymen and incidentally see something of the world, and amuse herself. She was being bored in Paris.

Then she thought of Marguerite St. Just, once of the Maison Molière, who had captivated an English milor of enormous wealth. Demoiselle Candeille had never been of the Maison Molière; she had been the leading star of one of the minor—yet much-frequented—theatres of Paris, but she felt herself quite able and ready to captivate some other unattached milor, who would load her with English money and incidentally bestow an English name upon her.

So she went to London.

The experiment, however, had not proved an unmitigated success. At first she and her company did obtain a few engagements at one or two of the minor theatres, to give representations of some of the French classical comedies in the original language.

But these never quite became the fashion. The feeling against France and all her doings was far too keen in that very set, which Demoiselle Candeille had desired to captivate with her talents, to allow of the English *jeunesse dorée* to flock and see Molière played in French, by a French troupe, whilst Candeille's own compatriots resident in England had given her but scant support.

One section of these—the aristocrats and émigrés—looked upon the actress who was a friend of all the Jacobins in Paris as nothing better than *canaille*. They sedulously ignored her presence in this country, and snubbed her whenever they had an opportunity.

The other section—chiefly consisting of agents and spies of

the Revolutionary Government—she would gladly have ignored. They had at first made a constant demand on her purse,
her talents and her time: then she grew tired of them, and felt
more and more chary of being identified with a set which was in
such ill-odour with that very same *jeunesse dorée* whom
Candeille had desired to please.

In her own country she was and always had been a good republican: Marat had given her her first start in life by his violent
praises of her talent in his widely-circulated paper; she had been
associated in Paris with the whole coterie of artists and actors:
every one of them republican to a man. But in London, although
one might be snubbed by the émigrés and aristocrats—it did not
do to be mixed up with the sans-culotte journalists and pam-
phleteers who haunted the Socialistic clubs of the English capi-
tal, and who were the prime organizers of all those seditious
gatherings and treasonable unions that caused Mr. Pitt and his
colleagues so much trouble and anxiety.

One by one, Désirée Candeille's comrades, male and female,
who had accompanied her to England, returned to their own
country. When war was declared, some of them were actually
sent back under the provisions of the Aliens Bill.

But Désirée had stayed on.

Her old friends in Paris had managed to advise her that she
would not be very welcome there just now. The sans-culotte
journalists of England, the agents and spies of the Revolutionary
Government, had taken their revenge of the frequent snubs inflicted upon them by the young actress, and in those days the
fact of being unwelcome in France was apt to have a more lurid
and more dangerous significance.

Candeille did not dare return: at any rate not for the present.

She trusted to her own powers of intrigue, and her well-
known fascinations, to re-conquer the friendship of the Jacobin
clique, and she once more turned her attention to the affiliated
Socialistic clubs of England. But between the proverbial two
stools, Demoiselle Candeille soon came to the ground. Her
machinations became known in official quarters, her connection
with all the seditious clubs of London was soon bruited abroad,

and one evening Désirée found herself confronted with a document addressed to her: "From the Office of His Majesty's Privy Seal," wherein it was set forth that, pursuant to the statute 33 George III. cap. 5, she, Désirée Candeille, a French subject now resident in England, was required to leave this kingdom by order of His Majesty within seven days, and that in the event of the said Désirée Candeille refusing to comply with this order, she would be liable to commitment, brought to trial and sentenced to imprisonment for a month, and afterwards to removal within a limited time under pain of transportation for life.

This meant that Demoiselle Candeille had exactly seven days in which to make complete her reconciliation with her former friends who now ruled Paris and France with a relentless and perpetually bloodstained hand. No wonder that during the night which followed the receipt of this momentous document, Demoiselle Candeille suffered gravely from insomnia.

She dared not go back to France, she was ordered out of England! What was to become of her?

This was just three days before the eventful afternoon of the Richmond Gala, and twenty-four hours after ex-Ambassador Chauvelin had landed in England. Candeille and Chauvelin had since then met at the "Cercle des Jacobins Français" in Soho Street, and now fair Désirée found herself in lodgings in Richmond, the evening of the day following the Gala, feeling that her luck had not altogether deserted her.

One conversation with Citizen Chauvelin had brought the fickle jade back to Demoiselle Candeille's service. Nay, more, the young actress saw before her visions of intrigue, of dramatic situations, of pleasant little bits of revenge;—all of which was meat and drink and air to breathe for Mademoiselle Désirée.

She was to sing in one of the most fashionable salons in England: that was very pleasant. The Prince of Wales would hear and see her! that opened out a vista of delightful possibilities! And all she had to do was to act a part dictated to her by Citizen Chauvelin, to behave as he directed, to move in the way he wished! Well! that was easy enough, since the part which she would have to play was one peculiarly suited to her talents.

She looked at herself critically in the glass. Her maid Fanchon—a little French waif picked up in the slums of Soho—helped to readjust a stray curl which had rebelled against the comb.

"Now for the necklace, Mademoiselle," said Fanchon with suppressed excitement.

It had just arrived by messenger: a large morocco case, which now lay open on the dressing table, displaying its dazzling contents.

Candeille scarcely dared to touch it, and yet it was for her. Citizen Chauvelin had sent a note with it.

"Citizeness Candeille will please accept this gift from the government of France in acknowledgment of useful services past and to come."

The note was signed with Robespierre's own name, followed by that of Citizen Chauvelin. The morocco case contained a necklace of diamonds worth the ransom of a king.

"For useful services past and to come!" and there were promises of still further rewards, a complete pardon for all defalcations, a place within the charmed circle of the Comédie Française, a grand pageant and apotheosis with Citizeness Candeille impersonating the Goddess of Reason, in the midst of a grand national fête, and the acclamations of excited Paris: and all in exchange for the enactment of a part—simple and easy—outlined for her by Chauvelin! . . .

How strange! how inexplicable! Candeille took the necklace up in her trembling fingers and gazed musingly at the priceless gems. She had seen the jewels before, long, long ago! round the neck of the Duchesse de Marny, in whose service her own mother had been. She—as a child—had often gazed at and admired the great lady, who seemed like a wonderful fairy from an altogether different world, to the poor little kitchen slut.

How wonderful are the vagaries of fortune! Désirée Candeille, the kitchen-maid's daughter, now wearing her ex-mistress' jewels. She supposed that these had been confiscated when the last of the Marnys—the girl, Juliette—had escaped from France! confiscated and now sent to her—Candeille—as a reward or as a bribe!

In either case they were welcome. The actress' vanity was soothed. She knew Juliette Marny was in England, and that she would meet her to-night at Lady Blakeney's. After the many snubs which she had endured from the French aristocrats settled in England, the actress felt that she was about to enjoy an evening of triumph.

The intrigue excited her. She did not quite know what schemes Chauvelin was aiming at, what ultimate end he had had in view when he commanded her services and taught her the part which he wished her to play.

That the schemes were vast and the end mighty, she could not doubt. The reward she had received was proof enough of that.

Little Fanchon stood there in speechless admiration, whilst her mistress still fondly fingered the magnificent necklace.

"Mademoiselle will wear the diamond to-night?" she asked with evident anxiety: she would have been bitterly disappointed to have seen the beautiful thing once more relegated to its dark morocco case.

"Oh, yes, Fanchon!" said Candeille with a sigh of great satisfaction; "see that they are fastened quite securely, my girl."

She put the necklace round her shapely neck and Fanchon looked to see that the clasp was quite secure.

There came the sound of loud knocking at the street door.

"That is M. Chauvelin come to fetch me with the chaise. Am I quite ready, Fanchon?" asked Désirée Candeille.

"Oh, yes, Mademoiselle!" sighed the little maid; "and Mademoiselle looks very beautiful to-night."

"Lady Blakeney is very beautiful too, Fanchon," rejoined the actress naïvely, "but I wonder if she will wear anything as fine as the Marny necklace?"

The knocking at the street door was repeated. Candeille took a final, satisfied survey of herself in the glass. She knew her part and felt that she had dressed well for it. She gave a final, affectionate little tap to the diamonds round her neck, took her cloak and hood from Fanchon, and was ready to go.

CHAPTER X

Lady Blakeney's Rout

There are several accounts extant, in the fashionable chronicles of the time, of the gorgeous reception given that autumn by Lady Blakeney in her magnificent riverside home.

Never had the spacious apartments of Blakeney Manor looked more resplendent than on this memorable occasion—memorable because of the events which brought the brilliant evening to a close.

The Prince of Wales had come over by water from Carlton House; the Royal Princesses came early, and all fashionable London was there, chattering and laughing, displaying elaborate gowns and priceless jewels, dancing, flirting, listening to the strains of the string band, or strolling listlessly in the gardens, where the late roses and clumps of heliotrope threw soft fragrance on the balmy air.

But Marguerite was nervous and agitated. Strive how she might, she could not throw off that foreboding of something evil to come, which had assailed her from the first moment when she met Chauvelin face to face.

That unaccountable feeling of unreality was still upon her, that sense that she, and the woman Candeille, Percy and even His Royal Highness were, for the time being, the actors in a play written and stage-managed by Chauvelin. The ex-ambassador's humility, his offers of friendship, his quietude under Sir Percy's good-humoured banter, everything was a sham. Marguerite knew it; her womanly instinct, her passionate love, all cried out to her in warning: but there was that in her husband's nature which rendered her powerless in the face of such dangers, as, she felt sure, were now threatening him.

Just before her guests had begun to assemble, she had been alone with him for a few minutes. She had entered the room in which he sat, looking radiantly beautiful in a shimmering gown of white and silver, with diamonds in her golden hair and round her exquisite neck.

Moments like this, when she was alone with him, were the joy of her life. Then and then only did she see him as he really was, with that wistful tenderness in his deep-set eyes, that occasional flash of passion from beneath the lazily-drooping lids. For a few minutes—seconds, mayhap—the spirit of the reckless adventurer was laid to rest, relegated into the furthermost background of his senses by the powerful emotions of the lover.

Then he would seize her in his arms, and hold her to him, with a strange longing to tear from out his heart all other thoughts, feelings and passions save those which made him a slave to her beauty and her smiles.

"Percy!" she whispered to him to-night when freeing herself from his embrace she looked up at him, and for this one heavenly second felt him all her own. "Percy, you will do nothing rash, nothing foolhardy to-night. That man had planned all that took place yesterday. He hates you, and . . ."

In a moment his face and attitude had changed, the heavy lids drooped over the eyes, the rigidity of the mouth relaxed, and that quaint, half-shy, half-inane smile played around the firm lips.

"Of course he does, m'dear," he said in his usual affected, drawly tones, "of course he does, but that is so demmed amusing. He does not really know what or how much he knows, or what I know. . . . In fact . . . er . . . we none of us know anything . . . just at present. . . ."

He laughed lightly and carelessly, then deliberately readjusted the set of his lace tie.

"Percy!" she said reproachfully.

"Yes, m'dear."

"Lately when you brought Déroulède and Juliette Marny to

England . . . I endured agonies of anxiety . . . and . . ."

He sighed, a quick, short, wistful sigh, and said very gently:

"I know you did, m'dear, and that is where the trouble lies. I know that you are fretting, so I have to be so demmed quick about the business, so as not to keep you in suspense too long. . . . And now I can't take Ffoulkes away from his young wife, and Tony and the others are so mighty slow."

"Percy!" she said once more with tender earnestness.

"I know, I know," he said with a slight frown of self-reproach. "La! but I don't deserve your solicitude. Heaven knows what a brute I was for years, whilst I neglected you, and ignored the noble devotion which I, alas! do even now so little to deserve.

She would have said something more, but was interrupted by the entrance of Juliette Marny into the room.

"Some of your guests have arrived, Lady Blakeney," said the young girl, apologising for her seeming intrusion. "I thought you would wish to know."

Juliette looked very young and girlish in a simple white gown, without a single jewel on her arms or neck. Marguerite regarded her with unaffected approval.

"You look charming to-night, Mademoiselle, does she not, Sir Percy?"

"Thanks to your bounty," smiled Juliette, a trifle sadly. "Whilst I dressed to-night, I felt how I should have loved to wear my dear mother's jewels, of which she used to be so proud."

"We must hope that you will recover them, dear, some day," said Marguerite vaguely, as she led the young girl out of the small study towards the larger reception rooms.

"Indeed I hope so," sighed Juliette. "When times became so troublous in France after my dear father's death, his confessor and friend, the Abbé Foucquet, took charge of all my mother's jewels for me. He said they would be safe with the ornaments of his own little church at Boulogne. He feared no sacrilege, and thought they would be most effectually hidden there, for no one would dream of looking for the Marny diamonds in the crypt of a country church."

Marguerite said nothing in reply. Whatever her own doubts

might be upon such a subject, it could serve no purpose to disturb the young girl's serenity.

"Dear Abbé Foucquet," said Juliette after a while, "his is the kind of devotion which I feel sure will never be found under the new régimes of anarchy and of so-called equality. He would have laid down his life for my father or for me. And I know that he would never part with the jewels which I entrusted to his care, whilst he had breath and strength to defend them."

Marguerite would have wished to pursue the subject a little further. It was very pathetic to witness poor Juliette's hopes and confidences, which she felt sure would never be realised.

Lady Blakeney knew so much of what was going on in France just now: spoliations, confiscations, official thefts, open robberies, all in the name of equality, of fraternity and of patriotism. She knew nothing, of course, of the Abbé Foucquet, but the tender little picture of the devoted old man, painted by Juliette's loving words, had appealed strongly to her sympathetic heart.

Instinct and knowledge of the political aspect of France told her that by entrusting valuable family jewels to the old Abbé, Juliette had most unwittingly placed the man she so much trusted in danger of persecution at the hands of a government which did not even admit the legality of family possessions. However, there was neither time nor opportunity now to enlarge upon the subject. Marguerite resolved to recur to it a little later, when she would be alone with Mlle. de Marny, and above all when she could take counsel with her husband as to the best means of recovering the young girl's property for her, whilst relieving a devoted old man from the dangerous responsibility which he had so selflessly undertaken.

In the meanwhile the two women had reached the first of the long line of state apartments wherein the brilliant fête was to take place. The staircase and the hall below were already filled with the early arrivals. Bidding Juliette to remain in the ballroom, Lady Blakeney now took up her stand on the exquisitely decorated landing, ready to greet her guests. She had a smile and a pleasant word for all, as, in a constant stream, the élite of London fashionable society began to file past her, exchanging the elaborate greetings which the stilted mode of the day prescribed to this butterfly-world.

The lacqueys in the hall shouted the names of the guests as they passed up the stairs: names celebrated in politics, in worlds of sport, of science or of art, great historic names, humble, newly-made ones, noble illustrious titles. The spacious rooms were filling fast. His Royal Highness, so 'twas said, had just stepped out of his barge. The noise of laughter and chatter was incessant, like unto a crowd of gaily-plumaged birds.

Huge bunches of apricot-coloured roses in silver vases made the air heavy with their subtle perfume. Fans began to flutter. The string band struck the preliminary cords of the gavotte.

At that moment the lacqueys at the foot of the stairs called out in stentorian tones:

"Mademoiselle Désirée Candeille! and Monsieur Chauvelin!"

Marguerite's heart gave a slight flutter; she felt a sudden tightening of the throat. She did not see Candeille at first, only the slight figure of Chauvelin dressed all in black, as usual, with head bent and hands clasped behind his back; he was slowly mounting the wide staircase, between a double row of brilliantly attired men and women, who looked with no small measure of curiosity at the ex-ambassador from revolutionary France.

Demoiselle Candeille was leading the way up the stairs. She paused on the landing in order to make before her hostess a most perfect and most elaborate curtsey. She looked smiling and radiant, beautifully dressed, a small wreath of wrought gold leaves in her hair, her only jewel an absolutely regal one, a magnificent necklace of diamonds round her shapely throat.

CHAPTER XI

THE CHALLENGE

It all occurred just before midnight, in one of the smaller rooms, which lead in enfilade from the principal ballroom.

Dancing had been going on for some time, but the evening was close, and there seemed to be a growing desire on the part of Lady Blakeney's guests to wander desultorily through the gardens and glasshouses, or sit about where some measure of coolness could be obtained.

There was a rumour that a new and charming French artiste was to sing a few peculiarly ravishing songs, unheard in England before. Close to the main ballroom was the octagon music-room which was brilliantly illuminated, and in which a large number of chairs had been obviously disposed for the comfort of an audience. Into this room many of the guests had already assembled. It was quite clear that a chamber-concert—select and attractive as were all Lady Blakeney's entertainments—was in contemplation.

Marguerite herself, released for a moment from her constant duties near her royal guests, had strolled through the smaller rooms, accompanied by Juliette, in order to search for Mademoiselle Candeille and to suggest the commencement of the improvised concert.

Désirée Candeille had kept herself very much aloof throughout the evening, only talking to the one or two gentlemen whom her hostess had presented to her on her arrival, and with M. Chauvelin always in close attendance upon her every movement.

Presently, when dancing began, she retired to a small boudoir, and there sat down, demurely waiting, until Lady Blakeney should require her services.

When Marguerite and Juliette Marny entered the little room, she rose and came forward a few steps.

"I am ready, Madame," she said pleasantly, "whenever you wish me to begin. I have thought out a short programme,—shall I start with the gay or the sentimental songs?"

But before Marguerite had time to utter a reply, she felt her arm nervously clutched by a hot and trembling hand.

"Who . . . who is this woman?" murmured Juliette Marny close to her ear.

The young girl looked pale and very agitated, and her large eyes were fixed in unmistakable wrath upon the French actress before her. A little startled, not understanding Juliette's attitude, Marguerite tried to reply lightly:

"This is Mademoiselle Candeille, Juliette dear," she said, affecting the usual formal introduction, "of the Variétés Theatre of Paris—Mademoiselle Désirée Candeille, who will sing some charming French ditties for us to-night."

While she spoke she kept a restraining hand on Juliette's quivering arm. Already, with the keen intuition which had been on the qui-vive the whole evening, she scented some mystery in this sudden outburst on the part of her young protégée.

But Juliette did not heed her: she felt surging up in her young, overburdened heart all the wrath and the contempt of the persecuted, fugitive aristocrat against the triumphant usurper. She had suffered so much from that particular class of the risen kitchen-wench of which the woman before her was so typical an example: years of sorrow, of poverty were behind her: loss of fortune, of kindred, of friends—she, even now a pauper, living on the bounty of strangers.

And all this through no fault of her own: the fault of her class mayhap! but not hers!

She had suffered much, and was still overwrought and nerve-strung: for some reason she could not afterwards have explained, she felt spiteful and uncontrolled, goaded into stupid fury by the look of insolence and of triumph with which Candeille calmly regarded her.

Afterwards she would willingly have bitten out her tongue for her vehemence, but for the moment she was absolutely incapable of checking the torrent of her own emotions.

"Mademoiselle Candeille, indeed?" she said in wrathful scorn, "Désirée Candeille, you mean, Lady Blakeney! my mother's kitchen-maid, flaunting shamelessly my dear mother's jewels which she has stolen mayhap . . ."

The young girl was trembling from head to foot, tears of anger obscured her eyes; her voice, which fortunately remained low—not much above a whisper—was thick and husky.

"Juliette! Juliette! I entreat you," admonished Marguerite, "you must control yourself, you must, indeed you must. Mademoiselle Candeille, I beg of you to retire. . . ."

But Candeille—well-schooled in the part she had to play— had no intention of quitting the field of battle. The more wrathful and excited Mademoiselle de Marny became the more insolent and triumphant waxed the young actress' whole attitude. An ironical smile played round the corners of her mouth, her almond-shaped eyes were half-closed, regarding through drooping lashes the trembling figure of the young impoverished aristocrat. Her head was thrown well back, in obvious defiance of the social conventions, which should have forbidden a fracas in Lady Blakeney's hospitable house, and her fingers provocatively toyed with the diamond necklace which glittered and sparkled round her throat.

She had no need to repeat the words of a well-learnt part: her own wit, her own emotions and feelings helped her to act just as her employer would have wished her to do. Her native vulgarity helped her to assume the very bearing which he would have desired. In fact, at this moment Désirée Candeille had forgotten everything save the immediate present: a more than contemptuous snub from one of those penniless aristocrats, who had rendered her own sojourn in London so unpleasant and unsuccessful.

She had suffered from these snubs before, but had never

had the chance of forcing an esclandre, as a result of her own humiliation. That spirit of hatred for the rich and idle classes, which was so characteristic of revolutionary France, was alive and hot within her: she had never had an opportunity—she, the humble fugitive actress from a minor Paris theatre—to retort with forcible taunts to the ironical remarks made at and before her by the various poverty-stricken but haughty émigrés who swarmed in those very same circles of London society into which she herself had vainly striven to penetrate.

Now at last, one of this same hated class, provoked beyond self-control, was allowing childish and unreasoning fury to outstrip the usual calm irony of aristocratic rebuffs.

Juliette had paused awhile, in order to check the wrathful tears which, much against her will, were choking the words in her throat and blinding her eyes.

"Hoity! toity!" laughed Candeille, "hark at the young baggage!"

But Juliette had turned to Marguerite and began explaining volubly:

"My mother's jewels!" she said in the midst of her tears, "ask her how she came by them. When I was obliged to leave the home of my fathers,—stolen from me by the Revolutionary Government—I contrived to retain my mother's jewels . . . you remember, I told you just now. . . . The Abbé Foucquet—dear old man! Saved them for me . . . that and a little money which I had . . . he took charge of them . . . he said he would place them in safety with the ornaments of his church, and now I see them round that woman's neck . . . I know that he would not have parted with them save with his life."

All the while that the young girl spoke in a voice half-choked with sobs, Marguerite tried with all the physical and mental will at her command to drag her out of the room and thus to put a summary ending to this unpleasant scene. She ought to have felt angry with Juliette for this childish and senseless outburst, were it not for the fact that somehow she knew within her innermost heart that all this had been arranged and preordained: not by

Fate—not by a Higher Hand, but by the most skilful intriguer present-day France had ever known.

And even now, as she was half succeeding in turning Juliette away from the sight of Candeille, she was not the least surprised or startled at seeing Chauvelin standing in the very doorway through which she had hoped to pass. Once glance at his face had made her fears tangible and real: there was a look of satisfaction and triumph in his pale, narrow eyes, a flash in them of approbation directed at the insolent attitude of the French actress: he looked like the stage-manager of a play, content with the effect his own well-arranged scenes were producing.

What he hoped to gain by this—somewhat vulgar—quarrel between the two women, Marguerite of course could not guess: that something was lurking in his mind, inimical to herself and to her husband, she did not for a moment doubt, and at this moment she felt that she would have given her very life to induce Candeille and Juliette to cease this passage of arms, without further provocation on either side.

But though Juliette might have been ready to yield to Lady Blakeney's persuasion, Désirée Candeille, under Chauvelin's eye, and fired by her own desire to further humiliate this overbearing aristocrat, did not wish the little scene to end so tamely just yet.

"Your old calotin was made to part with his booty, m'dear," she said, with a contemptuous shrug of her bare shoulders. "Paris and France have been starving these many years past: a paternal government seized all it could with which to reward those that served it well, whilst all that would have been brought bread and meat for the poor was being greedily stowed away by shameless traitors!"

Juliette winced at the insult.

"Oh!" she moaned, as she buried her flaming face in her hands.

Too late now did she realise that she had deliberately stirred up a mud-heap and sent noisome insects buzzing about her ears.

"Mademoiselle," said Marguerite authoritatively, "I must ask you to remember that Mlle. de Marny is my friend and that you are a guest in my house."

"Aye! I try not to forget it," rejoined Candeille lightly, "but of a truth you must admit, Citizeness, that it would require the patience of a saint to put up with the insolence of a penniless baggage, who but lately has had to stand her trial in her own country for impurity of conduct."

There was a moment's silence, whilst Marguerite distinctly heard a short sigh of satisfaction escaping from the lips of Chauvelin. Then a pleasant laugh broke upon the ears of the four actors who were enacting the dramatic little scene, and Sir Percy Blakeney, immaculate in his rich white satin coat and filmy lace ruffles, exquisite in manners and courtesy, entered the little boudoir, and with his long back slightly bent, his arm outstretched in a graceful and well-studied curve, he approached Mademoiselle Désirée Candeille.

"May I have the honour," he said with his most elaborate air of courtly deference, "of conducting Mademoiselle to her chaise?"

In the doorway just behind him stood His Royal Highness the Prince of Wales chatting with apparent carelessness to Sir Andrew Ffoulkes and Lord Anthony Dewhurst. A curtain beyond the open door was partially drawn aside, disclosing one or two brilliantly dressed groups, strolling desultorily through the further rooms.

The four persons assembled in the little boudoir had been so absorbed by their own passionate emotions and the violence of their quarrel that they had not noticed the approach of Sir Percy Blakeney and of his friends. Juliette and Marguerite certainly were startled and Candeille was evidently taken unawares. Chauvelin alone seemed quite indifferent and stood back a little when Sir Percy advanced, in order to allow him to pass.

But Candeille recovered quickly enough from her surprise: without heeding Blakeney's proffered arm, she turned with all the airs of an insulted tragedy queen towards Marguerite.

"So 'tis I," she said with affected calm, "who am to bear every insult in a house in which I was bidden as a guest. I am turned out like some intrusive and importunate beggar, and I, the stranger in this land, am destined to find that amidst all these brilliant English gentlemen there is not one man of honour.

"M. Chauvelin," she added loudly, "our beautiful country has, meseems, deputed you to guard the honour as well as the worldly goods of your unprotected compatriots. I call upon you, in the name of France, to avenge the insults offered to me to-night."

She looked round defiantly from one to the other of the several faces which were now turned towards her, but no one, for the moment, spoke or stirred. Juliette, silent and ashamed, had taken Marguerite's hand in hers, and was clinging to it as if wishing to draw strength of character and firmness of purpose through the pores of the other woman's delicate skin.

Sir Percy with backbone still bent in a sweeping curve had not relaxed his attitude of uttermost deference. The Prince of Wales and his friends were viewing the scene with slightly amused aloofness.

For a moment—seconds at most—there was dead silence in the room, during which time it almost seemed as if the beating of several hearts could be distinctly heard.

Then Chauvelin, courtly and urbane, stepped calmly forward.

"Believe me, Citizeness," he said, addressing Candeille directly and with marked emphasis, "I am entirely at your command, but am I not helpless, seeing that those who have so grossly insulted you are of your own irresponsible, if charming, sex?"

Like a great dog after a nap, Sir Percy Blakeney straightened his long back and stretched it out to its full length.

"La!" he said pleasantly, "my ever engaging friend from Calais. Sir, your servant. Meseems we are ever destined to discuss amiable matters, in an amiable spirit. . . . A glass of punch, Monsieur . . . er . . . Chauvelin?"

"I must ask you, Sir Percy," rejoined Chauvelin sternly, "to view this matter with becoming seriousness."

"Seriousness is never becoming, sir," said Blakeney, politely smothering a slight yawn, "and it is vastly unbecoming in the presence of ladies."

"Am I to understand then, Sir Percy," said Chauvelin, "that you are prepared to apologize to Mademoiselle Candeille for the insults offered to her by Lady Blakeney?"

Sir Percy again tried to smother that tiresome little yawn, which seemed most distressing, when he desired to be most polite. Then he flicked off a grain of dust from his immaculate lace ruffle and buried his long, slender hands in the capacious pockets of his white satin breeches; finally he said with the most good-natured of smiles:

"Sir, have you seen the latest fashion in cravats? I would wish to draw your attention to the novel way in which we in England tie a Mechlin-edged bow."

"Sir Percy," retorted Chauvelin firmly, "since you will not offer Mademoiselle Candeille the apology which she has the right to expect from you, are you prepared that you and I should cross swords like honourable gentlemen?"

Blakeney laughed his usual pleasant, somewhat shy laugh, shook his powerful frame and looked from his altitude of six feet three inches down on the small, sable-clad figure of ex-Ambassador Chauvelin.

"The question is, sir," he said slowly, "should we then be two honourable gentlemen crossing swords?"

"Sir Percy . . ."

"Sir?"

Chauvelin, who for one moment had seemed ready to lose his temper, now made a sudden effort to resume a calm and easy attitude and said quietly:

"Of course, if one of us is coward enough to shirk the contest . . ."

He did not complete the sentence, but shrugged his shoulders expressive of contempt. The other side of the curtained doorway a little crowd had gradually assembled, attracted hither by the loud and angry voices which came from that small boudoir. Host and hostess had been missed from the reception rooms for some time, His Royal Highness, too, had not been seen for the last quarter of an hour: like flies attracted by the light, one by one, or in small isolated groups, some of Lady Blakeney's guests had found their way to the room adjoining the royal presence.

As His Highness was standing in the doorway itself, no one could of course cross the threshold, but everyone could see into the room, and could take stock of the various actors in the little comedy. They were witnessing a quarrel between the French envoy and Sir Percy Blakeney wherein the former was evidently in deadly earnest and the latter merely politely bored. Amused comments flew to and fro: laughter and a babel of irresponsible chatter made an incessant chirruping accompaniment to the duologue between the two men.

But at this stage, the Prince of Wales, who hitherto had seemingly kept aloof from the quarrel, suddenly stepped forward and abruptly interposed the weight of his authority and of his social position between the bickering adversaries.

"Tush, man!" he said impatiently, turning more especially towards Chauvelin, "you talk at random. Sir Percy Blakeney is an English gentleman, and the laws of this country do not admit of duelling, as you understand it in France; and I for one certainly could not allow . . ."

"Pardon, your Royal Highness," interrupted Sir Percy with irresistible bonhomie, "your Highness does not understand the situation. My engaging friend here does not propose that I should transgress the laws of this country, but that I should go over to France with him, and fight him there, where duelling and . . . er . . . other little matters of that sort are allowed."

"Yes! quite so!" rejoined the Prince, "I understand M. Chauvelin's desire. . . . But what about you, Blakeney?"

"Oh!" replied Sir Percy lightly, "I have accepted his challenge, of course!"

CHAPTER XII

TIME—PLACE—CONDITIONS

It would be very difficult indeed to say why—at Blakeney's lightly spoken words—an immediate silence should have fallen upon all those present. All the actors in the little drawing-room drama, who had played their respective parts so unerringly up to now, had paused a while, just as if an invisible curtain had come down, marking the end of a scene, and the interval during which the players might recover strength and energy to resume their rôles. The Prince of Wales as foremost spectator said nothing for the moment, and beyond the doorway, the audience there assembled seemed suddenly to be holding its breath, waiting—eager, expectant, palpitating—for what would follow now.

Only here and there the gentle frou-frou of a silk skirt, the rhythmic flutter of a fan, broke those few seconds' deadly, stony silence.

Yet it was all simple enough. A fracas between two ladies, the gentlemen interposing, a few words of angry expostulation, then the inevitable suggestion of Belgium or of some other country where the childish and barbarous custom of settling such matters with a couple of swords had not been as yet systematically stamped out.

The whole scene—with but slight variations—had occurred scores of times in London drawing-rooms, English gentlemen had scores of times crossed the Channel for the purpose of settling similar quarrels in continental fashion.

Why should the present situation appear so abnormal? Sir

Percy Blakeney—an accomplished gentleman—was past master in the art of fence, and looked more than a match in strength and dexterity for the meagre, sable-clad little opponent who had so summarily challenged him to cross over to France, in order to fight a duel.

But somehow everyone had a feeling at this moment that this proposed duel would be unlike any other combat every fought between two antagonists. Perhaps it was the white, absolutely stony and unexpressive face of Marguerite which suggested a latent tragedy: perhaps it was the look of unmistakable horror in Juliette's eyes, or that of triumph in those of Chauvelin, or even that certain something in His Royal Highness' face, which seemed to imply that the Prince, careless man of the world as he was, would have given much to prevent this particular meeting from taking place.

Be that as it may, there is no doubt that a certain wave of electrical excitement swept over the little crowd assembled there, the while the chief actor in the little drama, the inimitable dandy, Sir Percy Blakeney himself, appeared deeply engrossed in removing a speck of powder from the wide black satin ribbon which held his gold-rimmed eye-glass.

"Gentlemen!" said His Royal Highness suddenly, "we are forgetting the ladies. My lord Hastings," he added, turning to one of the gentlemen who stood close to him, "I pray you to remedy this unpardonable neglect. Men's quarrels are not fit for ladies' dainty ears."

Sir Percy looked up from his absorbing occupation. His eyes met those of his wife; she was like a marble statue, hardly conscious of what was going on round her. But he, who knew every emotion which swayed that ardent and passionate nature, guessed that beneath that stony calm there lay a mad, almost unconquerable impulse: and that was to shout to all these puppets here, the truth, the awful, the unanswerable truth, to tell them what this challenge really meant; a trap wherein one man consumed with hatred and desire for revenge hoped to entice a brave and fearless foe into a death-dealing snare.

Full well did Percy Blakeney guess that for the space of one second his most cherished secret hovered upon his wife's lips, one turn of the balance of Fate, one breath from the mouth of an unseen sprite, and Marguerite was ready to shout:

"Do not allow this monstrous thing to be! The Scarlet Pimpernel, whom you all admire for his bravery, and love for his daring, stands before you now, face to face with his deadliest enemy, who is here to lure him to his doom!"

For that momentous second therefore Percy Blakeney held his wife's gaze with the magnetism of his own; all there was in him of love, of entreaty, of trust, and of command went out to her through that look with which he kept her eyes riveted upon his face.

Then he saw the rigidity of her attitude relax. She closed her eyes in order to shut out the whole world from her suffering soul. She seemed to be gathering all the mental force of which her brain was capable, for one great effort of self-control. Then she took Juliette's hand in hers, and turned to go out of the room; the gentlemen bowed as she swept past them, her rich silken gown making a soft hush-sh-sh as she went. She nodded to some, curtseyed to the Prince, and had at the last moment the supreme courage and pride to turn her head once more towards her husband, in order to reassure him finally that his secret was as safe with her now, in this hour of danger, as it had been in the time of triumph.

She smiled and passed out of his sight, preceded by Désirée Candeille, who, escorted by one of the gentlemen, had become singularly silent and subdued.

In the little room now there only remained a few men. Sir Andrew Ffoulkes had taken the precaution of closing the door after the ladies had gone.

Then His Royal Highness turned once more to Monsieur Chauvelin and said with an obvious show of indifference:

"Faith, Monsieur! meseems we are all enacting a farce, which can have no final act. I vow that I cannot allow my friend Blakeney to go over to France at your bidding. Your government now will not allow my father's subjects to land on your shores without a special passport, and then only for a specific purpose."

"La, your Royal Highness," interposed Sir Percy, "I pray you have no fear for me on that score. My engaging friend here has—an I mistake not—a passport ready for me in the pocket of his sable-hued coat, and as we are hoping effectually to spit one another over there . . . gadzooks! but there's the specific purpose. . . . Is it not true, sir," he added, turning once more to Chauvelin, "that in the pocket of that exquisitely cut coat of yours, you have a passport—name in blank perhaps—which you had specially designed for me?"

It was so carelessly, so pleasantly said, that no one save Chauvelin guessed the real import of Sir Percy's words. Chauvelin, of course, knew their inner meaning: he understood that Blakeney wished to convey to him the fact that he was well aware that the whole scene to-night had been prearranged, and that it was willingly and with eyes wide open that he walked into the trap which the revolutionary patriot had so carefully laid for him.

"The passport will be forthcoming in due course, sir," retorted Chauvelin evasively, "when our seconds have arranged all formalities."

"Seconds be demmed, sir," rejoined Sir Percy placidly, "you do not propose, I trust, that we travel a whole caravan to France."

"Time, place and conditions must be settled, Sir Percy," replied Chauvelin; "you are too accomplished a cavalier, I feel sure, to wish to arrange such formalities yourself."

"Nay! neither you nor I, Monsieur . . . er . . . Chauvelin," quoth Sir Percy blandly, "could, I own, settle such things with persistent good-humour; and good-humour in such cases is the most important of all formalities. Is it not so?"

"Certainly, Sir Percy."

"As for seconds? Perish the thought. One second only, I entreat, and that one a lady—the most adorable—the most detestable—the most true—the most fickle amidst all her charming sex. . . . Do you agree, sir?"

"You have not told me her name, Sir Percy?"

"Chance, Monsieur, Chance. . . . With His Royal Highness' permission let the wilful jade decide."

"I do not understand."

"Three throws of the dice, Monsieur. . . . Time . . . Place . . . Conditions, you said—three throws and the winner names them. . . . Do you agree?"

Chauvelin hesitated. Sir Percy's bantering mood did not quite fit in with his own elaborate plans, moreover the ex-ambassador feared a pitfall of some sort, and did not quite like to trust to this arbitration of the dice-box.

He turned, quite involuntarily, in appeal to the Prince of Wales and the other gentlemen present.

But the Englishman of those days was a born gambler. He lived with the dice-box in one pocket and a pack of cards in the other. The Prince himself was no exception to this rule, and the first gentleman in England was the most avowed worshipper of Hazard in the land.

"Chance, by all means," quoth His Highness gaily.

"Chance! Chance!" repeated the others eagerly.

In the midst of so hostile a crowd, Chauvelin felt it unwise to resist. Moreover, one second's reflection had already assured him that this throwing of the dice could not seriously interfere with the success of his plans. If the meeting took place at all— and Sir Percy now had gone too far to draw back—then of necessity it would have to take place in France.

The question of time and conditions of the fight, which at best would be only a farce—only a means to an end—could not be of paramount importance.

Therefore he shrugged his shoulders with well-marked indifference, and said lightly:

"As you please."

There was a small table in the centre of the room with a settee and two or three chairs arranged close to it. Around this table now an eager little group had congregated: the Prince of Wales in the forefront, unwilling to interfere, scarce knowing what madcap plans were floating through Blakeney's adventurous brain, but excited in spite of himself at this momentous game of hazard the issues of which seemed so nebulous, so vaguely fraught with dangers. Close to him were Sir Andrew Ffoulkes, Lord Anthony Dewhurst, Lord Grenville and perhaps a half score gentlemen, young men about town mostly, gay and giddy butterflies of fashion, who did not even attempt to seek in this strange game of chance any hidden meaning save that it was one of Blakeney's irresponsible pranks.

And in the centre of the compact group, Sir Percy Blakeney in his gorgeous suit of shimmering white satin, one knee bent upon a chair, and leaning with easy grace—dice-box in hand—across the small gilt-legged table; beside him ex-Ambassador Chauvelin, standing with arms folded behind his back, watching every movement of his brilliant adversary like some dark-plumaged hawk hovering near a bird of paradise.

"Place first, Monsieur?" suggested Sir Percy.

"As you will, sir," assented Chauvelin.

He took up a dice-box which one of the gentlemen handed to him and the two men threw.

"'Tis mine, Monsieur," said Blakeney carelessly, "mine to name the place where shall occur this historic encounter, 'twixt the busiest man in France and the most idle fop that e'er disgraced these three kingdoms. . . . Just for the sake of argument, sir, what place would you suggest?"

"Oh! the exact spot is immaterial, Sir Percy," replied Chauvelin coldly, "the whole of France stands at your disposal."

"Aye! I thought as much, but could not be quite sure of such boundless hospitality," retorted Blakeney imperturbably.

"Do you care for the woods around Paris, sir?"

"Too far from the coast, sir. I might be sea-sick crossing over the Channel, and glad to get the business over as soon as possible. . . . No, not Paris, sir—rather let us say Boulogne. . . . Pretty little place, Boulogne . . . do you not think so . . . ?"

"Undoubtedly, Sir Percy."

"Then Boulogne it is . . . the ramparts, as you will, on the south side of the town."

"As you please," rejoined Chauvelin drily. "Shall we throw again?"

A murmur of merriment had accompanied this brief colloquy between the adversaries, and Blakeney's bland sallies were received with shouts of laughter. Now the dice rattled again and once more the two men threw.

"'Tis yours this time, Monsieur Chauvelin," said Blakeney, after a rapid glance at the dice. "See how evenly Chance favours us both. Mine, the choice of place . . . admirably done you'll confess. . . . Now yours the choice of time. I wait upon your pleasure, sir. . . . The southern ramparts at Boulogne—when?"

"The fourth day from this, sir, at the hour when the Cathedral bell chimes the evening Angelus," came Chauvelin's ready reply.

"Nay! but methought that your demmed government had abolished Cathedrals, and bells and chimes. . . . The people of France have now to go to hell their own way . . . for the way to heaven has been barred by the National Convention. . . . Is that not so? . . . Methought the Angelus was forbidden to be rung."

"Not at Boulogne, I think, Sir Percy," retorted Chauvelin drily, "and I'll pledge you my word that the evening Angelus shall be rung that night."

"At what hour is that, sir?"

"One hour after sundown."

"But why four days after this? Why not two or three?"

"I might have asked, why the southern ramparts, Sir Percy; why not the western? I chose the fourth day—does it not suit you?" asked Chauvelin ironically.

"Suit me! Why, sir, nothing could suit me better," rejoined Blakeney with his pleasant laugh. "Zounds! but I call it marvellous . . . demmed marvellous . . . I wonder now," he added blandly, "what made you think of the Angelus?"

Everyone laughed at this, a little irrelevantly perhaps.

"Ah!" continued Blakeney gaily, "I remember now. . . . Faith! to think that I was nigh forgetting that when last you and I met, sir, you had just taken or were about to take Holy Orders. . . . Ah! how well the thought of the Angelus fits in with your clerical garb. . . . I recollect that the latter was mightily becoming to you, sir . . ."

"Shall we proceed to settle the conditions of the fight, Sir Percy?" said Chauvelin, interrupting the flow of his antagonist's gibes, and trying to disguise his irritation beneath a mask of impassive reserve.

"The choice of weapons you mean," here interposed His Royal Highness, "but I thought that swords had already been decided on."

"Quite so, your Highness," assented Blakeney, "but there are various little matters in connection with this momentous encounter which are of vast importance. . . . Am I not right, Monsieur? . . . Gentlemen, I appeal to you. . . . Faith! one never knows . . . my engaging opponent here might desire that I should fight him in green socks, and I that he should wear a scarlet flower in his coat."

"The Scarlet Pimpernel, Sir Percy?"

"Why not, Monsieur? It would look so well in your button-hole, against the black of the clerical coat, which I understand you sometimes affect in France . . . and when it is withered and quite dead you would find that it would leave an overpowering odour in your nostrils, far stronger than that of incense."

There was general laughter after this. The hatred which every member of the French revolutionary government—including, of course, ex-Ambassador Chauvelin—bore to the national hero was well known.

"The conditions then, Sir Percy," said Chauvelin, without seeming to notice the taunt conveyed in Blakeney's last words. "Shall we throw again?"

"After you, sir," acquiesced Sir Percy.

For the third and last time the two opponents rattled the dice-box and threw. Chauvelin was now absolutely unmoved. These minor details quite failed to interest him. What mattered the conditions of the fight which was only intended as a bait with which to lure his enemy in the open? The hour and place were decided on and Sir Percy would not fail to come. Chauvelin knew enough of his opponent's boldly adventurous spirit not to feel in the least doubtful on that point. Even now, as he gazed with grudging admiration at the massive, well-knit figure of his arch-enemy, noted the thin nervy hands and square jaw, the low, broad forehead and deep-set, half-veiled eyes, he knew that in this matter wherein Percy Blakeney was obviously playing with his very life, the only emotion that really swayed him at this moment was his passionate love of adventure.

The ruling passion strong in death!

Yes! Sir Percy would be on the southern ramparts of Boulogne one hour after sunset on the day named, trusting, no doubt, in his usual marvellous good-fortune, his own presence of mind and his great physical and mental strength, to escape from the trap into which he was so ready to walk.

That remained beyond a doubt! Therefore what mattered details?

But even at this moment, Chauvelin had already resolved on one great thing: namely, that on that eventful day, nothing what-ever should be left to Chance; he would meet his cunning enemy not only with cunning, but also with power, and if the en-tire force of the republican army then available in the north of France had to be requisitioned for the purpose, the ramparts of Boulogne would be surrounded and no chance of escape left for the daring Scarlet Pimpernel.

His wave of meditation, however, was here abruptly stemmed by Blakeney's pleasant voice.

"Lud! Monsieur Chauvelin," he said, "I fear me your luck has deserted you. Chance, as you see, has turned to me once more."

"Then it is for you, Sir Percy," rejoined the Frenchman, "to name the conditions under which we are to fight."

"Ah! that is so, is it not, Monsieur?" quoth Sir Percy lightly. "By my faith! I'll not plague you with formalities. . . . We'll fight with our coats on if it be cold, in our shirtsleeves if it be sultry. . . . I'll not demand either green socks or scarlet ornaments. I'll even try and be serious for the space of two minutes, sir, and confine my whole attention—the product of my infinitesimal brain—to thinking out some pleasant detail for this duel, which might be acceptable to you. Thus, sir, the thought of weapons springs to my mind. . . . Swords you said, I think. Sir! I will e'en restrict my choice of conditions to that of the actual weapons with which we are to fight. . . . Ffoulkes, I pray you," he added, turning to his friend, "the pair of swords which lie across the top of my desk at this moment. . . .

"We'll not ask a menial to fetch them, eh, Monsieur?" he continued gaily, as Sir Andrew Ffoulkes at a sign from him had quickly left the room. "What need to bruit our pleasant quarrel abroad? You will like the weapons, sir, and you shall have your own choice from the pair. . . . You are a fine fencer, I feel sure . . . and you shall decide if a scratch or two or a more serious wound shall be sufficient to avenge Mademoiselle Candeille's wounded vanity."

Whilst he prattled so gaily on, there was dead silence among all those present. The Prince had his shrewd eyes steadily fixed upon him, obviously wondering what this seemingly irresponsible adventurer held at the back of his mind. There is no doubt that everyone felt oppressed, and that a strange murmur of anticipatory excitement went round the little room, when, a few seconds later, Sir Andrew Ffoulkes returned, with two sheathed swords in his hand.

Blakeney took them from his friend and placed them on the little table in front of ex-Ambassador Chauvelin. The spectators strained their necks to look at the two weapons. They were exactly similar one to the other: both encased in plain black leather sheaths, with steel ferrules polished to shine like silver; the handles too were of plain steel, with just the grip fashioned in a twisted basket pattern of the same highly-tempered metal.

"What think you of these weapons, Monsieur?" asked Blakeney, who was carelessly leaning against the back of a chair.

Chauvelin took up one of the two swords and slowly drew it from out its scabbard, carefully examining the brilliant, narrow steel blade as he did so.

"A little old-fashioned in style and make, Sir Percy," he said, closely imitating his opponent's easy demeanour, "a trifle heavier, perhaps, than we in France have been accustomed to lately, but, nevertheless, a beautifully tempered piece of steel."

"Of a truth there's not much the matter with the tempering, Monsieur," quoth Blakeney, "the blades were fashioned at Toledo just two hundred years ago."

"Ah! here I see an inscription," said Chauvelin, holding the sword close to his eyes, the better to see the minute letters engraved in the steel.

"The name of the original owner. I myself bought them—when I travelled in Italy—from one of his descendants."

"Lorenzo Giovanni Cenci," said Chauvelin, spelling the Italian names quite slowly.

"The greatest blackguard that ever trod this earth. You, no doubt, Monsieur, know his history better than we do. Rapine, theft, murder, nothing came amiss to Signor Lorenzo . . . neither the deadly drug in the cup nor the poisoned dagger."

He had spoken lightly, carelessly, with that same tone of easy banter which he had not forsaken throughout the evening, and the same drawly manner which was habitual to him. But at these last words of his, Chauvelin gave a visible start, and then abruptly replaced the sword—which he had been examining—upon the table.

He threw a quick, suspicious glance at Blakeney, who, leaning back against the chair and one knee resting on the cushioned seat, was idly toying with the other blade, the exact pair to the one which the ex-ambassador had so suddenly put down.

"Well, Monsieur," quoth Sir Percy after a slight pause, and meeting with a swift glance of lazy irony his opponent's fixed gaze. "Are you satisfied with the weapons? Which of the two shall be yours, and which mine?"

"Of a truth, Sir Percy . . ." murmured Chauvelin, still hesitating.

"Nay, Monsieur," interrupted Blakeney with pleasant bonhomie, "I know what you would say . . . of a truth, there is no choice between this pair of perfect twins: one is as exquisite as the other. . . . And yet you must take one and I the other . . . this or that, whichever you prefer. . . . You shall take it home with you to-night and practise thrusting at a haystack or at a bobbin, as you please. . . . The sword is yours to command until you have

used it against my unworthy person . . . yours until you bring it
out four days hence—on the southern ramparts of Boulogne,
when the cathedral bells chime the evening Angelus; then you
shall cross it against its faithless twin. . . . There, Monsieur—
they are of equal length . . . of equal strength and temper . . . a
perfect pair . . . Yet I pray you choose."

He took up both the swords in his hands and carefully bal-
ancing them by the extreme tip of their steel-bound scabbards,
he held them out towards the Frenchman. Chauvelin's eyes
were fixed upon him, and he from his towering height was looking down at the little sable-clad figure before him.

The Terrorist seemed uncertain what to do. Though he was
one of those men whom by the force of their intellect, the
strength of their enthusiasm, the power of their cruelty, had
built a new anarchical France, had overturned a throne and
murdered a king, yet now, face to face with this affected fop, this
lazy and debonnair adventurer, he hesitated—trying in vain to
read what was going on behind that low, smooth forehead or
within the depths of those lazy, blue eyes.

He would have given several years of his life at this moment
for one short glimpse into the innermost brain cells of this daring mind, to see the man start, quiver but for the fraction of a
second, betray himself by a tremor of the eyelid. What counterplan was lurking in Percy Blakeney's head, as he offered to his
opponent the two swords which had once belonged to Lorenzo
Cenci?

Did any thought of foul play, of dark and deadly poisonings
linger in the fastidious mind of this accomplished English gentleman?

Surely not!

Chauvelin tried to chide himself for such fears. It seemed
madness even to think of Italian poisons, of the Cencis or the
Borgias in the midst of this brilliantly lighted English drawing-
room.

But because he was above all a diplomatist, a fencer with
words and with looks, the envoy of France determined to know,
to probe and to read. He forced himself once more to careless

laughter and nonchalance of manner and schooled his lips to smile up with gentle irony at the good-humoured face of his arch-enemy.

He tapped one of the swords with his long pointed finger.

"Is this the one you choose, sir?" asked Blakeney.

"Nay! which do you advise, Sir Percy," replied Chauvelin lightly. "Which of those two blades think you is most like to hold after two hundred years the poison of the Cenci?"

But Blakeney neither started nor winced. He broke into a laugh, his own usual pleasant laugh, half shy and somewhat inane, then said in tones of lively astonishment:

"Zounds! sir, but you are full of surprises. . . . Faith! I never would have thought of that. . . . Marvellous, I call it . . . demmed marvellous. . . . What say you, gentlemen? . . . Your Royal Highness, what think you? . . . Is not my engaging friend here of a most original turn of mind. . . . Will you have this sword or that, Monsieur? . . . Nay, I must insist—else we shall weary our friends if we hesitate too long. . . . This one then, sir, since you have chosen it," he continued, as Chauvelin finally took one of the swords in his hand. "And now for a bowl of punch. . . . Nay, Monsieur, 'twas demmed smart what you said just now . . . I must insist on your joining us in a bowl. . . . Such wit as yours, Monsieur, must need whetting at times. . . . I pray you repeat that same sally again. . . ."

Then finally turning to the Prince and to his friends, he added:

"And after that bowl, gentlemen, shall we rejoin the ladies?"

CHAPTER XIII

REFLECTIONS

It seemed indeed as if the incident were finally closed, the chief actors in the drama having deliberately vacated the centre of the stage.

The little crowd which had stood in a compact mass round the table, began to break up into sundry small groups: laughter and desultory talk, checked for a moment by that oppressive sense of unknown danger, which had weighed on the spirits of those present, once more became general. Blakeney's light-heartedness had put everyone into good-humour; since he evidently did not look upon the challenge as a matter of serious moment, why then, no one else had any cause for anxiety, and the younger men were right glad to join in that bowl of punch which their genial host had offered with so merry a grace.

Lacqueys appeared, throwing open the doors. From a distance the sound of dance music once more broke upon the ear.

A few of the men only remained silent, deliberately holding aloof from the renewed mirthfulness. Foremost amongst these was His Royal Highness, who was looking distinctly troubled, and who had taken Sir Percy by the arm, and was talking to him with obvious earnestness. Lord Anthony Dewhurst and Lord Hastings were holding converse in a secluded corner of the room, whilst Sir Andrew Ffoulkes, as being the host's most intimate friend, felt it incumbent on him to say a few words to ex-Ambassador Chauvelin.

The latter was desirous of effecting a retreat. Blakeney's invitation to join in the friendly bowl of punch could not be taken seriously, and the Terrorist wanted to be alone, in order to think out the events of the past hour.

A lacquey waited on him, took the momentous sword from his hand, found his hat and cloak and called his coach for him: Chauvelin having taken formal leave of his host and acquaintances, quickly worked his way to the staircase and hall, through the less frequented apartments.

He sincerely wished to avoid meeting Lady Blakeney face to face. Not that the slightest twinge of remorse disturbed his mind, but he feared some impulsive action on her part, which indirectly might interfere with his future plans. Fortunately no one took much heed of the darkly-clad, insignificant little figure that glided so swiftly by, obviously determined to escape attention.

In the hall he found Demoiselle Candeille waiting for him. She, too, had evidently been desirous of leaving Blakeney Manor as soon as possible. He saw her to her chaise; then escorted her as far as her lodgings, which were close by: there were still one or two things which he wished to discuss with her, one or two final instructions which he desired to give.

On the whole, he was satisfied with his evening's work: the young actress had well supported him, and had played her part so far with marvellous sang-froid and skill. Sir Percy, whether willingly or blindly, had seemed only too ready to walk into the trap which was being set for him.

This fact alone disturbed Chauvelin not a little, and as half an hour or so later, having taken final leave of his ally, he sat alone in the coach, which was conveying him back to town, the sword of Lorenzo Cenci close to his hand, he pondered very seriously over it.

That the adventurous Scarlet Pimpernel should have guessed all along, that sooner or later the French Revolutionary Government—whom he had defrauded of some of its most important victims,—would desire to be even with him, and to bring him to the scaffold, was not to be wondered at. But that he should be so blind as to imagine that Chauvelin's challenge was anything else but a lure to induce him to go to France, could not possibly be supposed. So bold an adventurer, so keen an intriguer was sure to have scented the trap immediately, and if he appeared ready to fall into it, it was because there had already sprung up in his resourceful mind some bold coup or subtle counterplan, with which he hoped to gratify his own passionate love of sport, whilst once more bringing his enemies to discomfiture and humiliation.

Undoubtedly Sir Percy Blakeney, as an accomplished gentleman of the period, could not very well under the circumstances which had been so carefully stage-managed and arranged by Chauvelin, refuse the latter's challenge to fight him on the other side of the Channel. Any hesitation on the part of the leader of that daring Scarlet Pimpernel League would have covered him with a faint suspicion of pusillanimity, and a subtle breath of ridicule, and in a moment the prestige of the unknown and elusive hero would have vanished forever.

But apart from the necessity of the fight, Blakeney seemed to enter into the spirit of the plot directed against his own life, with such light-hearted merriment, such zest and joy, that Chauvelin could not help but be convinced that the capture of the Scarlet Pimpernel at Boulogne or elsewhere would not prove quite so easy a matter as he had at first anticipated.

That same night he wrote a long and circumstantial letter to his colleague, Citizen Robespierre, shifting thereby, as it were, some of the responsibility of coming events from his own shoulders on to the executive of the Committee of Public Safety.

"I guarantee to you, Citizen Robespierre," he wrote, "and to the members of the Revolutionary Government who have entrusted me with the delicate mission, that four days from this date at one hour after sunset, the man who goes by the mysterious name of the Scarlet Pimpernel, will be on the ramparts of Boulogne on the south side of the town. I have done what has been asked of me. On that day and at that hour, I shall have brought the enemy of the Revolution, the intriguer against the policy of the Republic, within the power of the government which he has flouted and outraged. Now look to it, citizens all, that the fruits of my diplomacy and of my skill be not lost to

France again. The man will be there at my bidding, 'tis for you to see that he does not escape this time."

This letter he sent by the special courier which the National Convention had placed at his disposal in case of emergency. Having sealed it and entrusted it to the man, Chauvelin felt at peace with the world and with himself. Although he was not so sure of success as he would have wished, he yet could not see *how* failure could possibly come about: and the only regret which he felt to-night, when he finally in the early dawn sought a few hours' troubled rest, was that that momentous fourth day was still so very far distant.

CHAPTER XIV

The Ruling Passion

In the meanwhile silence had fallen over the beautiful old manorial house. One by one the guests had departed, leaving that peaceful sense of complete calm and isolation which follows the noisy chatter of any great throng bent chiefly on enjoyment.

The evening had been universally acknowledged to have been brilliantly successful. True, the much talked of French artiste had not sung the promised ditties, but in the midst of the whirl and excitement of dances, of the inspiriting tunes of the string band, the elaborate supper and recherché wines, no one had paid much heed to this change in the programme of entertainments.

And everyone had agreed that never had Lady Blakeney looked more radiantly beautiful than on this night. She seemed absolutely indefatigable; a perfect hostess, full of charming little attentions towards every one, although more than ordinarily absorbed by her duties towards her many royal guests.

The dramatic incidents which had taken place in the small boudoir had not been much bruited abroad. It was always considered bad form in those courtly days to discuss men's quarrels before ladies, and in this instance, those who were present when it all occurred instinctively felt that their discretion would be appreciated in high circles, and held their tongues accordingly.

Thus the brilliant evening was brought to a happy conclusion without a single cloud to mar the enjoyment of the guests. Marguerite performed a veritable miracle of fortitude, forcing her very smiles to seem natural and gay, chatting pleasantly, even wittily, upon every known fashionable topic of the day, laughing merrily the while her poor, aching heart was filled with unspeakable misery.

Now, when everybody had gone, when the last of her guests had bobbed before her the prescribed curtsey, to which she had invariably responded with the same air of easy self-possession, now at last she felt free to give rein to her thoughts, to indulge in the luxury of looking her own anxiety straight in the face and to let the tension of her nerves relax.

Sir Andrew Ffoulkes had been the last to leave and Percy had strolled out with him as far as the garden gate, for Lady Ffoulkes had left in her chaise some time ago, and Sir Andrew meant to walk to his home, not many yards distant from Blakeney Manor.

In spite of herself Marguerite felt her heartstrings tighten as she thought of this young couple so lately wedded. People smiled a little when Sir Andrew Ffoulkes' name was mentioned, some called him effeminate, others uxorious, his fond attachment for his pretty little wife was thought to pass the bounds of decorum. There was no doubt that since his marriage the young man had greatly changed. His love of sport and adventure seemed to have died out completely, yielding evidently to the great, more overpowering love, that for his young wife.

Suzanne was nervous for her husband's safety. She had sufficient influence over him to keep him at home, when other members of the brave little League of The Scarlet Pimpernel followed their leader with mad zest, on some bold adventure.

Marguerite too at first had smiled in kindly derision when Suzanne Ffoulkes, her large eyes filled with tears, had used her wiles to keep Sir Andrew tied to her own dainty apronstrings. But somehow, lately, with that gentle contempt which she felt for the weaker man, there had mingled a half-acknowledged sense of envy.

How different 'twixt her and her husband.

Percy loved her truly and with a depth of passion proportionate to his own curious dual personality: it were sacrilege, almost, to doubt the intensity of his love. But nevertheless she had at all times a feeling as if he were holding himself and his emotions in check, as if his love, as if she, Marguerite, his wife, were but secondary matters in his life; as if her anxieties, her sorrow when he left her, her fears for his safety were but small episodes in the great book of life which he had planned out and conceived for himself.

Then she would hate herself for such thoughts: they seemed like doubts of him. Did any man ever love a woman, she asked herself, as Percy loved her? He was difficult to understand, and perhaps—oh! that was an awful "perhaps"—perhaps there lurked somewhere in his mind a slight mistrust of her. She had betrayed him once! unwittingly 'tis true! did he fear she might do so again?

And to-night after her guests had gone she threw open the great windows that gave on the beautiful terrace, with its marble steps leading down to the cool river beyond. Everything now seemed so peaceful and still; the scent of the heliotrope made the midnight air swoon with its intoxicating fragrance: the rhythmic murmur of the waters came gently echoing from below, and from far away there came the melancholy cry of a night-bird on the prowl.

That cry made Marguerite shudder: her thoughts flew back to the episodes of this night and to Chauvelin, the dark bird of prey with his mysterious death-dealing plans, his subtle intrigues which all tended towards the destruction of one man: his enemy, the husband whom Marguerite loved.

Oh! how she hated these wild adventures which took Percy away from her side. Is not a woman who loves—be it husband or child—the most truly selfish, the most cruelly callous creature in the world, there, where the safety and the well-being of the loved one is in direct conflict with the safety and well-being of others.

She would right gladly have closed her eyes to every horror perpetrated in France, she would not have known what went on in Paris, she wanted her husband! And yet month after month, with but short intervals, she saw him risk that precious life of his, which was the very essence of her own soul, for others! for others! always for others!

And she! she! Marguerite, his wife, was powerless to hold him back! powerless to keep him beside her, when that mad fit of passion seized him to go on one of those wild quests, wherefrom she always feared he could not return alive: and this, although she might use every noble artifice, every tender wile of which a loving and beautiful wife is capable.

At times like those her own proud heart was filled with hatred and with envy towards everything that took him away from her: and to-night all these passionate feelings which she felt were quite unworthy of her and of him seemed to surge within her soul more tumultuously than ever. She was longing to throw herself in his arms, to pour out into his loving ear all that she suffered, in fear and anxiety, and to make one more appeal to his tenderness and to that passion which had so often made him forget the world at her feet.

And so instinctively she walked along the terrace towards that more secluded part of the garden just above the river bank, where she had so oft wandered hand in hand with him, in the honeymoon of their love. There great clumps of old-fashioned cabbage roses grew in untidy splendour, and belated lilies sent intoxicating odours into the air, whilst the heavy masses of Egyptian and Michaelmas daisies looked like ghostly constellations in the gloom.

She thought Percy must soon be coming this way. Though it was so late, she knew that he would not go to bed. After the events of the night, his ruling passion, strong in death, would be holding him in its thrall.

She too felt wide awake and unconscious of fatigue; when she reached the secluded path beside the river, she peered eagerly up and down, and listened for a sound.

Presently it seemed to her that above the gentle clapper of the waters she could hear a rustle and the scrunching of the fine gravel under carefully measured footsteps. She waited a while. The footsteps seemed to draw nearer, and soon, although the starlit night was very dark, she perceived a cloaked and hooded figure approaching cautiously towards her.

"Who goes there?" she called suddenly.

The figure paused: then came rapidly forward, and a voice said timidly:

"Ah! Lady Blakeney!"

"Who are you?" asked Marguerite peremptorily.

"It is I . . . Désirée Candeille," replied the midnight prowler.

"Demoiselle Candeille!" ejaculated Marguerite, wholly taken by surprise. "What are you doing here? alone? and at this hour?"

"Sh-sh-sh . . ." whispered Candeille eagerly, as she approached quite close to Marguerite and drew her hood still lower over her eyes. "I am all alone . . . I wanted to see someone—you if possible, Lady Blakeney . . . for I could not rest . . . I wanted to know what had happened."

"What had happened? When? I don't understand."

"What happened between Citizen Chauvelin and your husband?" asked Candeille.

"What is that to you?" replied Marguerite haughtily.

"I pray you do not misunderstand me . . ." pleaded Candeille eagerly. "I know my presence in your house . . . the quarrel which I provoked must have filled your heart with hatred and suspicion towards me . . . but oh! how can I persuade you? . . . I acted unwillingly . . . will you not believe me? . . . I was that man's tool . . . and . . . Oh God!" she added with sudden, wild vehemence, "if only you could know what tyranny that accursed government of France exercises over poor helpless women or men who happen to have fallen within reach of its relentless clutches . . ."

Her voice broke down in a sob. Marguerite hardly knew what to say or think. She had always mistrusted this woman with her theatrical ways and stagy airs, from the very first moment she saw her in the tent on the green: and she did not wish to run counter against her instinct, in anything pertaining to the present crisis. And yet in spite of her mistrust the actress' vehement words found an echo in the depths of her own heart. How well she knew that tyranny of which Candeille spoke with such bitterness! Had she not suffered from it, endured terrible sorrow and humiliation, when under the ban of that same appalling

tyranny she had betrayed the identity—then unknown to her—
of the Scarlet Pimpernel?

Therefore when Candeille paused after those last excited
words, she said with more gentleness than she had shown hitherto, though still quite coldly:

"But you have not yet told me why you came back here to-
night? If Citizen Chauvelin was your taskmaster, then you must
know all that has occurred."

"I had a vague hope that I might see you."

"For what purpose?"

"To warn you if I could."

"I need no warning."

"Or are too proud to take one. . . . Do you know, Lady
Blakeney, that Citizen Chauvelin has a personal hatred against
your husband?"

"How do you know that?" asked Marguerite, with her suspi-
cions once more on the qui-vive. She could not understand
Candeille's attitude. This midnight visit, the vehemence of her
language, the strange mixture of knowledge and ignorance
which she displayed. What did this woman know of Chauvelin's
secret plans? Was she his open ally, or his helpless tool? And was
she even now playing a part taught her or commanded her by
that prince of intriguers?

Candeille, however, seemed quite unaware of the spirit of an-
tagonism and mistrust which Marguerite took but little pains
now to disguise. She clasped her hands together, and her voice
shook with the earnestness of her entreaty.

"Oh!" she said eagerly, "have I not seen that look of hatred in
Chauvelin's cruel eyes? . . . He hates your husband, I tell you.
. . . Why I know not . . . but he hates him . . . and means that
great harm shall come to Sir Percy through this absurd duel. . . .
Oh! Lady Blakeney, do not let him go . . . I entreat you, do not
let him go!"

But Marguerite proudly drew back a step or two, away from
the reach of those hands, stretched out towards her in such vehement appeal.

"You are overwrought, Mademoiselle," she said coldly. "Believe me, I have no need either of your entreaties or of your warning. . . . I should like you to think that I have no wish to be ungrateful . . . that I appreciate any kind thought you may have harboured for me in your mind. . . . But beyond that . . . please forgive me if I say it somewhat crudely—I do not feel that the matter concerns you in the least. . . . The hour is late," she added more gently, as if desiring to attenuate the harshness of her last words. "Shall I send my maid to escort you home? She is devoted and discreet . . ."

"Nay!" retorted the other in tones of quiet sadness, "there is no need of discretion . . . I am not ashamed of my visit to you to-night. . . . You are very proud, and for your sake I will pray to God that sorrow and humiliation may not come to you, as I feared. . . . We are never likely to meet again, Lady Blakeney . . . you will not wish it, and I shall have passed out of your life as swiftly as I had entered into it. . . . But there was another thought lurking in my mind when I came to-night. . . . In case Sir Percy goes to France . . . the duel is to take place in or near Boulogne . . . this much I do know . . . would you not wish to go with him?"

"Truly, Mademoiselle, I must repeat to you . . ."

"That 'tis no concern of mine . . . I know . . . I own that. . . . But, you see when I came back here to-night in the silence and the darkness—I had not guessed that you would be so proud . . . I thought that I, a woman, would know how to touch your womanly heart. . . . I was clumsy, I suppose. . . . I made so sure that you would wish to go with your husband, in case . . . in case he insisted on running his head into the noose, which I feel sure Chauvelin has prepared for him. . . . I myself start for France shortly. Citizen Chauvelin has provided me with the necessary passport for myself and my maid, who was to have accompanied me. . . . Then, just now, when I was all alone . . . and thought over all the mischief which that fiend had forced me to do for him, it seemed to me that perhaps . . ."

She broke off abruptly, and tried to read the other woman's face in the gloom. But Marguerite, who was taller than the

Frenchwoman, was standing, very stiff and erect, giving the young actress neither discouragement nor confidence. She did not interrupt Candeille's long and voluble explanation: vaguely she wondered what it was all about, and even now when the Frenchwoman paused, Marguerite said nothing, but watched her quietly as she took a folded paper from the capacious pocket of her cloak and then held it out with a look of timidity towards Lady Blakeney.

"My maid need not come with me," said Désirée Candeille humbly. "I would far rather travel alone . . . this is her passport and . . . Oh! you need not take it out of my hand," she added in tones of bitter self-deprecation, as Marguerite made no sign of taking the paper from her. "See! I will leave it here among the roses! . . . You mistrust me now . . . it is only natural . . . presently, perhaps, calmer reflection will come . . . you will see that my purpose now is selfless . . . that I only wish to serve you and him."

She stooped and placed the folded paper in the midst of a great clump of centifolium roses, and then without another word she turned and went her way. For a few moments, whilst Marguerite still stood there, puzzled and vaguely moved, she could hear the gentle frou-frou of the other woman's skirts against the soft sand of the path, and then a long-drawn sigh that sounded like a sob.

Then all was still again. The gentle midnight breeze caressed the tops of the ancient oaks and elms behind her, drawing murmurs from their dying leaves like unto the whisperings of ghosts.

Marguerite shuddered with a slight sense of cold. Before her, amongst the dark clump of leaves and the roses, invisible in the gloom, there fluttered with a curious, melancholy flapping, the folded paper placed there by Candeille. She watched it for awhile, as, disturbed by the wind, it seemed ready to take its flight towards the river. Anon it fell to the ground, and Marguerite with sudden overpowering impulse, stooped and picked it up. Then clutching it nervously in her hand, she walked rapidly back towards the house.

CHAPTER XV

Farewell

As she neared the terrace, she became conscious of several forms moving about at the foot of the steps, some few feet below where she was standing. Soon she saw the glimmer of lanthorns, heard whispering voices, and the lapping of the water against the side of a boat.

Anon a figure, laden with cloaks and sundry packages, passed down the steps close beside her. Even in the darkness Marguerite recognized Benyon, her husband's confidential valet. Without a moment's hesitation, she flew along the terrace towards the wing of the house occupied by Sir Percy. She had not gone far before she discerned his tall figure walking leisurely along the path which here skirted part of the house.

He had on his large caped coat, which was thrown open in front, displaying a grey travelling suit of fine cloth; his hands were as usual buried in the pockets of his breeches, and on his head he wore the folding chapeau-bras which he habitually affected.

Before she had time to think, or to realize that he was going, before she could utter one single word, she was in his arms, clinging to him with passionate intensity, trying in the gloom to catch every expression of his eyes, every quiver of the face now bent down so close to her.

"Percy, you cannot go . . . you cannot go! . . ." she pleaded.

She had felt his strong arms closing round her, his lips seeking hers, her eyes, her hair, her clinging hands, which dragged at his shoulders in a wild agony of despair.

"If you really loved me, Percy," she murmured, "you would not go, you would not go . . ."

He would not trust himself to speak; it well-nigh seemed as if his sinews cracked with the violent effort at self-control. Oh! how she loved him, when she felt in him the passionate lover, the wild, untamed creature that he was at heart, on whom the frigid courtliness of manner sat but as a thin veneer. This was his own real personality, and there was little now of the elegant and accomplished gentleman of fashion, schooled to hold every emotion in check, to hide every thought, every desire save that for amusement or for display.

She—feeling her power and his weakness now—gave herself wholly to his embrace, not grudging one single, passionate caress, yielding her lips to him, the while she murmured:

"You cannot go . . . you cannot . . . why should you go? . . . It is madness to leave me . . . I cannot let you go . . ."

Her arms clung tenderly round him, her voice was warm and faintly shaken with suppressed tears, and as he wildly murmured: "Don't! for pity's sake!" she almost felt that her love would be triumphant.

"For pity's sake, I'll go on pleading, Percy!" she whispered. "Oh! my love, my dear! do not leave me! . . . we have scarce had time to savour our happiness . . . we have such arrears of joy to make up. . . . Do not go, Percy . . . there's so much I want to say to you. . . . Nay! you shall not! you shall not!" she added with sudden vehemence. "Look me straight in the eyes, my dear, and tell me if you can leave now?"

He did not reply, but, almost roughly, he placed his hand over her tear-dimmed eyes, which were turned up to his, in an agony of tender appeal. Thus he blindfolded her with that wild caress. She should not see—no, not even she!—that for the space of a few seconds stern manhood was well-nigh vanquished by the magic of her love.

All that was most human in him, all that was weak in this strong and untamed nature, cried aloud for peace and luxury and idleness: for long summer afternoons spent in lazy content, for the companionship of horses and dogs and of flowers, with no thought or cares save those for the next evening's gavotte, no graver occupation save that of sitting at *her* feet.

And during these few seconds, whilst his hand lay across her eyes, the lazy, idle fop of fashionable London was fighting a hand-to-hand fight with the bold leader of a band of adventurers: and his own passionate love for his wife ranged itself with fervent intensity on the side of his weaker self. Forgotten were the horrors of the guillotine, the calls of the innocent, the appeal of the helpless; forgotten the daring adventures, the excitements, the hair's-breadth escapes; for those few seconds, heavenly in themselves, he only remembered her—his wife—her beauty and her tender appeal to him.

She would have pleaded again, for she felt that she was winning in this fight: her instinct—that unerring instinct of the woman who loves and feels herself beloved—told her that for the space of an infinitesimal fraction of time, his iron will was inclined to bend; but he checked her pleading with a kiss.

Then there came a change.

Like a gigantic wave carried inwards by the tide, his turbulent emotion seemed suddenly to shatter itself against a rock of self-control. Was it a call from the boatmen below? a distant scrunching of feet upon the gravel?—who knows, perhaps only a sigh in the midnight air, a ghostly summons from the land of dreams that recalled him to himself.

Even as Marguerite was still clinging to him, with the ardent fervour of her own passion, she felt the rigid tension of his arms relax, the power of his embrace weaken, the wild love-light become dim in his eyes.

He kissed her fondly, tenderly, and with infinite gentleness smoothed away the little damp curls from her brow. There was a wistfulness now in his caress, and in his kiss there was the finality of a long farewell.

"'Tis time I went," he said, "or we shall miss the tide."

These were the first coherent words he had spoken since first she had met him here in this lonely part of the garden, and his voice was perfectly steady, conventional and cold. An icy pang shot through Marguerite's heart. It was as if she had been abruptly wakened from a beautiful dream.

"You are not going, Percy!" she murmured, and her own voice now sounded hollow and forced. "Oh! if you loved me you would not go!"

"If I loved you!"

Nay! in this at least there was no dream! no coldness in his voice when he repeated those words with such a sigh of tenderness, such a world of longing, that the bitterness of her great pain vanished, giving place to tears. He took her hand in his. The passion was momentarily conquered, forced within his innermost soul, by his own alter ego, that second personality in him, the cold-blooded and coolly-calculating adventurer who juggled with his life and tossed it recklessly upon the sea of chance 'twixt a doggerel and a smile. But the tender love lingered on, fighting the enemy a while longer, the wistful desire was there for her kiss, the tired longing for the exquisite repose of her embrace.

He took her hand in his, and bent his lips to it, and with the warmth of his kiss upon it, she felt a moisture like a tear.

"I must go, dear," he said, after a little while.

"Why? Why?" she repeated obstinately. "Am I nothing then? Is my life of no account? My sorrows? My fears? My misery? Oh!" she added with vehement bitterness, "why should it always be others? What are others to you and to me, Percy? . . . Are we not happy here? . . . Have you not fulfilled to its uttermost that self-imposed duty to people who can be nothing to us? . . . Is not your life ten thousand times more precious to me than the lives of ten thousand others?"

Even through the darkness, and because his face was so close to hers, she could see a quaint little smile playing round the corners of his mouth.

"Nay, m'dear," he said gently, "'tis not ten thousand lives that call to me to-day . . . only one at best. . . . Don't you hate to think of that poor little old curé sitting in the midst of his ruined pride and hopes: the jewels so confidently entrusted to his care, stolen from him, he waiting, perhaps, in his little presbytery for the day when those brutes will march him to prison and to death. . . .

Nay! I think a little sea voyage and English country air would suit the Abbé Foucquet, m'dear, and I only mean to ask him to cross the Channel with me! . . ."

"Percy!" she pleaded.

"Oh! I know! I know!" he rejoined with that short deprecatory sigh of his, which seemed always to close any discussion between them on that point, "you are thinking of that absurd duel . . ." He laughed lightly, good-humouredly, and his eyes gleamed with merriment.

"La, m'dear!" he said gaily, "will you not reflect a moment? Could I refuse the challenge before His Royal Highness and the ladies? I couldn't. . . . Faith! that was it. . . . Just a case of couldn't. . . . Fate did it all . . . the quarrel . . . my interference . . . the challenge. . . . *He* had planned it all of course. . . . Let us own that he is a brave man, seeing that he and I are not even yet, for that beating he gave me on the Calais cliffs."

"Yes! he has planned it all," she retorted vehemently. "The quarrel to-night, your journey to France, your meeting with him face to face at a given hour and place where he can most readily, most easily close the death-trap upon you."

This time he broke into a laugh. A good, hearty laugh, full of the joy of living, of the madness and intoxication of a bold adventure, a laugh that had not one particle of anxiety or of tremor in it.

"Nay! m'dear!" he said, "but your ladyship is astonishing. . . . Close a death-trap upon your humble servant? . . . Nay! the governing citizens of France will have to be very active and mighty wide-awake ere they succeed in stealing a march on me. . . . Zounds! but we'll give them an exciting chase this time. . . . Nay! little woman, do not fear!" he said with sudden infinite gentleness, "those demmed murderers have not got me yet."

Oh! how often she had fought with him thus: with him, the adventurer, the part of his dual nature that was her bitter enemy, and which took him, the lover, away from her side. She knew so well the finality of it all, the amazing hold which that unconquerable desire for these mad adventures had upon him. Impulsive, ardent as she was, Marguerite felt in her very soul an overwhelming fury against herself for her own weakness, her own powerlessness in the face of that which forever threatened to ruin her life and her happiness.

Yes! and his also! for he loved her! he loved her! he loved her! the thought went on hammering in her mind, for she knew of its great truth. He loved her and went away! And she, poor, puny weakling, was unable to hold him back; the tendrils which fastened his soul to hers were not so tenacious as those which made him cling to suffering humanity, over there in France, where men and women were in fear of death and torture, and looked upon the elusive and mysterious Scarlet Pimpernel as a heaven-born hero sent to save them from their doom. To them at these times his very heartstrings seemed to turn with unconquerable force, and when, with all the ardour of her own passion, she tried to play upon the cords of his love for her, he could not respond, for they—the strangers—had the stronger claim.

And yet through it all she knew that this love of humanity, this mad desire to serve and to help, in no way detracted from his love for her. Nay, it intensified it, made it purer and better, adding to the joy of perfect intercourse the poetic and subtle fragrance of ever-recurring pain.

But now at last she felt weary of the fight: her heart was aching, bruised and sore. An infinite fatigue seemed to weigh like lead upon her very soul. This seemed so different to any other parting, that had perforce been during the past year. The presence of Chauvelin in her house, the obvious planning of this departure for France, had filled her with a foreboding, nay, almost a certitude of a gigantic and deadly cataclysm.

Her senses began to reel; she seemed not to see anything very distinctly: even the loved form took on a strange and ghostlike shape. He now looked preternaturally tall, and there was a mist between her and him.

She thought that he spoke to her again, but she was not quite sure, for his voice sounded like some weird and mysterious echo. A bosquet of climbing heliotrope close by threw a fragrance into the evening air, which turned her giddy with its overpowering sweetness.

She closed her eyes, for she felt as if she must die, if she held them open any longer; and as she closed them it seemed to her as if he folded her in one last, long, heavenly embrace.

He felt her graceful figure swaying in his arms like a tall and slender lily bending to the wind. He saw that she was but half-conscious, and thanked heaven for this kindly solace to this heart-breaking farewell.

There was a sloping, mossy bank close by, there where the marble terrace yielded to the encroaching shrubbery: a tangle of pale pink monthly roses made a bower overhead. She was just sufficiently conscious to enable him to lead her to this soft green couch. There he laid her amongst the roses, kissed the dear, tired eyes, her hands, her lips, her tiny feet, and went.

CHAPTER XVI

THE PASSPORT

The rhythmic clapper of oars roused Marguerite from this trance-like swoon.

In a moment she was on her feet, all her fatigue gone, her numbness of soul and body vanished as in a flash. She was fully conscious now! conscious that he had gone! that according to every probability under heaven and every machination concocted in hell, he would never return from France alive, and that she had failed to hear the last words which he spoke to her, had failed to glean his last look or to savour his final kiss.

Though the night was starlit and balmy it was singularly dark, and vainly did Marguerite strain her eyes to catch sight of that boat which was bearing him away so swiftly now: she strained her ears, vaguely hoping to catch one last, lingering echo of his voice. But all was silence, save that monotonous clapper, which seemed to beat against her heart like a rhythmic knell of death.

She could hear the oars distinctly: there were six or eight, she thought: certainly no fewer. Eight oarsmen probably, which meant the larger boat, and undoubtedly the longer journey . . . not to London only with a view to posting to Dover, but to Tilbury Fort, where the "Day Dream" would be in readiness to start with a favourable tide.

Thought was returning to her, slowly and coherently: the pain of the last farewell was still there, bruising her very senses with its dull and heavy weight, but it had become numb and dead, leaving her, herself, her heart and soul, stunned and apathetic, whilst her brain was gradually resuming its activity.

And the more she thought it over, the more certain she grew that her husband was going as far as Tilbury by river and would embark on the "Day Dream" there. Of course he would go to Boulogne at once. The duel was to take place there, Candeille had told her that . . . adding that she thought she, Marguerite, would wish to go with him.

To go with him!

Heavens above! was not that the only real, tangible thought in that whirling chaos which was raging in her mind?

To go with him! Surely there must be some means of reaching him yet! Fate, Nature, God Himself would never permit so monstrous a thing as this: that she should be parted from her husband, now when his life was not only in danger, but forfeited already . . . lost . . . a precious thing all but gone from this world.

Percy was going to Boulogne . . . she must go too. By posting at once to Dover, she could get the tidal boat on the morrow and reach the French coast quite as soon as the "Day Dream." Once at Boulogne, she would have no difficulty in finding her husband, of that she felt sure. She would have but to dog Chauvelin's footsteps, find out something of his plans, of the orders he gave to troops or to spies,—oh! she would find him! of that she was never for a moment in doubt!

How well she remembered her journey to Calais just a year ago, in company with Sir Andrew Ffoulkes! Chance had favoured her then, had enabled her to be of service to her husband if only by distracting Chauvelin's attention for awhile to herself. Heaven knows! she had but little hope of being of use to him now: an aching sense was in her that fate had at last been too strong! that the daring adventurer had staked once too often, had cast the die and had lost.

In the bosom of her dress she felt the sharp edge of the paper left for her by Désirée Candeille among the roses in the park. She had picked it up almost mechanically then, and tucked it away, hardly heeding what she was doing. Whatever the motive of the French actress had been in placing the passport at her disposal, Marguerite blessed her in her heart for it. To the woman she had mistrusted, she would owe the last supreme happiness of her life.

Her resolution never once wavered. Percy would not take her with him: that was understandable. She could neither expect it nor think it. But she, on the other hand, could not stay in England, at Blakeney Manor, whilst any day, any hour, the death-trap set by Chauvelin for the Scarlet Pimpernel might be closing upon the man whom she worshipped. She would go mad if she stayed. As there could be no chance of escape for Percy now, as he had agreed to meet his deadly enemy face to face at a given place, and a given hour, she could not be a hindrance to him: and she knew enough subterfuges, enough machinations and disguises by now, to escape Chauvelin's observation, unless . . . unless Percy wanted her, and then she would be there.

No! she could not be a hindrance. She had a passport in her pocket, everything en règle, nobody could harm her, and she could come and go as she pleased. There were plenty of swift horses in the stables, plenty of devoted servants to do her bidding quickly and discreetly: moreover, at moments like these, conventionalities and the possible conjectures and surmises of others became of infinitesimally small importance. The household of Blakeney Manor were accustomed to the master's sudden journeys and absences of several days, presumably on some shooting or other sporting expeditions, with no one in attendance on him, save Benyon, his favourite valet. These passed without any comments now! Bah! let everyone marvel for once at her ladyship's sudden desire to go to Dover, and let it all be a nine days' wonder; she certainly did not care. Skirting the house, she reached the stables beyond. One or two men were still astir. To these she gave the necessary orders for her coach and four, then she found her way back to the house.

Walking along the corridor, she went past the room occupied by Juliette de Marny. For a moment she hesitated, then she turned and knocked at the door.

Juliette was not yet in bed, for she went to the door herself and opened it. Obviously she had been quite unable to rest, her

hair was falling loosely over her shoulders, and there was a look
of grave anxiety on her young face.

"Juliette," said Marguerite in a hurried whisper, the moment
she had closed the door behind her and she and the young girl
were alone, "I am going to France to be near my husband. He
has gone to meet that fiend in a duel which is nothing but a trap,
set to capture him, and lead him to his death. I want you to be
of help to me, here in my house, in my absence."

"I would give my life for you, Lady Blakeney." said Juliette
simply, "is it not *his* since he saved it?"

"It is only a little presence of mind, a little coolness and patience, which I will ask of you, dear," said Marguerite. "You of
course know who your rescuer was, therefore you will understand my fears. Until to-night, I had vague doubts as to how
much Chauvelin really knew, but now these doubts have naturally vanished. He and the French Revolutionary Government
know that the Scarlet Pimpernel and Percy Blakeney are one
and the same. The whole scene to-night was prearranged: you
and I and all the spectators, and that woman Candeille—we
were all puppets piping to that devil's tune. The duel, too, was
prearranged! . . . that woman wearing your mother's jewels! . . .
Had you not provoked her, a quarrel between her and me, or
one of my guests would have been forced somehow . . . I wanted
to tell you this, lest you should fret, and think that you were in
any way responsible for what has happened. . . . You were not.
. . . He had arranged it all. . . . You were only the tool . . . just as
I was. . . . You must understand and believe that. . . . Percy
would hate to think that you felt yourself to blame . . . you are
not that, in any way. . . . The challenge was bound to come. . . .
Chauvelin had arranged that it should come, and if you had
failed him as a tool, he soon would have found another! Do you
believe that?"

"I believe that you are an angel of goodness, Lady Blakeney,"
replied Juliette, struggling with her tears, "and that you are the
only woman in the world worthy to be his wife."

"But," insisted Marguerite firmly, as the young girl took her
cold hand in her own, and gently fondling it, covered it with

grateful kisses, "but if . . . if anything happens . . . anon . . . you will believe firmly that you were in no way responsible? . . . that you were innocent . . . and merely a blind tool? . . ."

"God bless you for that!"

"You will believe it?"

"I will."

"And now for my request," rejoined Lady Blakeney in a more quiet, more matter-of-fact tone of voice. "You must represent me, here, when I am gone: explain as casually and as naturally as you can, that I have gone to join my husband on his yacht for a few days. Lucie, my maid, is devoted and a tower of secrecy; she will stand between you and the rest of the household, in concocting some plausible story. To every friend who calls, to anyone of our world whom you may meet, you must tell the same tale, and if you note an air of incredulity in anyone, if you hear whispers of there being some mystery, well! let the world wag its busy tongue—I care less than naught: it will soon tire of me and my doings, and having torn my reputation to shreds will quickly leave me in peace. But to Sir Andrew Ffoulkes," she added earnestly, "tell the whole truth from me. He will understand and do as he thinks right."

"I will do all you ask, Lady Blakeney, and am proud to think that I shall be serving you, even in so humble and easy a capacity. When do you start?"

"At once. Good-bye, Juliette."

She bent down to the young girl and kissed her tenderly on the forehead, then she glided out of the room as rapidly as she had come. Juliette, of course, did not try to detain her, or to force her help of companionship on her when obviously she would wish to be alone.

Marguerite quickly reached her room. Her maid Lucie was already waiting for her. Devoted and silent as she was, one glance at her mistress' face told her that trouble—grave and imminent—had reached Blakeney Manor.

Marguerite, whilst Lucie undressed her, took up the passport and carefully perused the personal description of one, Céline Dumont, maid to Citizeness Désirée Candeille, which was given therein: tall, blue eyes, light hair, age about twenty-five. It all might have been vaguely meant for her. She had a dark cloth gown, and long black cloak with hood to come well over the head. These she now donned, with some thick shoes, and a dark-coloured handkerchief tied over her head under the hood, so as to hide the golden glory of her hair.

She was quite calm and in no haste. She made Lucie pack a small hand valise with some necessaries for the journey, and provided herself plentifully with money—French and English notes—which she tucked well away inside her dress.

Then she bade her maid, who was struggling with her tears, a kindly farewell, and quickly went down to her coach.

CHAPTER XVII

BOULOGNE

During the journey Marguerite had not much leisure to think. The discomforts and petty miseries incidental on cheap travelling had the very welcome effect of making her forget, for the time being, the soul-rendering crisis through which she was now passing.

For, of necessity, she had to travel at the cheap rate, among the crowd of poorer passengers who were herded aft the packet boat, leaning up against one another, sitting on bundles and packages of all kinds; that part of the deck, reeking with the smell of tar and sea-water, damp, squally and stuffy, was an abomination of hideous discomfort to the dainty, fastidious lady of fashion, yet she almost welcomed the intolerable propinquity, the cold douches of salt water, which every now and then wetted her through and through, for it was the consequent sense of physical wretchedness that helped her to forget the intolerable anguish of her mind.

And among these poorer travellers she felt secure from observation. No one took much notice of her. She looked just like one of the herd, and in the huddled-up little figure, in the dark bedraggled clothes, no one would for a moment have recognized the dazzling personality of Lady Blakeney.

Drawing her hood well over her head, she sat in a secluded corner of the deck, upon the little black valise which contained the few belongings she had brought with her. Her cloak and dress, now mud-stained and dank with splashings of salt-water, attracted no one's attention. There was a keen northeasterly breeze, cold and penetrating, but favourable to a rapid crossing. Marguerite, who had gone through several hours of weary travelling by coach, before she had embarked at Dover in the late afternoon, was unspeakably tired. She had watched the golden sunset out at sea until her eyes were burning with pain, and as the dazzling crimson and orange and purple gave place to the soft grey tones of evening, she descried the round cupola of the church of Our Lady of Boulogne against the dull background of the sky.

After that her mind became a blank. A sort of torpor fell over her senses: she was wakeful and yet half-asleep, unconscious of everything around her, seeing nothing but the distant massive towers of old Boulogne churches gradually detaching themselves one by one from out the fast gathering gloom.

The town seemed like a dream city, a creation of some morbid imagination, presented to her mind's eye as the city of sorrow and of death.

When the boat finally scraped her sides along the rough wooden jetty, Marguerite felt as if she were being forcibly awakened. She was numb and stiff and thought she must have fallen asleep during the last half hour of the journey. Everything round her was dark. The sky was overcast, and the night seemed unusually sombre. Figures were moving all around her, there was noise and confusion of voices, and a general pushing and shouting which seemed strangely weird in this gloom. Here among the poorer passengers, there had not been thought any necessity for a light: one solitary lantern fixed to a mast only enhanced the intense blackness of everything around. Now and then a face would come within range of this meagre streak of yellow light, looking strangely distorted, with great, elongated shadows across the brow and chin, a grotesque, ghostly apparition which quickly vanished again, scurrying off like some frightened gnome, giving place to other forms, other figures all equally grotesque and equally weird.

Marguerite watched them all half stupidly and motionlessly for awhile. She did not quite know what she ought to do, and did not like to ask any questions: she was dazed and the darkness blinded her. Then gradually things began to detach themselves more clearly. On looking straight before her, she began to discern the landing place, the little wooden bridge across which the passengers walked one by one from the boat onto the jetty. The first-class passengers were evidently all alighting now: the crowd of which Marguerite formed a unit, had been pushed back in a more compact herd, out of the way for the moment, so that their betters might get along more comfortably.

Beyond the landing stage a little booth had been erected, a kind of tent, open in front and lighted up within by a couple of lanthorns. Under this tent there was a table, behind which sat a man dressed in some sort of official looking clothes, and wearing the tricolour scarf across his chest.

All the passengers from the boat had apparently to file past this tent. Marguerite could see them now quite distinctly, the profiles of the various faces, as they paused for a moment in front of the table, being brilliantly illuminated by one of the lanterns. Two sentinels wearing the uniform of the National Guard stood each side of the table. The passengers one by one took out their passport as they went by, handed it to the man in the official dress, who examined it carefully, very lengthily, then signed it and returned the paper to its owner: but at times, he appeared doubtful, folded the passport and put it down in front of him: the passenger would protest; Marguerite could not hear what was said, but she could see that some argument was attempted, quickly dismissed by a peremptory order from the official. The doubtful passport was obviously put on one side for further examination, and the unfortunate owner thereof detained, until he or she had been able to give more satisfactory references to the representatives of the Committee of Public Safety, stationed at Boulogne.

This process of examination necessarily took a long time. Marguerite was getting horribly tired, her feet ached and she scarcely could hold herself upright: yet she watched all these people mechanically, making absurd little guesses in her weary mind as to whose passport would find favour in the eyes of the official, and whose would be found suspect and inadequate.

Suspect! a terrible word these times! since Merlin's terrible law decreed now that every man, woman or child, who was suspected by the Republic of being a traitor, was a traitor in fact.

How sorry she felt for those whose passports were detained: who tried to argue—so needlessly!—and who were finally led off by a soldier, who had stepped out from somewhere in the dark, and had to await further examination, probably imprisonment and often death.

As to herself, she felt quite safe: the passport given to her by Chauvelin's own accomplice was sure to be quite en règle.

Then suddenly her heart seemed to give a sudden leap and then to stop in its beating for a second or two. In one of the passengers, a man who was just passing in front of the tent, she had recognized the form and profile of Chauvelin.

He had no passport to show, but evidently the official knew who he was, for he stood up and saluted, and listened deferentially whilst the ex-ambassador apparently gave him a few instructions. It seemed to Marguerite that these instructions related to two women who were close behind Chauvelin at the time, and who presently seemed to file past without going through the usual formalities of showing their passports. But of this she could not be quite sure. The women were closely hooded and veiled and her own attention had been completely absorbed by this sudden appearance of her deadly enemy.

Yet what more natural than that Chauvelin should be here now? His object accomplished, he had no doubt posted to Dover, just as she had done. There was no difficulty in that, and a man of his type and importance would always have unlimited means and money at his command to accomplish any journey he might desire to undertake.

There was nothing strange or even unexpected in the man's presence here; and yet somehow it had made the whole, awful reality more tangible, more wholly unforgettable. Marguerite remembered his abject words to her, when first she had seen him at the Richmond fête: he said that he had fallen into disgrace, that, having failed in his service to the Republic, he had

been relegated to a subordinate position, pushed aside with contumely to make room for better, abler men.

Well! all that was a lie, of course, a cunning method of gain-
ing access into her house; of that she had already been convinced, when Candeille provoked the esclandre which led to the
challenge.

That on French soil he seemed in anything but a subsidiary
position, that he appeared to rule rather than to obey, could in
no way appear to Marguerite in the nature of surprise.

As the actress had been a willing tool in the cunning hands of
Chauvelin, so were probably all these people around her. Where
others cringed in the face of officialism, the ex-ambassador had
stepped forth as a master: he had shown a badge, spoken a word
mayhap, and the man in the tent who had made other people
tremble, stood up deferentially and obeyed all commands.

It was all very simple and very obvious: but Marguerite's mind
had been asleep, and it was the sight of the sable-clad little figure which had roused it from its happy torpor.

In a moment now her brain was active and alert, and
presently it seemed to her as if another figure—taller than those
around—had crossed the barrier immediately in the wake of
Chauvelin. Then she chided herself for her fancies!

It could not be her husband. Not yet! He had gone by water,
and would scarce be in Boulogne before the morning!

Ah! now at last came the turn of the second-class passengers!
There was a general bousculade and the human bundle began
to move. Marguerite lost sight of the tent and its awe-inspiring
appurtenances: she was a mere unit again in this herd on the
move. She too progressed along slowly, one step at a time; it was
wearisome and she was deadly tired. She was beginning to form
plans now that she had arrived in France. All along she had
made up her mind that she would begin by seeking out the
Abbé Foucquet, for he would prove a link 'twixt her husband
and herself. She knew that Percy would communicate with the
abbé; had he not told her that the rescue of the devoted old man
from the clutches of the Terrorists would be one of the chief ob-

jects of his journey? It had never occurred to her what she would do if she found the Abbé Foucquet gone from Boulogne.

"Hé! la mère! your passport!"

The rough words roused her from her meditations. She had moved forward, quite mechanically, her mind elsewhere, her thoughts not following the aim of her feet. Thus she must have crossed the bridge along with some of the crowd, must have landed on the jetty, and reached the front of the tent, without really knowing what she was doing.

Ah yes! her passport! She had quite forgotten that! But she had it by her, quite in order, given to her in a fit of tardy remorse by Demoiselle Candeille, the intimate friend of one of the most influential members of the Revolutionary Government of France.

She took the passport from the bosom of her dress and handed it to the man in the official dress.

"Your name?" he asked peremptorily.

"Céline Dumont," she replied unhesitatingly, for had she not rehearsed all this in her mind dozens of times, until her tongue could rattle off the borrowed name as easily as it could her own; "servitor to Citizeness Désirée Candeille!"

The man who had very carefully been examining the paper the while, placed it down on the table deliberately in front of him, and said:

"Céline Dumont! Eh! la mère! what tricks are you up to now?"

"Tricks? I don't understand!" she said quietly, for she was not afraid. The passport was en règle: she knew she had nothing to fear.

"Oh! but I think you do!" retorted the official with a sneer, "and 'tis a mighty clever one, I'll allow. Céline Dumont, ma foi! Not badly imagined, ma petite mère: and all would have passed off splendidly; unfortunately, Céline Dumont, servitor to Citizeness Désirée Candeille, passed through these barriers along with her mistress not half an hour ago."

And with long, grimy finger he pointed to an entry in the large book which lay open before him, and wherein he had apparently been busy making notes of the various passengers who had filed past him.

Then he looked up with a triumphant leer at the calm face of Marguerite. She still did not feel really frightened, only puzzled and perturbed; but all the blood had rushed away from her face, leaving her cheeks ashen white, and pressing against her heart, until it almost choked her.

"You are making a mistake, Citizen," she said very quietly. "I am Citizeness Candeille's maid. She gave me the passport herself, just before I left England; if you will ask her the question, she will confirm what I say, and she assured me that it was quite en règle."

But the man only shrugged his shoulders and laughed derisively. The incident evidently amused him, yet he must have seen many of the same sort; in the far corner of the tent Marguerite seemed to discern a few moving forms, soldiers, she thought, for she caught sight of a glint like that of steel. One or two men stood close behind the official at the desk, and the sentinels were to the right and left of the tent.

With an instinctive sense of appeal, Marguerite looked round from one face to the other: but each looked absolutely impassive and stolid, quite uninterested in this little scene, the exact counterpart of a dozen others, enacted on this very spot within the last hour.

"Hé! là! là! petite mère!" said the official in the same tone of easy persiflage which he had adopted all along, "but we do know how to concoct a pretty lie, aye! and so circumstantially too! Unfortunately it was Citizeness Désirée Candeille herself who happened to be standing just where you are at the present moment, along with her maid, Céline Dumont, both of whom were specially signed for and recommended as perfectly trustworthy, by no less a person than Citoyen Chauvelin of the Committee of Public Safety."

"But I assure you that there is a mistake," pleaded Marguerite earnestly, "'Tis the other woman who lied, I have my passport and . . ."

"A truce on this," retorted the man peremptorily. "If everything is as you say, and if you have nothing to hide, you'll be at liberty to continue your journey to-morrow, after you have explained yourself before the citizen governor. Next one now, quick!"

Marguerite tried another protest, just as those others had done, whom she had watched so mechanically before. But already she knew that that would be useless, for she had felt that a heavy hand was being placed on her shoulder, and that she was being roughly led away.

In a flash she had understood and seen the whole sequel of the awful trap which had all along been destined to engulf her as well as her husband.

What a clumsy, blind fool she had been!

What a miserable antagonist the subtle schemes of a past master of intrigue as was Chauvelin. To have enticed the Scarlet Pimpernel to France was a great thing! The challenge was clever, the acceptance of it by the bold adventurer a foregone conclusion, but the master stroke of the whole plan was done, when she, the wife, was enticed over too with the story of Candeille's remorse and the offer of the passport.

Fool! fool that she was!

And how well did Chauvelin know feminine nature! How cleverly he had divined her thoughts, her feelings, the impulsive way in which she would act; how easily he had guessed that, knowing her husband's danger, she, Marguerite, would immediately follow him.

Now the trap had closed on her—and she saw it all, when it was too late.

Percy Blakeney in France! His wife a prisoner! Her freedom and safety in exchange for his life!

The hopelessness of it all struck her with appalling force, and her senses reeled with the awful finality of the disaster.

Yet instinct in her still struggled for freedom. Ahead of her, and all around, beyond the tent and in the far distance there was a provocative alluring darkness: if she only could get away, only could reach the shelter of that remote and sombre distance, she would hide, and wait, not blunder again, oh no! she would be prudent and wary, if only she could get away!

One woman's struggles, against five men! It was pitiable, sublime, absolutely useless.

The man in the tent seemed to be watching her with much amusement for a moment or two, as her whole graceful body stiffened for that absurd and unequal physical contest. He seemed vastly entertained at the sight of this good-looking young woman striving to pit her strength against five sturdy soldiers of the Republic.

"Allons! that will do now!" he said at last roughly. "We have no time to waste! Get the jade away, and let her cool her temper in No. 6, until the citizen governor gives further orders.

"Take her away!" he shouted more loudly, banging a grimy fist down on the table before him, as Marguerite still struggled on with the blind madness of despair. "Pardi! can none of you rid us of that turbulent baggage?"

The crowd behind were pushing forward: the guard within the tent were jeering at those who were striving to drag Marguerite away: these latter were cursing loudly and volubly, until one of them, tired out, furious and brutal, raised his heavy fist and with an obscene oath brought it crashing down upon the unfortunate woman's head.

Perhaps, though it was the work of a savage and cruel creature, the blow proved more merciful than it had been intended: it had caught Marguerite full between the eyes; her aching senses, wearied and reeling already, gave way beneath this terrible violence; her useless struggles ceased, her arms fell inert by her side: and losing consciousness completely, her proud, unbendable spirit was spared the humiliating knowledge of her final removal by the rough soldiers, and of the complete wreckage of her last, lingering hopes.

CHAPTER XVIII

No. 6

Consciousness returned very slowly, very painfully.
It was night when last Marguerite had clearly known what was going on around her; it was daylight before she realized that she still lived, that she still knew and suffered.

Her head ached intolerably: that was the first conscious sensation which came to her; then she vaguely perceived a pale ray of sunshine, very hazy and narrow, which came from somewhere in front of her and struck her in the face. She kept her eyes tightly shut, for that filmy light caused her an increase of pain.

She seemed to be lying on her back, and her fingers wandering restlessly around felt a hard paillasse, beneath their touch, then a rough pillow, and her own cloak laid over her: thought had not yet returned, only the sensation of great suffering and of infinite fatigue.

Anon she ventured to open her eyes, and gradually one or two objects detached themselves from out the haze which still obscured her vision.

Firstly, the narrow aperture—scarcely a window—filled in with tiny squares of coarse, unwashed glass, through which the rays of the morning sun were making kindly efforts to penetrate, then the cloud of dust illumined by those same rays, and made up—so it seemed to the poor tired brain that strove to perceive—of myriads of abnormally large molecules, over-abundant, and over-active, for they appeared to be dancing a kind of wild saraband before Marguerite's aching eyes, advancing and retreating, forming themselves into groups and taking on funny shapes of weird masques and grotesque faces which grinned at the unconscious figure lying helpless on the rough paillasse.

Through and beyond them Marguerite gradually became aware of three walls of a narrow room, dank and grey, half covered with whitewash and half with greenish mildew! Yes! and there, opposite to her and immediately beneath that semblance of a window, was another paillasse, and on it something dark, that moved.

The words: "Liberté, Egalité, Fraternité ou la Mort!" stared out at her from somewhere beyond those active molecules of dust, but she also saw just above the other paillasse the vague outline of a dark crucifix.

It seemed a terrible effort to co-ordinate all these things, and to try and realize what the room was, and what was the meaning of the paillasse, the narrow window and the stained walls, too much altogether for the aching head to take in save very slowly, very gradually.

Marguerite was content to wait and to let memory creep back as reluctantly as it would.

"Do you think, my child, you could drink a little of this now?"

It was a gentle, rather tremulous voice which struck upon her ear. She opened her eyes, and noticed that the dark something which had previously been on the opposite paillasse was no longer there, and that there appeared to be a presence close to her only vaguely defined, someone kindly and tender who had spoken to her in French, with that soft sing-song accent peculiar to the Normandy peasants, and who now seemed to be pressing something cool and soothing to her lips.

"They gave me this for you!" continued the tremulous voice close to her ear. "I think it would do you good, if you tried to take it."

A hand and arm was thrust underneath the rough pillow, causing her to raise her head a little. A glass was held to her lips and she drank.

The hand that held the glass was all wrinkled, brown and dry, and trembled slightly, but the arm which supported her head was firm and very kind.

"There! I am sure you feel better now. Close your eyes and try to go to sleep."

She did as she was bid, and was ready enough to close her eyes. It seemed to her presently as if something had been interposed between her aching head and that trying ray of white September sun.

Perhaps she slept peacefully for a little while after that, for though her head was still very painful, her mouth and throat felt less parched and dry. Through this sleep or semblance of sleep, she was conscious of the same pleasant voice softly droning Paters and Aves close to her ear.

Thus she lay, during the greater part of that day. Not quite fully conscious, not quite awake to the awful memories which anon would crowd upon her thick and fast.

From time to time the same kind and trembling hands would with gentle pressure force a little liquid food through her unwilling lips: some warm soup, or anon a glass of milk. Beyond the pain in her head, she was conscious of no physical ill; she felt at perfect peace, and an extraordinary sense of quiet and repose seemed to pervade this small room, with its narrow window through which the rays of the sun came gradually in more golden splendour as the day drew towards noon, and then they vanished altogether.

The drony voice close beside her acted as a soporific upon her nerves. In the afternoon she fell into a real and beneficent sleep. . . .

But after that, she woke to full consciousness!

Oh! the horror, the folly of it all!

It came back to her with all the inexorable force of an appalling certainty.

She was a prisoner in the hands of those who long ago had sworn to bring The Scarlet Pimpernel to death!

She! his wife, a hostage in their hands! her freedom and safety offered to him as the price of his own! Here there was no question of dreams or of nightmares: no illusions as to the ultimate intentions of her husband's enemies. It was all a reality, and even now, before she had the strength fully to grasp the whole nature of this horrible situation, she knew that by her own act of mad and passionate impulse, she had hopelessly jeopardized the life of the man she loved.

For with that sublime confidence in him begotten of her love, she never for a moment doubted which of the two alternatives he would choose, when once they were placed before him. He would sacrifice himself for her; he would prefer to die a thousand deaths so long as they set her free.

For herself, her own sufferings, her danger or humiliation she cared nothing! Nay! at this very moment she was conscious of a wild passionate desire for death. . . . In this sudden onrush of memory and of thought she wished with all her soul and heart and mind to die here suddenly, on this hard paillasse, in this lonely and dark prison . . . so that she should be out of the way once and for all . . . so that she should *not* be the hostage to be bartered against his precious life and freedom.

He would suffer acutely, terribly at her loss, because he loved her above everything else on earth, he would suffer in every fibre of his passionate and ardent nature, but he would not then have to endure the humiliations, the awful alternatives, the galling impotence and miserable death, the relentless "either—or" which his enemies were even now preparing for him.

And then came a revulsion of feeling. Marguerite's was essentially a buoyant and active nature, a keen brain which worked and schemed and planned, rather than one ready to accept the inevitable.

Hardly had these thoughts of despair and of death formulated themselves in her mind, than with brilliant swiftness, a new train of ideas began to take root.

What if matters were not so hopeless after all?

Already her mind had flown instinctively to thoughts of escape. Had she the right to despair? She, the wife and intimate companion of the man who had astonished the world with his daring, his prowess, his amazing good luck, she to imagine for a moment that in this all-supreme moment of adventurous life the Scarlet Pimpernel would fail!

Was not English society peopled with men, women and children whom his ingenuity had rescued from plights quite as seemingly hopeless as her own, and would not all the resources of that inventive brain be brought to bear upon this rescue which touched him nearer and more deeply than any which he had attempted hitherto.

Now Marguerite was chiding herself for her doubts and for her fears. Already she remembered that amongst the crowd on the landing stage she had perceived a figure—unusually tall—following in the wake of Chauvelin and his companions. Awakened hope had already assured her that she had not been mistaken, that Percy, contrary to her own surmises, had reached Boulogne last night: he always acted so differently to what anyone might expect, that it was quite possible that he had crossed over in the packet-boat after all, unbeknown to Marguerite as well as to his enemies.

Oh yes! the more she thought about it all, the more sure was she that Percy was already in Boulogne, and that he knew of her capture and her danger.

What right had she to doubt even for a moment that he would know how to reach her, how—when the time came—to save himself and her?

A warm glow began to fill her veins, she felt excited and alert, absolutely unconscious now of pain or fatigue, in this radiant joy of reawakened hope.

She raised herself slightly, leaning on her elbow: she was still very weak and the slight movement had made her giddy, but soon she would be strong and well . . . she must be strong and well and ready to do his bidding when the time for escape would have come.

"Ah! you are better, my child, I see . . ." said that quaint, tremulous voice again, with its soft sing-song accent, "but you must not be so venturesome, you know. The physician said that you had received a cruel blow. The brain has been rudely shaken . . . and you must lie quite still all to-day, or your poor little head will begin to ache again."

Marguerite turned to look at the speaker, and in spite of her excitement, of her sorrow and of her anxieties, she could not help smiling at the whimsical little figure which sat opposite to her, on a very rickety chair, solemnly striving with slow and measured movement of hand and arm, and a large supply of breath, to get up a polish on the worn-out surface of an ancient pair of buckled shoes.

The figure was slender and almost wizened, the thin shoulders round with an habitual stoop, the lean shanks were encased in a pair of much-darned, coarse black stockings. It was the figure of an old man, with a gentle, clear-cut face furrowed by a forest of wrinkles, and surmounted by scanty white locks above a smooth forehead which looked yellow and polished like an ancient piece of ivory.

He had looked across at Marguerite as he spoke, and a pair of innately kind and mild blue eyes were fixed with tender reproach upon her. Marguerite thought that she had never seen quite so much goodness and simple-heartedness portrayed on any face before. It literally beamed out of those pale blue eyes, which seemed quite full of unshed tears.

The old man wore a tattered garment, a miracle of shining cleanliness, which had once been a soutane of smooth black cloth, but was now a mass of patches and threadbare at shoulders and knees. He seemed deeply intent in the task of polishing his shoes, and having delivered himself of his little admonition, he very solemnly and earnestly resumed his work.

Marguerite's first and most natural instinct had, of course, been one of dislike and mistrust of anyone who appeared to be in some way on guard over her. But when she took in every detail of the quaint figure of the old man, his scrupulous tidiness of apparel, the resigned stoop of his shoulders, and met in full the gaze of those moist eyes, she felt that the whole aspect of the man, as he sat there polishing his shoes, was infinitely pathetic and, in its simplicity, commanding of respect.

"Who are you?" asked Lady Blakeney at last, for the old man after looking at her with a kind of appealing wonder, seemed to be waiting for her to speak.

"A priest of the good God, my dear child," replied the old man with a deep sigh and a shake of his scanty locks, "who is not allowed to serve his divine Master any longer. A poor old fellow, very harmless and very helpless, who has been set here to watch over you.

"You must not look upon me as a jailer because of what I say, my child," he added with a quaint air of deference and apology. "I am very old and very small, and only take up a very little room. I can make myself very scarce; you shall hardly know that I am here. They forced me to it much against my will. . . . But they are strong and I am weak, how could I deny them since they put me here. After all," he concluded naively, "perhaps it is the will of le bon Dieu, and He knows best, my child, He knows best."

The shoes evidently refused to respond any further to the old man's efforts at polishing them. He contemplated them now, with a whimsical look of regret on his furrowed face, then set them down on the floor and slipped his stockinged feet into them.

Marguerite was silently watching him, still leaning on her elbow. Evidently her brain was still numb and fatigued, for she did not seem able to grasp all that the old man said. She smiled to herself too as she watched him. How could she look upon him as a jailer? He did not seem at all like a Jacobin or a Terrorist, there was nothing of the dissatisfied democrat, of the snarling anarchist ready to lend his hand to any act of ferocity directed against a so-called aristocrat, about this pathetic little figure in the ragged soutane and worn shoes.

He seemed singularly bashful too and ill at ease, and loath to meet Marguerite's great, ardent eyes, which were fixed questioningly upon him.

"You must forgive me, my daughter," he said shyly, "for concluding my toilet before you. I had hoped to be quite ready before you woke, but I had some trouble with my shoes; except for a little water and soap the prison authorities will not provide us poor captives with any means of cleanliness and tidiness, and le bon Dieu does love a tidy body as well as a clean soul.

"But there, there," he added fussily, "I must not continue to gossip like this. You would like to get up, I know, and refresh your face and hands with a little water. Oh! you will see how well I have thought it out. I need not interfere with you at all, and when you make your little bit of toilette, you will feel quite alone . . . just as if the old man was not there."

He began busying himself about the room, dragging the rickety, rush-bottomed chairs forward. There were four of these in the room, and he began forming a kind of bulwark with them, placing two side by side, then piling the two others up above.

"You will see, my child, you will see!" he kept repeating at intervals as the work of construction progressed. It was no easy matter, for he was of low stature, and his hands were unsteady from apparently uncontrollable nervousness.

Marguerite, leaning slightly forward, her chin resting in her hand, was too puzzled and anxious to grasp the humour of this comical situation. She certainly did not understand. This old man had in some sort of way, and for a hitherto unexplained reason, been set as a guard over her; it was not an unusual device on the part of the inhuman wretches who now ruled over France, to add to the miseries and terrors of captivity, where a woman of refinement was concerned, the galling outrage of never leaving her alone for a moment.

That peculiar form of mental torture, surely the invention of brains rendered mad by their own ferocious cruelty, was even now being inflicted on the hapless, dethroned Queen of France. Marguerite, in far-off England, had shuddered when she heard of it, and in her heart had prayed, as indeed every pure-minded woman did then, that proud, unfortunate Marie Antoinette might soon find release from such torments in death.

There was evidently some similar intention with regard to Marguerite herself in the minds of those who now held her prisoner. But this old man seemed so feeble and so helpless, his very delicacy of thought as he built up a screen to divide the squalid room in two, proved him to be singularly inefficient for the task of a watchful jailer.

When the four chairs appeared fairly steady, and in comparatively little danger of toppling, he dragged the paillasse forward and propped it up against the chairs. Finally he drew the table along, which held the cracked ewer and basin, and placed it against this improvised partition: then he surveyed the whole construction with evident gratification and delight.

"There now!" he said, turning a face beaming with satisfaction to Marguerite, "I can continue my prayers on the other side of the fortress. Oh! it is quite safe . . ." he added, as with a fearsome hand he touched his engineering feat with gingerly pride, "and you will be quite private. . . . Try and forget that the old abbé is in the room. . . . He does not count . . . really he does not count . . . he has ceased to be of any moment these many months now that Saint Joseph is closed and he may no longer say Mass."

He was obviously prattling on in order to hide his nervous bashfulness. He ensconced himself behind his own finely constructed bulwark, drew a breviary from his pocket and having found a narrow ledge on one of the chairs, on which he could sit, without much danger of bringing the elaborate screen onto the top of his head, he soon became absorbed in his orisons.

Marguerite watched him for a little while longer: he was evidently endeavouring to make her think that he had become oblivious of her presence, and his transparent little manœuvers amused and puzzled her not a little.

He looked so comical with his fussy and shy ways, yet withal so gentle and so kindly that she felt completely reassured and quite calm.

She tried to raise herself still further and found the process astonishingly easy. Her limbs still ached and the violent, intermittent pain in her head certainly made her feel sick and giddy at times, but otherwise she was not ill. She sat up on the paillasse, then put her feet to the ground and presently walked up to the improvised dressing-room and bathed her face and hands. The rest had done her good, and she felt quite capable of co-ordinating her thoughts, of moving about without too much pain, and of preparing herself both mentally and physically for the grave events which she knew must be imminent.

While she busied herself with her toilet her thoughts dwelt on the one all-absorbing theme: Percy was in Boulogne, he knew that she was here, in prison, he would reach her without fail, in fact he might communicate with her at any moment now, and had without a doubt already evolved a plan of escape for her, more daring and ingenious than any which he had conceived hitherto; therefore, she must be ready, and prepared for any eventuality, she must be strong and eager, in no way despondent, for if he were here, would he not chide her for her want of faith?

By the time she had smoothed her hair and tidied her dress, Marguerite caught herself singing quite cheerfully to herself.

So full of buoyant hope was she.

CHAPTER XIX

The Strength of the Weak

"M L'Abbé! . . ." said Marguerite gravely.
"Yes, mon enfant."

The old man looked up from his breviary, and saw Marguerite's great earnest eyes fixed with obvious calm and trust upon him. She had finished her toilet as well as she could, had shaken up and tidied the paillasse, and was now sitting on the edge of it, her hands clasped between her knees. There was something which still puzzled her, and impatient and impulsive as she was, she had watched the abbé as he calmly went on reading the Latin prayers for the last five minutes, and now she could contain her questionings no longer.

"You said just now that they set you to watch over me . . ."

"So they did, my child, so they did . . ." he replied with a sigh, as he quietly closed his book and slipped it back into his pocket. "Ah! they are very cunning . . . and we must remember that they have the power. No doubt," added the old man, with his own, quaint philosophy, "no doubt le bon Dieu meant them to have the power, or they would not have it, would they?"

"By 'they' you mean the Terrorists and Anarchists of France, M. l'Abbé. . . . The Committee of Public Safety who pillage and murder, outrage women, and desecrate religion. . . . Is that not so?"

"Alas! my child!" he sighed.

"And it is 'they' who have set you to watch over me? . . . I confess I don't understand. . . ."

She laughed, quite involuntarily indeed, for in spite of the reassurance in her heart her brain was still in a whirl of passionate anxiety.

"You don't look at all like one of 'them,' M. l'Abbé," she said.

"The good God forbid!" ejaculated the old man, raising protesting hands up towards the very distant, quite invisible sky. "How could I, a humble priest of the Lord, range myself with those who would flout and defy Him."

"Yet I am a prisoner of the Republic and you are my jailer, M. l'Abbé."

"Ah, yes!" he sighed. "But I am very helpless. This was my cell. I had been here with François and Félicité, my sister's children, you know. Innocent lambs, whom those fiends would lead to slaughter. Last night," he continued, speaking volubly, "the soldiers came in and dragged François and Félicité out of this room, where, in spite of the danger before us, in spite of what we suffered, we had contrived to be quite happy together. I could read the Mass, and the dear children would say their prayers night and morning at my knee."

He paused awhile. The unshed tears in his mild blue eyes struggled for freedom now, and one or two flowed slowly down his wrinkled cheek. Marguerite, though heartsore and full of agonizing sorrow herself, felt her whole noble soul go out to this kind old man, so pathetic, so high and simple-minded in his grief.

She said nothing, however, and the Abbé continued after a few seconds' silence.

"When the children had gone, they brought you in here, mon enfant, and laid you on the paillasse where Félicité used to sleep. You looked very white, and stricken down, like one of God's lambs attacked by the ravening wolf. Your eyes were closed and you were blissfully unconscious. I was taken before the governor of the prison, and he told me that you would share the cell with me for a time, and that I was to watch you night and day, because . . ."

The old man paused again. Evidently what he had to say was very difficult to put into words. He groped in his pockets and brought out a large bandana handkerchief, red and yellow and green, with which he began to mop his moist forehead. The quaver in his voice and the trembling of his hands became more apparent and pronounced.

"Yes, M. l'Abbé? Because? . . ." queried Marguerite gently.

"They said that if I guarded you well, Félicité and François would be set free," replied the old man after a while, during which he made vigorous efforts to overcome his nervousness, "and that if you escaped the children and I would be guillotined the very next day."

There was silence in the little room now. The Abbé was sitting quite still, clasping his trembling fingers, and Marguerite neither moved nor spoke. What the old man had just said was very slowly finding its way to the innermost cells of her brain. Until her mind had thoroughly grasped the meaning of it all, she could not trust herself to make a single comment.

It was some seconds before she fully understood it all, before she realized what it meant not only to her, but indirectly to her husband. Until now she had not been fully conscious of the enormous wave of hope which almost in spite of herself had risen triumphant above the dull, grey sea of her former despair; only now when it had been shattered against this deadly rock of almost superhuman devilry and cunning did she understand what she had hoped, and what she must now completely forswear.

No bolts and bars, no fortified towers or inaccessible fortresses could prove so effectual a prison for Marguerite Blakeney as the dictum which morally bound her to her cell.

"If you escape the children and I would be guillotined the very next day."

This meant that even if Percy knew, even if he could reach her, he could never set her free, since her safety meant death to two innocent children and to this simple hearted man.

It would require more than the ingenuity of the Scarlet Pimpernel himself to untie this Gordian knot.

"I don't mind for myself, of course," the old man went on with gentle philosophy. "I have lived my life. What matters if I die tomorrow, or if I linger on until my earthly span is legitimately run out? I am ready to go home whenever my Father calls me. But it is the children, you see. I have to think of them. François is his mother's only son, the bread-winner of the household, a good lad and studious too, and Félicité has always been very delicate. She is blind from birth and . . ."

"Oh! don't . . . for pity's sake, don't . . ." moaned Marguerite in an agony of helplessness. "I understand . . . you need not fear for your children, M. l'Abbé: no harm shall come to them through me."

"It is as the good God wills!" replied the old man quietly.

Then, as Marguerite had once more relapsed into silence, he fumbled for his beads, and his gentle voice began droning the Paters and Aves wherein no doubt his childlike heart found peace and solace.

He understood that the poor woman would not wish to speak, he knew as well as she did the overpowering strength of his helpless appeal. Thus the minutes sped on, the jailer and the captive, tied to one another by the strongest bonds that hand of man could forge, had nothing to say to one another: he, the old priest, imbued with the traditions of his calling, could pray and resign himself to the will of the Almighty, but she was young and ardent and passionate, she loved and was beloved, and an impassable barrier was built up between her and the man she worshipped!

A barrier fashioned by the weak hands of children, one of whom was delicate and blind. Outside was air and freedom, reunion with her husband, an agony of happy remorse, a kiss from his dear lips, and trembling hands held her back from it all, because of François who was the bread-winner and of Félicité who was blind.

Mechanically now Marguerite rose again, and like an automaton—lifeless and thoughtless—she began putting the dingy, squalid room to rights. The Abbé helped her to demolish the improvised screen; with the same gentle delicacy of thought which had caused him to build it up, he refrained from speaking to her now: he would not intrude himself on her grief and her despair.

Later on, she forced herself to speak again, and asked the old man his name.

"My name is Foucquet," he replied, "Jean Baptiste Marie Foucquet, late parish priest of the Church of Saint Joseph, the patron saint of Boulogne."

Foucquet! This was l'Abbé Foucquet! the faithful friend and servant of the de Marny family.

Marguerite gazed at him with great, questioning eyes.

What a wealth of memories crowded in on her mind at sound of that name! Her beautiful home at Richmond, her brilliant array of servants and guests, His Royal Highness at her side! life in free, joyous, happy England—how infinitely remote it now seemed. Her ears were filled with the sound of a voice, drawly and quaint and gentle, a voice and a laugh half shy, wholly mirthful, and oh! so infinitely dear:

"I think a little sea voyage and English country air would suit the Abbé Foucquet, m'dear, and I only mean to ask him to cross the Channel with me . . ."

Oh! the joy and confidence expressed in those words! the daring, the ambition! the pride! and the soft, languorous air of the old-world garden round her then, the passion of his embrace! the heavy scent of late roses and of heliotrope, which caused her to swoon in his arms!

And now a narrow prison cell, and that pathetic, tender little creature there, with trembling hands and tear-dimmed eyes, the most powerful and most relentless jailer which the ferocious cunning of her deadly enemies could possibly have devised.

Then she talked to him of Juliette Marny.

The Abbé did not know that Mlle. de Marny had succeeded in reaching England safely and was overjoyed to hear it.

He recounted to Marguerite the story of the Marny jewels: how he had put them safely away in the crypt of his little church, until the Assembly of the Convention had ordered the closing of the churches, and placed before every minister of le bon Dieu the alternative of apostasy or death.

"With me it has only been prison so far," continued the old man simply, "but prison has rendered me just as helpless as the guillotine would have done, for the enemies of le bon Dieu have ransacked the Church of Saint Joseph and stolen the jewels which I should have guarded with my life."

But it was obvious joy for the Abbé to talk of Juliette Marny's happiness. Vaguely, in his remote little provincial cure, he had heard of the prowess and daring of the Scarlet Pimpernel and liked to think that Juliette owed her safety to him.

"The good God will reward him and those whom he cares for," added Abbé Foucquet with that earnest belief in divine interference which seemed so strangely pathetic under these present circumstances.

Marguerite sighed, and for the first time in this terrible soul-stirring crisis through which she was passing so bravely, she felt a beneficent moisture in her eyes: the awful tension of her nerves relaxed. She went up to the old man, took his wrinkled hand in hers and falling on her knees beside him she eased her overburdened heart in a flood of tears.

CHAPTER XX

Triumph

The day that Citizen Chauvelin's letter was received by the members of the Committee of Public Safety was indeed one of great rejoicing.

The Moniteur tells us that in the Séance of September 22nd, 1793, or Vendemiaire 1st of the Year I. it was decreed that sixty prisoners, not absolutely proved guilty of treason against the Republic—only suspected—were to be set free.

Sixty! . . . at the mere news of the possible capture of the Scarlet Pimpernel.

The Committee was inclined to be magnanimous. Ferocity yielded for the moment to the elusive joy of anticipatory triumph.

A glorious prize was about to fall into the hands of those who had the welfare of the people at heart.

Robespierre and his decemvirs rejoiced, and sixty persons had cause to rejoice with them. So be it! There were plans evolved already as to national fêtes and wholesale pardons when that impudent and meddlesome Englishman at last got his deserts.

Wholesale pardons which could easily be rescinded afterwards. Even with those sixty it was a mere respite. Those of le Salut Public only loosened their hold for awhile, were nobly magnanimous for a day, quite prepared to be doubly ferocious the next.

In the meanwhile let us heartily rejoice!

The Scarlet Pimpernel is in France or will be very soon, and on an appointed day he will present himself conveniently to the soldiers of the Republic for capture and for subsequent guillotine. England is at war with us, there is nothing therefore further to fear from her. We might hang every Englishman we can lay hands on, and England could do no more than she is doing at the present moment: bombard our ports, bluster and threaten, join hands with Flanders, and Austria and Sardinia, and the devil if she choose.

Allons! vogue la galère! The Scarlet Pimpernel is perhaps on our shores at this very moment! Our most stinging, most irritating foe is about to be delivered into our hands.

Citizen Chauvelin's letter is very categorical:

"I guarantee to you, Citizen Robespierre, and to the Members of the Revolutionary Government who have entrusted me with the delicate mission . . ."

Robespierre's sensuous lips curl into a sarcastic smile. Citizen Chauvelin's pen was ever florid in its style: "entrusted me with the delicate mission," is hardly the way to describe an order given under penalty of death.

But let it pass.

". . . that four days from this date, at one hour after sunset, the man who goes by the mysterious name of the Scarlet Pimpernel will be on the southern ramparts of Boulogne, at the extreme southern corner of the town."

"Four days from this date . . ." and Citizen Chauvelin's letter is dated the nineteenth of September, 1793.

"Too much of an aristocrat—Monsieur le Marquis Chauvelin . . ." sneers Merlin, the Jacobin. "He does not know that all good citizens had called that date the 28th Fructidor, Year I. of the Republic."

"No matter," retorts Robespierre with impatient frigidity, "whatever we may call the day it was forty-eight hours ago, and in forty-eight hours more that damned Englishman will have run his head into a noose, from which, an I mistake not, he'll not find it easy to extricate himself."

"And you believe in Citizen Chauvelin's assertion," commented Danton with a lazy shrug of the shoulders.

"Only because he asks for help from us," quoth Robespierre drily; "he is sure that the man will be there, but not sure if he can tackle him."

But many were inclined to think that Chauvelin's letter was an idle boast. They knew nothing of the circumstances which had caused that letter to be written: they could not conjecture how it was that the ex-ambassador could be so precise in naming the day and hour when the enemy of France would be at the mercy of those whom he had outraged and flouted.

Nevertheless Citizen Chauvelin asks for help, and help must not be denied him. There must be no shadow of blame upon the actions of the Committee of Public Safety.

Chauvelin had been weak once, had allowed the prize to slip through his fingers; it must not occur again. He has a wonderful head for devising plans, but he needs a powerful hand to aid him, so that he may not fail again.

Collot d'Herbois, just home from Lyons and Tours, is the right man in an emergency like this. Citizen Collot is full of ideas; the inventor of the "Noyades" is sure to find a means of converting Boulogne into one gigantic prison out of which the mysterious English adventurer will find it impossible to escape.

And whilst the deliberations go on, whilst this committee of butchers are busy slaughtering in imagination the game they have not yet succeeded in bringing down, there comes another messenger from Citizen Chauvelin.

He must have ridden hard on the other one's heels, and something very unexpected and very sudden must have occurred to cause the Citizen to send this second note.

This time it is curt and to the point. Robespierre unfolds it and reads it to his colleagues.

"We have caught the woman—his wife—there may be murder attempted against my person, send me some one at once who will carry out my instructions in case of my sudden death."

Robespierre's lips curl in satisfaction, showing a row of yellowish teeth, long and sharp like the fangs of a wolf. A murmur like unto the snarl of a pack of hyenas rises round the table, as Chauvelin's letter is handed round.

Everyone has guessed the importance of this preliminary capture: "the woman—his wife." Chauvelin evidently thinks much of it, for he anticipates an attempt against his life, nay! he is quite prepared for it, ready to sacrifice it for the sake of his revenge.

Who had accused him of weakness?

He only thinks of his duty, not of his life; he does not fear for himself, only that the fruits of his skill might be jeopardized through assassination.

Well! this English adventurer is capable of any act of desperation to save his wife and himself, and Citizen Chauvelin must not be left in the lurch.

Thus, Citizen Collot d'Herbois is despatched forthwith to Boulogne to be a helpmeet and counsellor to Citizen Chauvelin.

Everything that can humanly be devised must be done to keep the woman secure and to set the trap for that elusive Pimpernel.

Once he is caught the whole of France shall rejoice, and Boulogne, who had been instrumental in running the quarry to earth, must be specially privileged on that day.

A general amnesty for all prisoners the day the Scarlet Pimpernel is captured. A public holiday and a pardon for all natives of Boulogne who are under sentence of death: they shall be allowed to find their way to the various English boats—trading and smuggling craft—that always lie at anchor in the roads there.

The Committee of Public Safety feel amazingly magnanimous towards Boulogne; a proclamation embodying the amnesty and the pardon is at once drawn up and signed by Robespierre and his bloodthirsty Council of Ten, it is entrusted to Citizen Collot d'Herbois to be read out at every corner of the ramparts as an inducement to the little town to do its level best. The Englishman and his wife—captured in Boulogne—will both be subsequently brought to Paris, formally tried on a charge of conspiring against the Republic and guillotined as English spies, but Boulogne shall have the greater glory and shall reap the first and richest reward.

And armed with the magnanimous proclamation, the orders for general rejoicings and a grand local fête, armed also with any and every power over the entire city, its municipality, its garrisons, its forts, for himself and his colleague Chauvelin, Citizen Collot d'Herbois starts for Boulogne forthwith.

Needless to tell him not to let the grass grow under his horse's hoofs. The capture of the Scarlet Pimpernel, though not absolutely an accomplished fact, is nevertheless a practical certainty, and no one rejoices over this great event more than the man who is to be present and see all the fun.

Riding and driving, getting what relays of horses or waggons from roadside farms that he can, Collot is not likely to waste much time on the way.

It is 157 miles to Boulogne by road, and Collot, burning with ambition to be in at the death, rides or drives as no messenger of good tidings has ever ridden or driven before.

He does not stop to eat, but munches chunks of bread and cheese in the recess of the lumbering chaise or waggon that bears him along whenever his limbs refuse him service and he cannot mount a horse.

The chronicles tell us that twenty-four hours after he left Paris, half-dazed with fatigue, but ferocious and eager still, he is borne to the gates of Boulogne by an old cart horse requisitioned from some distant farm, and which falls down, dead, at the Porte Gayole, whilst its rider, with a last effort, loudly clamours for admittance into the town "in the name of the Republic."

CHAPTER XXI

SUSPENSE

In his memorable interview with Robespierre, the day before he left for England, Chauvelin had asked that absolute power be given him, in order that he might carry out the plans for the capture of the Scarlet Pimpernel, which he had in his mind. Now that he was back in France he had no cause to complain that the revolutionary government had grudged him this power for which he had asked.

Implicit obedience had followed whenever he had commanded.

As soon as he heard that a woman had been arrested in the act of uttering a passport in the name of Céline Dumont, he guessed at once that Marguerite Blakeney had, with characteristic impulse, fallen into the trap which, with the aid of the woman Candeille, he had succeeded in laying for her.

He was not the least surprised at that. He knew human nature, feminine nature, far too well, ever to have been in doubt for a moment that Marguerite would follow her husband without calculating either costs or risks.

Ye gods! the irony of it all! Had she not been called the cleverest woman in Europe at one time? Chauvelin himself had thus acclaimed her, in those olden days, before she and he became such mortal enemies, and when he was one of the many satellites that revolved round brilliant Marguerite St. Just. And to-night, when a sergeant of the town guard brought him news of her capture, he smiled grimly to himself; the cleverest woman in

Europe had failed to perceive the trap laid temptingly open for her.

Once more she had betrayed her husband into the hands of those who would not let him escape a second time. And now she had done it with her eyes open, with loving, passionate heart which ached for self-sacrifice, and only succeeded in imperilling the loved one more hopelessly than before.

The sergeant was waiting for orders. Citizen Chauvelin had come to Boulogne, armed with more full and more autocratic powers than any servant of the new republic had ever been endowed with before. The governor of the town, the captain of the guard, the fort and municipality were all as abject slaves before him.

As soon as he had taken possession of the quarters organized for him in the town hall, he had asked for a list of prisoners who for one cause or another were being detained pending further investigations.

The list was long and contained many names which were of not the slightest interest to Chauvelin: he passed them over impatiently.

"To be released at once," he said curtly.

He did not want the guard to be burdened with unnecessary duties, nor the prisons of the little sea-port town to be inconveniently encumbered. He wanted room, space, air, the force and intelligence of the entire town at his command for the one capture which meant life and revenge to him.

"A woman—name unknown—found in possession of a forged passport in the name of Céline Dumont, maid to the Citizeness Désirée Candeille—attempted to land—was interrogated and failed to give satisfactory explanation of herself—detained in room No. 6 of the Gayole prison.

This was one of the last names on the list, the only one of any importance to Citizen Chauvelin. When he read it he nearly drove his nails into the palms of his hands, so desperate an effort did he make not to betray before the sergeant by look or sigh the exultation which he felt.

For a moment he shaded his eyes against the glare of the

lamp, but it was not long before he had formulated a plan and was ready to give his orders.

He asked for a list of prisoners already detained in the various forts. The name of l'Abbé Foucquet with those of his niece and nephew attracted his immediate attention. He asked for further information respecting these people, heard that the boy was a widow's only son, the sole supporter of his mother's declining years: the girl was ailing, suffering from incipient phthisis, and was blind.

Pardi! the very thing! L'Abbé himself, the friend of Juliette Marny, the pathetic personality around which this final adventure of the Scarlet Pimpernel was intended to revolve! and these two young people! his sister's children! one of them blind and ill, the other full of vigour and manhood.

Citizen Chauvelin had soon made up his mind.

A few quick orders to the sergeant of the guard, and l'Abbé Foucquet, weak, helpless and gentle, became the relentless jailer who would guard Marguerite more securely than a whole regiment of loyal soldiers could have done.

Then, having despatched a messenger to the Committee of Public Safety, Chauvelin laid himself down to rest. Fate had not deceived him. He had thought and schemed and planned, and events had shaped themselves exactly as foreseen, and the fact that Marguerite Blakeney was at the present moment a prisoner in his hands was merely the result of his own calculations.

As for the Scarlet Pimpernel, Chauvelin could not very well conceive what he would do under these present circumstances. The duel on the southern ramparts had of course become a farce, not likely to be enacted now that Marguerite's life was at stake. The daring adventurer was caught in a network at last, from which all his ingenuity, all his wit, his impudence and his amazing luck could never extricate him.

And in Chauvelin's mind there was still something more. Revenge was the sweetest emotion his bruised and humbled pride could know: he had not yet tasted its complete intoxicating joy: but every hour now his cup of delight became more and more full: in a few days it would overflow.

In the meanwhile he was content to wait. The hours sped by and there was no news yet of that elusive Pimpernel. Of Marguerite he knew nothing save that she was well guarded; the sentry who passed up and down outside room No. 6 had heard her voice and that of the Abbé Foucquet, in the course of the afternoon.

Chauvelin had asked the Committee of Public Safety for aid in his difficult task, but forty-eight hours at least must elapse before such aid could reach him. Forty-eight hours, during which the hand of an assassin might be lurking for him, and might even reach him ere his vengeance was fully accomplished.

That was the only thought which really troubled him. He did not want to die before he had seen the Scarlet Pimpernel a withered abject creature, crushed in fame and honour, too debased to find glorification even in death.

At this moment he only cared for his life because it was needed for the complete success of his schemes. No one else he knew would have that note of personal hatred towards the enemy of France which was necessary now in order to carry out successfully the plans which he had formed.

Robespierre and all the others only desired the destruction of a man who had intrigued against the reign of terror which they had established; his death on the guillotine, even if it were surrounded with the halo of martyrdom, would have satisfied them completely. Chauvelin looked further than that. He hated the man! He had suffered humiliation through him individually. He wished to see him as an object of contempt rather than of pity. And because of the anticipation of this joy, he was careful of his life, and throughout those two days which elapsed between the capture of Marguerite and the arrival of Collot d'Herbois at Boulogne, Chauvelin never left his quarters at the Hotel de Ville, and requisitioned a special escort consisting of proved soldiers of the town guard to attend his every footstep.

On the evening of the 22nd, after the arrival of Citizen Collot in Boulogne, he gave orders that the woman from No. 6 cell be brought before him in the ground floor room of the Fort Gayole.

CHAPTER XXII

NOT DEATH

Two days of agonizing suspense, of alternate hope and despair, had told heavily on Marguerite Blakeney.

Her courage was still indomitable, her purpose firm and her faith secure, but she was without the slightest vestige of news, entirely shut off from the outside world, left to conjecture, to scheme, to expect and to despond alone.

The Abbé Foucquet had tried in his gentle way to be of comfort to her, and she in her turn did her very best not to render his position more cruel than it already was.

A message came to him twice during those forty-eight hours from François and Félicité, a little note scribbled by the boy, or a token sent by the blind girl, to tell the Abbé that the children were safe and well, that they would be safe and well so long as the Citizeness with the name unknown remained closely guarded by him in room No. 6.

When these messages came, the old man would sigh and murmur something about the good God: and hope, which perhaps had faintly risen in Marguerite's heart within the last hour or so, would once more sink back into the abyss of uttermost despair.

Outside the monotonous walk of the sentry sounded like the perpetual thud of a hammer beating upon her bruised temples.

"What's to be done? My God? what's to be done?"

Where was Percy now?

"How to reach him! . . . Oh, God! grant me light!"

The one real terror which she felt was that she would go mad.

Nay! that she was in a measure mad already. For hours now,—
or was it days? . . . or years? . . . she had heard nothing save that
rhythmic walk of the sentinel, and the kindly, tremulous voice of
the Abbé whispering consolations, or murmuring prayers in her
ears, she had seen nothing save that prison door, of rough deal,
painted a dull grey, with great old-fashioned lock, and hinges
rusty with the damp of ages.

She had kept her eyes fixed on that door until they burned
and ached with well-nigh intolerable pain; yet she felt that she
could not look elsewhere, lest she missed the golden moment
when the bolts would be drawn, and that dull, grey door would
swing slowly on its rusty hinges.

Surely, surely, that was the commencement of madness!

Yet for Percy's sake, because he might want her, because he
might have need of her courage and of her presence of mind,
she tried to keep her wits about her. But it was difficult! oh! terribly difficult! especially when the shades of evening began to
gather in, and peopled the squalid, whitewashed room with in-
numerable threatening ghouls.

Then when the moon came up, a silver ray crept in through
the tiny window and struck full upon that grey door, making it
look weird and spectral like the entrance to a house of ghosts.

Even now as there was a distinct sound of the pushing of bolts
and bars, Marguerite thought that she was the prey of halluci-
nations. The Abbé Foucquet was sitting in the remote and darkest corner of the room, quietly telling his beads. His serene
philosophy and gentle placidity could in no way be disturbed by
the opening or shutting of a door, or by the bearer of good or
evil tidings.

The room now seemed strangely gloomy and cavernous, with
those deep, black shadows all around and that white ray of the
moon which struck so weirdly on the door.

Marguerite shuddered with one of those unaccountable pre-
monitions of something evil about to come, which ofttimes as-
sail those who have a nervous and passionate temperament.

The door swung slowly open upon its hinges: there was a
quick word of command, and the light of a small oil lamp struck

full into the gloom. Vaguely Marguerite discerned a group of
men, soldiers no doubt, for there was a glint of arms and the
suggestion of tricolour cockades and scarves. One of the men
was holding the lamp aloft, another took a few steps forward
into the room. He turned to Marguerite, entirely ignoring the
presence of the old priest, and addressed her peremptorily.

"Your presence is desired by the citizen governor," he said
curtly; "stand up and follow me."

"Whither am I to go?" she asked.

"To where my men will take you. Now then, quick's the word.
The citizen governor does not like to wait."

At a word of command from him, two more soldiers now entered the room and placed themselves one on each side of
Marguerite, who, knowing that resistance was useless, had already risen and was prepared to go.

The Abbé tried to utter a word of protest and came quickly
forward towards Marguerite, but he was summarily and very
roughly pushed aside.

"Now then, calotin," said the first soldier with an oath, "this is
none of your business. Forward! march!" he added, addressing
his men, "and you, Citizeness, will find it wiser to come quietly
along and not to attempt any tricks with me, or the gag and man-
acles will have to be used."

But Marguerite had no intention of resisting. She was too
tired even to wonder as to what they meant to do with her or
whither they were going; she moved as in a dream and felt a
hope within her that she was being led to death: summary executions were the order of the day, she knew that, and sighed for
this simple solution of the awful problem which had been ha-
rassing her these past two days.

She was being led along a passage, stumbling ever and anon
as she walked, for it was but dimly lighted by the same little oil
lamp, which one of the soldiers was carrying in front, holding it
high up above his head: then they went down a narrow flight of
stone steps, until she and her escort reached a heavy oak door.

A halt was ordered at this point: and the man in command of
the little party pushed the door open and walked in. Marguerite

caught sight of a room beyond, dark and gloomy-looking, as was her own prison cell. Somewhere on the left there was obviously a window; she could not see it but guessed that it was there because the moon struck full upon the floor, ghost-like and spectral, well fitting in with the dream-like state in which Marguerite felt herself to be.

In the centre of the room she could discern a table with a chair close beside it, also a couple of tallow-candles, which flickered in the draught caused no doubt by that open window which she could not see.

All these little details impressed themselves on Marguerite's mind, as she stood there, placidly waiting until she should once more be told to move along. The table, the chair, that unseen window, trivial objects though they were, assumed before her overwrought fancy an utterly disproportionate importance. She caught herself presently counting up the number of boards visible on the floor, and watching the smoke of the tallow-candles rising up towards the grimy ceiling.

After a few minutes' weary waiting which seemed endless to Marguerite, there came a short word of command from within and she was roughly pushed forward into the room by one of the men. The cool air of a late September's evening gently fanned her burning temples. She looked round her and now perceived that someone was sitting at the table, the other side of the tallow-candles—a man, with head bent over a bundle of papers and shading his face against the light with his hand.

He rose as she approached, and the flickering flame of the candles played weirdly upon the slight, sable-clad figure, illumining the keen, ferret-like face, and throwing fitful gleams across the deep-set eyes and the narrow, cruel mouth.

It was Chauvelin.

Mechanically Marguerite took the chair which the soldier drew towards her, ordering her curtly to sit down. She seemed to have but little power to move. Though all her faculties had suddenly become preternaturally alert at sight of this man, whose very life now was spent in doing her the most grievous wrong that one human being can do to another, yet all these faculties were forcefully centred in the one mighty effort not to flinch before him, not to let him see for a moment that she was afraid.

She compelled her eyes to look at him fully and squarely, her lips not to tremble, her very heart to stop its wild, excited beating. She felt his keen eyes fixed intently upon her, but more in curiosity than in hatred or satisfied vengeance.

When she had sat down he came round the table and moved towards her. When he drew quite near, she instinctively recoiled. It had been an almost imperceptible action on her part and certainly an involuntary one, for she did not wish to betray a single thought or emotion, until she knew what he wished to say.

But he had noted her movement—a sort of drawing up and stiffening of her whole person as he approached. He seemed pleased to see it, for he smiled sarcastically but with evident satisfaction, and—as if his purpose was now accomplished—he immediately withdrew and went back to his former seat on the other side of the table. After that he ordered the soldiers to go.

"But remain at attention outside, you and your men," he added, "ready to enter if I call."

It was Marguerite's turn to smile at this obvious sign of a lurking fear on Chauvelin's part, and a line of sarcasm and contempt curled her full lips.

The soldiers having obeyed and the oak door having closed upon them, Marguerite was now alone with the man whom she hated and loathed beyond every living thing on earth.

She wondered when he would begin to speak and why he had sent for her. But he seemed in no hurry to begin. Still shading his face with his hand, he was watching her with utmost attention: she, on the other hand, was looking through and beyond him, with contemptuous indifference, as if his presence here did not interest her in the least.

She would give him no opening for this conversation which he had sought and which she felt would prove either purposeless or else deeply wounding to her heart and to her pride. She sat, therefore, quite still with the flickering and yellow light fully illumining her delicate face, with its child-like curves, and delicate features, the noble, straight brow, the great blue eyes and halo of golden hair.

"My desire to see you here to-night, must seem strange to you, Lady Blakeney," said Chauvelin at last.

Then, as she did not reply, he continued, speaking quite gently, almost deferentially:

"There are various matters of grave importance, which the events of the next twenty-four hours will reveal to your ladyship: and believe me that I am actuated by motives of pure friendship towards you in this my effort to mitigate the unpleasantness of such news as you might hear to-morrow perhaps, by giving you due warning of what its nature might be."

She turned great questioning eyes upon him, and in their expression she tried to put all the contempt which she felt, all the bitterness, all the defiance and the pride.

He quietly shrugged his shoulders.

"Ah! I fear me," he said, "that your ladyship, as usual, doth me grievous wrong. It is but natural that you should misjudge me, yet believe me . . ."

"A truce on this foolery, M. Chauvelin," she broke in, with sudden impatient vehemence, "pray leave your protestations of friendship and courtesy alone, there is no one here to hear them. I pray you proceed with what you have to say."

"Ah!" It was a sigh of satisfaction on the part of Chauvelin. Her anger and impatience even at this early stage of the interview proved sufficiently that her icy restraint was only on the surface.

And Chauvelin always knew how to deal with vehemence. He loved to play with the emotions of a passionate fellow-creature: it was only the imperturbably calm of a certain enemy of his that was wont to shake his own impenetrable armour of reserve.

"As your ladyship desires," he said, with a slight and ironical bow of the head. "But before proceeding according to your wish, I am compelled to ask your ladyship just one question."

"And that is?"

"Have you reflected what your present position means to that inimitable prince of dandies, Sir Percy Blakeney?"

Is it necessary for your present purpose, Monsieur, that you should mention my husband's name at all?" she asked.

"It is indispensable, fair lady," he replied suavely, "for is not the fate of your husband so closely intertwined with yours, that his actions will inevitably be largely influenced by your own."

Marguerite gave a start of surprise, and as Chauvelin had paused she tried to read what hidden meaning lay behind these last words of his. Was it his intention then to propose some bargain, one of those terrible "either–or's" of which he seemed to possess the malignant secret? Oh! if that was so, if indeed he had sent for her in order to suggest one of those terrible alternatives of his, then—be it what it may, be it the wildest conception which the insane brain of a fiend could invent, she would accept it, so long as the man she loved were given one single chance of escape.

Therefore she turned to her arch-enemy in a more conciliatory spirit now, and even endeavoured to match her own diplomatic cunning against his.

"I do not understand," she said tentatively. "How can my actions influence those of my husband? I am a prisoner in Boulogne: he probably is not aware of that fact yet and . . ."

"Sir Percy Blakeney may be in Boulogne at any moment now," he interrupted quietly. "An I mistake not, few places can offer such great attractions to that peerless gentleman of fashion than doth this humble provincial town of France just at this present. . . . Hath it not the honour of harbouring Lady Blakeney within its gates? . . . And your ladyship may indeed believe me when I say that the day that Sir Percy lands in our hospitable port, two hundred pairs of eyes will be fixed upon him, lest he should wish to quit it again."

"And if there were two thousand, sir," she said impulsively, "they would not stop his coming or going as he pleased."

"Nay, fair lady," he said, with a smile, "are you then endowing Sir Percy Blakeney with the attributes which, as popular fancy has it, belong exclusively to that mysterious English hero, the Scarlet Pimpernel?"

"A truce to your diplomacy, Monsieur Chauvelin," she retorted, goaded by his sarcasm, "why should we try to fence with one another? What was the object of your journey to England? of the farce which you enacted in my house, with the help of the woman Candeille? of that duel and that challenge, save that you desired to entice Sir Percy Blakeney to France?"

"And also his charming wife," he added with an ironical bow.

She bit her lip, and made no comment.

"Shall we say that I succeeded admirably?" he continued, speaking with persistent urbanity and calm, "and that I have strong cause to hope that the elusive Pimpernel will soon be a guest on our friendly shores? . . . There! you see I too have laid down the foils. . . . As you say, why should we fence? Your ladyship is now in Boulogne, soon Sir Percy will come to try and take you away from us, but believe me, fair lady, that it would take more than the ingenuity and the daring of the Scarlet Pimpernel magnified a thousandfold to get him back to England again . . . unless . . ."

"Unless? . . ."

Marguerite held her breath. She felt now as if the whole universe must stand still during the next supreme moment, until she had heard what Chauvelin's next words would be.

There was to be an "unless" then? An "either–or" more terrible no doubt than the one he had formulated before her just a year ago.

Chauvelin, she knew, was past master in the art of putting a knife at his victim's throat and of giving it just the necessary twist with his cruel and relentless "unless"!

But she felt quite calm, because her purpose was resolute. There is no doubt that during this agonizing moment of suspense she was absolutely firm in her determination to accept any and every condition which Chauvelin would put before her as the price of her husband's safety. After all, these conditions, since he placed them before *her*, could resolve themselves into questions of her own life against her husband's.

With that unreasoning impulse which was one of her most

salient characteristics, she never paused to think that, to Chauvelin, her own life or death were only the means to the great end which he had in view: the complete annihilation of the Scarlet Pimpernel.

That end could only be reached by Percy Blakeney's death—not by her own.

Even now as she was watching him with eyes glowing and lips tightly closed, lest a cry of impatient agony should escape her throat, he,—like a snail that has shown its slimy horns too soon, and is not ready to face the enemy as yet,—seemed suddenly to withdraw within his former shell of careless suavity. The earnestness of his tone vanished, giving place to light and easy conversation, just as if he were discussing social topics with a woman of fashion in a Paris drawing-room.

"Nay!" he said pleasantly, "is not your ladyship taking this matter in too serious a spirit? Of a truth you repeated my innocent word "unless" even as if I were putting a knife at your dainty throat. Yet I meant naught that need disturb you yet. Have I not said that I am your friend? Let me try and prove it to you."

"You will find that a difficult task, Monsieur," she said drily.

"Difficult tasks always have had a great fascination for your humble servant. May I try?"

"Certainly."

"Shall we then touch at the root of this delicate matter? Your ladyship, so I understand, is at this moment under the impression that I desire to encompass—shall I say?—the death of an English gentleman for whom, believe me, I have the greatest respect. That is so, is it not?"

"What is so, M. Chauvelin?" she asked almost stupidly, for truly she had not even begun to grasp his meaning. "I do not understand."

"You think that I am at this moment taking measures for sending the Scarlet Pimpernel to the guillotine? Eh?"

"I do."

"Never was so great an error committed by a clever woman.

Your ladyship must believe me when I say that the guillotine is the very last place in the world where I would wish to see that enigmatic and elusive personage."

"Are you trying to fool me, M. Chauvelin? If so, for what purpose? And why do you lie to me like that?"

"On my honour, 'tis the truth. The death of Sir Percy Blakeney—I may call him that, may I not?—would ill suit the purpose which I have in view."

"What purpose? You must pardon me, Monsieur Chauvelin," she added with a quick, impatient sigh, "but of a truth I am getting confused, and my wits must have become dull in the past few days. I pray you to add to your many protestations of friendship a little more clearness in your speech and, if possible, a little more brevity. What then is the purpose which you had in view when you enticed my husband to come over to France?"

"My purpose was the destruction of the Scarlet Pimpernel, not the death of Sir Percy Blakeney. Believe me, I have a great regard for Sir Percy. He is a most accomplished gentleman, witty, brilliant, an inimitable dandy. Why should he not grace with his presence the drawing-rooms of London or of Brighton for many years to come?"

She looked at him with puzzled inquiry. For one moment the thought flashed through her mind that, after all, Chauvelin might be still in doubt as to the identity of the Scarlet Pimpernel. . . . But no! that hope was madness. . . . It was preposterous and impossible. . . . But then, why? why? why? . . . Oh God! for a little more patience!

"What I have just said may seem a little enigmatic to your ladyship," he continued blandly, "but surely so clever a woman as yourself, so great a lady as is the wife of Sir Percy Blakeney, Baronet, will be aware that there are other means of destroying an enemy than the taking of his life."

"For instance, Monsieur Chauvelin?"

"There is the destruction of his honour," he replied slowly.

A long, bitter laugh, almost hysterical in its loud outburst, broke from the very depths of Marguerite's convulsed heart.

"The destruction of his honour! . . . ha! ha! ha! ha! . . . of a truth, Monsieur Chauvelin, your inventive powers have led you beyond the bounds of dreamland! . . . Ha! ha! ha! ha! . . . It is in the land of madness that you are wandering, sir, when you talk in one breath of Sir Percy Blakeney and the possible destruction of his honour!"

But he remained apparently quite unruffled, and when her laughter had somewhat subsided, he said placidly:

"Perhaps! . . ."

Then he rose from his chair, and once more approached her. This time she did not shrink from him. The suggestion which he had made just now, this talk of attacking her husband's honour rather than his life, seemed so wild and preposterous—the conception truly of a mind unhinged—that she looked upon it as a sign of extreme weakness on his part, almost as an acknowledgement of impotence.

But she watched him as he moved round the table more in curiosity now than in fright. He puzzled her, and she still had a feeling at the back of her mind that there must be something more definite and more evil lurking at the back of that tortuous brain.

"Will your ladyship allow me to conduct you to yonder window?" he said, "the air is cool, and what I have to say can best be done in sight of yonder sleeping city."

His tone was one of perfect courtesy, even of respectful deference through which not the slightest trace of sarcasm could be discerned, and she, still actuated by curiosity and interest, not in any way by fear, quietly rose to obey him. Though she ignored the hand which he was holding out towards her, she followed him readily enough as he walked up to the window.

All through this agonizing and soul-stirring interview she had felt heavily oppressed by the close atmosphere of the room, rendered nauseous by the evil smell of the smoky tallow-candles which were left to spread their grease and smoke abroad unchecked. Once or twice she had gazed longingly towards the suggestion of pure air outside.

Chauvelin evidently had still much to say to her: the torturing, mental rack to which she was being subjected had not yet fully done its work. It still was capable of one or two turns, a twist or so which might succeed in crushing her pride and her defiance. Well! so be it! she was in the man's power: had placed herself therein through her own unreasoning impulse. This interview was but one of the many soul-agonies which she had been called upon to endure, and if by submitting to it all she could in a measure mitigate her own faults and be of help to the man she loved, she would find the sacrifice small and the mental torture easy to bear.

Therefore when Chauvelin beckoned to her to draw near, she went up to the window, and leaning her head against the deep stone embrasure, she looked out into the night.

CHAPTER XXIII

THE HOSTAGE

Chauvelin, without speaking, extended his hand out towards the city as if to invite Marguerite to gaze upon it.

She was quite unconscious what hour of the night it might be, but it must have been late, for the little town, encircled by the stony arms of its forts, seemed asleep. The moon, now slowly sinking in the west, edged the towers and spires with filmy lines of silver. To the right Marguerite caught sight of the frowning Beffroi, which even as she gazed out began tolling its heavy bell. It sounded like the tocsin, dull and muffled. After ten strokes it was still.

Ten o'clock! At this hour in far-off England, in fashionable London, the play was just over, crowds of gaily dressed men and women poured out of the open gates of the theatres calling loudly for attendant or chaise. Thence to balls or routs, gaily fluttering like so many butterflies, brilliant and irresponsible. . . .

And in England also, in the beautiful gardens of her Richmond home, ofttimes at ten o'clock she had wandered alone with Percy, when he was at home, and the spirit of adventure in him momentarily laid to rest. Then, when the night was very dark and the air heavy with the scent of roses and lilies, she lay quiescent in his arms in that little arbour beside the river. The rhythmic lapping of the waves was the only sound that stirred the balmy air. He seldom spoke then, for his voice would shake whenever he uttered a word: but his impenetrable armour of flippancy was pierced through and he did not speak because his lips were pressed to hers, and his love had soared beyond the domain of speech.

A shudder of intense mental pain went through her now as she gazed on the sleeping city, and sweet memories of the past turned to bitterness in this agonizing present. One by one as the moon gradually disappeared behind a bank of clouds, the towers of Boulogne were merged in the gloom. In front of her far, far away, beyond the flat sand dunes, the sea seemed to be calling to her with a ghostly and melancholy moan.

The window was on the ground floor of the Fort, and gave direct onto the wide and shady walk which runs along the crest of the city walls; from where she stood Marguerite was looking straight along the ramparts, some thirty mètres wide at this point, flanked on either side by the granite balustrade, and adorned with a double row of ancient elms stunted and twisted into grotesque shapes by the persistent action of the wind.

"These wide ramparts are a peculiarity of this city . . ." said a voice close to her ear, "at times of peace they form an agreeable promenade under the shade of the trees, and a delightful meeting-place for lovers . . . or enemies. . . ."

The sound brought her back to the ugly realities of the present: the rose-scented garden at Richmond, the lazily flowing river, the tender memories which for that brief moment had confronted her from out a happy past, suddenly vanished from her ken. Instead of these the brine-laden sea-air struck her quivering nostrils, the echo of the old Beffroi died away in her ear, and now from out one of the streets or open places of the sleeping city there came the sound of a raucous voice, shouting in monotonous tones a string of words, the meaning of which failed to reach her brain.

Not many feet below the window, the southern ramparts of the town stretched away into the darkness. She felt unaccountably cold suddenly as she looked down upon them and, with aching eyes, tried to pierce the gloom. She was shivering in spite of the mildness of this early autumnal night: her overwrought fancy was peopling the lonely walls with unearthly shapes strolling along, discussing in spectral language a strange duel which was to take place here between a noted butcher of men and a mad Englishman overfond of adventure.

The ghouls seemed to pass and repass along in front of her and to be laughing audibly because that mad Englishman had been offered his life in exchange for his honour. They laughed and laughed, no doubt because he refused the bargain—Englishmen were always eccentric, and in these days of equality and other devices of a free and glorious revolution, honour was such a very marketable commodity that it seemed ridiculous to prize it quite so highly. Then they strolled away again and disappeared, whilst Marguerite distinctly heard the scrunching of the path beneath their feet. She leant forward to peer still further into the darkness, for this sound had seemed so absolutely real, but immediately a detaining hand was placed upon her arm and a sarcastic voice murmured at her elbow:

"The result, fair lady, would only be a broken leg or arm; the height is not great enough for picturesque suicides, and believe me these ramparts are only haunted by ghosts."

She drew back as if a viper had stung her; for the moment she had become oblivious of Chauvelin's presence. However, she would not take notice of his taunt, and, after a slight pause, he asked her if she could hear the town crier over in the public streets.

"Yes," she replied.

"What he says at this present moment is of vast importance to your ladyship," he remarked drily.

"How so?"

"Your ladyship is a precious hostage. We are taking measures to guard our valuable property securely."

Marguerite thought of the Abbé Foucquet, who no doubt was still quietly telling his beads, even if in his heart he had begun to wonder what had become of her. She thought of François, who was the breadwinner, and of Félicité, who was blind.

"Methinks you and your colleagues have done that already," she said.

"Not as completely as we would wish. We know the daring of the Scarlet Pimpernel. We are not even ashamed to admit that

we fear his luck, his impudence and his marvellous ingenuity.
. . . Have I not told you that I have the greatest possible respect
for that mysterious English hero. . . . An old priest and two
young children might be spirited away by that enigmatical adventurer, even whilst Lady Blakeney herself is made to vanish
from our sight."

"Ah! I see your ladyship is taking my simple words as a confession of weakness," he continued, noting the swift sigh of hope
which had involuntarily escaped her lips. "Nay! and it please
you, you shall despise me for it. But a confession of weakness is
the first sign of strength. The Scarlet Pimpernel is still at large,
and whilst we guard our hostage securely, he is bound to fall into
our hands."

"Aye! still at large!" she retorted with impulsive defiance.
"Think you that all your bolts and bars, the ingenuity of yourself
and your colleagues, the collaboration of the devil himself,
would succeed in outwitting the Scarlet Pimpernel, now that his
purpose will be to try and drag *me* from out your clutches."

She felt hopeful and proud. Now that she had the pure air of
heaven in her lungs, that from afar she could smell the sea, and
could feel that perhaps in a straight line of vision from where
she stood, the "Day-Dream" with Sir Percy on board, might be
lying out there in the roads, it seemed impossible that he should
fail in freeing her and those poor people—an old man and two
children—whose lives depended on her own.

But Chauvelin only laughed a dry, sarcastic laugh and said:

"Hm! perhaps not! . . . It of course will depend on you and
your personality . . . your feelings in such matters . . . and
whether an English gentleman likes to save his own skin at the
expense of others."

Marguerite shivered as if from cold.

"Ah! I see," resumed Chauvelin quietly, "that your ladyship
has not quite grasped the position. That public crier is a long
way off: the words have lingered on the evening breeze and have
failed to reach your brain. Do you suppose that I and my colleagues do not know that all the ingenuity of which the Scarlet
Pimpernel is capable will now be directed in piloting Lady

Blakeney, and incidentally the Abbé Foucquet with his nephew and niece, safely across the Channel. Four people! . . . Bah! a bagatelle, for this mighty conspirator, who but lately snatched twenty aristocrats from the prisons of Lyons. . . . Nay! nay! two children and an old man were not enough to guard our precious hostage, and I was not thinking of either the Abbé Foucquet or of the two children, when I said that an English gentleman would not save himself at the expense of others."

"Of whom then were you thinking, Monsieur Chauvelin? Whom else have you set to guard the prize which you value so highly?"

"The whole city of Boulogne," he replied simply.

"I do not understand."

"Let me make my point clear. My colleague, Citizen Collot d'Herbois, rode over from Paris yesterday; like myself he is a member of the Committee of Public Safety whose duty it is to look after the welfare of France by punishing all those who conspire against her laws and the liberties of the people. Chief among these conspirators, whom it is our duty to punish is, of course, that impudent adventurer who calls himself the Scarlet Pimpernel. He has given the government of France a great deal of trouble through his attempts—mostly successful, as I have already admitted,—at frustrating the just vengeance which an oppressed country has the right to wreak on those who have proved themselves to be tyrants and traitors."

"Is it necessary to recapitulate all this, Monsieur Chauvelin?" she asked impatiently.

"I think so," he replied blandly. "You see, my point is this. We feel that in a measure now the Scarlet Pimpernel is in our power. Within the next few hours he will land at Boulogne . . . Boulogne, where he has agreed to fight a duel with me . . . Boulogne, where Lady Blakeney happens to be at this present moment . . . as you see, Boulogne has a grave responsibility to bear: just now she is to a certain extent the proudest city in France, since she holds within her gates a hostage for the appearance on our shores of her country's most bitter enemy. But she must not fall from that high estate. Her double duty is clear before her: she must guard Lady Blakeney and capture the Scarlet Pimpernel; if she fail in the former she must be punished, if she succeed in the latter she shall be rewarded."

He paused and leaned out of the window again, whilst she watched him, breathless and terrified. She was beginning to understand.

"Hark!" he said, looking straight at her. "Do you hear the crier now? He is proclaiming the punishment and the reward. He is making it clear to the citizens of Boulogne that on the day when the Scarlet Pimpernel falls into the hands of the Committee of Public Safety a general amnesty will be granted to all natives of Boulogne who are under arrest at the present time, and a free pardon to all those who, born within these city walls, are to-day under sentence of death. . . . A noble reward, eh? well-deserved you'll admit. . . . Should you wonder then if the whole town of Boulogne were engaged just now in finding that mysterious hero, and delivering him into our hands? . . . How many mothers, sisters, wives, think you, at the present moment, would fail to lay hands on the English adventurer, if a husband's or a son's life or freedom happened to be at stake? . . . I have some records there," he continued, pointing in the direction of the table, "which tell me that there are five and thirty natives of Boulogne in the local prisons, a dozen more in the prisons of Paris; of these at least twenty have been tried already and are condemned to death. Every hour that the Scarlet Pimpernel succeeds in evading his captors so many deaths lie at his door. If he succeeds in once more reaching England safely three score lives mayhap will be the price of his escape. . . . Nay! but I see your ladyship is shivering with cold . . ." he added with a dry little laugh, "shall I close the window? or do you wish to hear what punishment will be meted out to Boulogne, if on the day that the Scarlet Pimpernel is captured, Lady Blakeney happens to have left the shelter of these city walls?"

"I pray you proceed, Monsieur," she rejoined with perfect calm.

"The Committee of Public Safety," he resumed, "would look upon this city as a nest of traitors if on the day that the Scarlet

Pimpernel becomes our prisoner Lady Blakeney herself, the wife of that notorious English spy, had already quitted Boulogne. The whole town knows by now that you are in our hands—you, the most precious hostage we can hold for the ultimate capture of the man whom we all fear and detest. Virtually the town-crier is at the present moment proclaiming to the inhabitants of this city: 'We want that man, but we already have his wife, see to it, citizens, that she does not escape! for if she do, we shall summarily shoot the breadwinner in every family in the town!'"

A cry of horror escaped Marguerite's parched lips.

"Are you devils then, all of you," she gasped, "that you should think of such things?"

"Aye! some of us are devils, no doubt," said Chauvelin drily; "but why should you honour us in this case with so flattering an epithet? We are mere men striving to guard our property and mean no harm to the citizens of Boulogne. We have threatened them, true! but is it not for you and that elusive Pimpernel to see that the threat is never put into execution?"

"You would not do it!" she repeated, horror-stricken.

"Nay! I pray you, fair lady, do not deceive yourself. At present the proclamation sounds like a mere threat, I'll allow, but let me assure you that if we fail to capture the Scarlet Pimpernel and if you on the other hand are spirited out of this fortress by that mysterious adventurer we shall undoubtedly shoot or guillotine every able-bodied man and woman in this town."

He had spoken quietly and emphatically, neither with bombast, nor with rage, and Marguerite saw in his face nothing but a calm and ferocious determination, the determination of an entire nation embodied in this one man, to be revenged at any cost. She would not let him see the depth of her despair, nor would she let him read in her face the unutterable hopelessness which filled her soul. It were useless to make an appeal to him: she knew full well that from him she could obtain neither gentleness nor mercy.

"I hope at last I have made the situation quite clear to your ladyship?" he was asking quite pleasantly now. "See how easy is your position: you have but to remain quiescent in room No. 6, and if any chance of escape be offered you ere the Scarlet Pimpernel is captured, you need but to think of all the families of Boulogne, who would be deprived of their bread-winner—fathers and sons mostly, but there are girls too, who support their mothers or sisters; the fish curers of Boulogne are mostly women, and there are the net-makers and the seamstresses, all would suffer if your ladyship were no longer to be found in No. 6 room of this ancient fort, whilst all would be included in the amnesty if the Scarlet Pimpernel fell into our hands . . ."

He gave a low, satisfied chuckle which made Marguerite think of the evil spirits in hell exulting over the torments of unhappy lost souls.

"I think, Lady Blakeney," he added drily and making her an ironical bow, "that your humble servant hath outwitted the elusive hero at last."

Quietly he turned on his heel and went back into the room, Marguerite remaining motionless beside the open window, where the soft, brine-laden air, the distant murmur of the sea, the occasional cry of a sea-mew, all seemed to mock her agonizing despair.

The voice of the town-crier came nearer and nearer now: she could hear the words he spoke quite distinctly: something about "amnesty" and pardon, the reward for the capture of the Scarlet Pimpernel, the lives of men, women and children in exchange for his.

Oh! she knew what all that meant! that Percy would not hesitate one single instant to throw his life into the hands of his enemies, in exchange for that of others. Others! others! always others! this sigh that had made her heart ache so often in England, what terrible significance it bore now!

And how he would suffer in his heart and in his pride, because of her whom he could not even attempt to save since it would mean the death of others! of others, always of others!

She wondered if he had already landed in Boulogne! Again she remembered the vision on the landing stage: his massive figure, the glimpse she had of the loved form, in the midst of the crowd!

The moment he entered the town he would hear the proclamation read, see it posted up no doubt on every public building, and realize that she had been foolish enough to follow him, that she was a prisoner and that he could do nothing to save her.

What would he do? Marguerite at the thought instinctively pressed her hands to her heart, the agony of it all had become physically painful. She hoped that perhaps this pain meant approaching death! oh! how easy would this simple solution be!

The moon peered out from beneath the bank of clouds which had obscured her for so long; smiling, she drew her pencilled silver lines along the edge of towers and pinnacles, the frowning Beffroi and those stony walls which seemed to Marguerite as if they encircled a gigantic graveyard.

The town-crier had evidently ceased to read the proclamation. One by one the windows in the public square were lighted up from within. The citizens of Boulogne wanted to think over the strange events which had occurred without their knowledge, yet which were apparently to have such direful or such joyous consequences for them.

A man to be captured! the mysterious English adventurer of whom they had all heard, but whom nobody had seen. And a woman—his wife—to be guarded until the man was safely under lock and key.

Marguerite felt as if she could almost hear them talking it over and vowing that she should not escape, and that the Scarlet Pimpernel should soon be captured.

A gentle wind stirred the old gnarled trees on the southern ramparts, a wind that sounded like the sigh of swiftly dying hope.

What could Percy do now? His hands were tied, and he was inevitably destined to endure the awful agony of seeing the woman he loved die a terrible death beside him.

Having captured him, they would not keep him long; no necessity for a trial, for detention, for formalities of any kind. A summary execution at dawn on the public place, a roll of drums, a public holiday to mark the joyful event, and a brave man will have ceased to live, a noble heart have stilled its beatings forever, whilst a whole nation gloried over the deed.

"Sleep, citizens of Boulogne! all is still!"

The night watchman had replaced the town-crier. All was quiet within the city walls: the inhabitants could sleep in peace, a beneficent government was wakeful and guarding their rest.

But many of the windows of the town remained lighted up, and at a little distance below her, round the corner so that she could not see it, a small crowd must have collected in front of the gateway which led into the courtyard of the Gayole Fort. Marguerite could hear a persistent murmur of voices, mostly angry and threatening, and once there were loud cries of: "English spies," and "à la lanterne!"

"The citizens of Boulogne are guarding the treasures of France!" commented Chauvelin drily, as he laughed again, that cruel, mirthless laugh of his.

Then she roused herself from her torpor: she did not know how long she had stood beside the open window, but the fear seized her that that man must have seen and gloated over the agony of her mind. She straightened her graceful figure, threw back her proud head defiantly, and quietly walked up to the table, where Chauvelin seemed once more absorbed in the perusal of his papers.

"Is this interview over?" she asked quietly, and without the slightest tremor in her voice. "May I go now?"

"As soon as you wish," he replied with gentle irony.

He regarded her with obvious delight, for truly she was beautiful: grand in this attitude of defiant despair. The man, who had spent the last half-hour in martyrizing her, gloried over the misery which he had wrought, and which all her strength of will could not entirely banish from her face.

"Will you believe me, Lady Blakeney?" he added, "that there is no personal animosity in my heart towards you or your husband? Have I not told you that I do not wish to compass his death?"

"Yet you propose to send him to the guillotine as soon as you have laid hands on him."

"I have explained to you the measures which I have taken in order to make sure that we *do* lay hands on the Scarlet Pimpernel. Once he is in our power, it will rest with him to walk to the guillotine or to embark with you on board his yacht."

"You propose to place an alternative before Sir Percy Blakeney?"

"Certainly."

"To offer him his life?"

"And that of his charming wife."

"In exchange for what?"

"His honour."

"He will refuse, Monsieur."

"We shall see."

Then he touched a handbell which stood on the table, and within a few seconds the door was opened and the soldier who had led Marguerite hither, re-entered the room.

The interview was at an end. It had served its purpose. Marguerite knew now that she must not even think of escape for herself, or hope for safety for the man she loved. Of Chauvelin's talk of a bargain which would touch Percy's honour she would not even think: and she was too proud to ask anything further from him.

Chauvelin stood up and made her a deep bow, as she crossed the room and finally went out of the door. The little company of soldiers closed in around her and she was once more led along the dark passages, back to her own prison cell.

CHAPTER XXIV

COLLEAGUES

As soon as the door had closed behind Marguerite, there came from somewhere in the room the sound of a yawn, a grunt and a volley of oaths.

The flickering light of the tallow candles had failed to penetrate into all the corners, and now from out one of these dark depths, a certain something began to detach itself, and to move forward towards the table at which Chauvelin had once more resumed his seat.

"Has the damned aristocrat gone at last?" queried a hoarse voice, as a burly body clad in loose-fitting coat and mud-stained boots and breeches appeared within the narrow circle of light.

"Yes," replied Chauvelin curtly.

"And a cursed long time you have been with the baggage," grunted the other surlily. "Another five minutes and I'd have taken the matter in my own hands."

"An assumption of authority," commented Chauvelin quietly, "to which your position here does not entitle you, Citizen Collot."

Collot d'Herbois lounged lazily forward, and presently he threw his ill-knit figure into the chair lately vacated by Marguerite. His heavy, square face bore distinct traces of the fatigue endured in the past twenty-four hours on horseback or in jolting market waggons. His temper too appeared to have suffered on the way, and, at Chauvelin's curt and dictatorial replies, he looked as surly as a chained dog.

"You were wasting your breath over that woman," he muttered, bringing a large and grimy fist heavily down on the table, "and your measures are not quite so sound as you fondly imagine, Citizen Chauvelin."

"They were mostly of your imagining, Citizen Collot," rejoined the other quietly, "and of your suggestion."

"I added a touch of strength and determination to your mild milk-and-water notions, Citizen," snarled Collot spitefully. "I'd have knocked that intriguing woman's brains out at the very first possible opportunity, had I been consulted earlier than this."

"Quite regardless of the fact that such violent measures would completely damn all our chances of success as far as the capture of the Scarlet Pimpernel is concerned," remarked Chauvelin drily, with a contemptuous shrug of the shoulders. "Once his wife is dead, the Englishman will never run his head into the noose which I have so carefully prepared for him."

"So you say, Citizen; and therefore I suggested to you certain measures to prevent the woman escaping which you will find adequate, I hope."

"You need have no fear, Citizen Collot," said Chauvelin curtly, "this woman will make no attempt at escape now."

"If she does . . ." and Collot d'Herbois swore an obscene oath.

"I think she understands that we mean to put our threat in execution."

"Threat? . . . It was no empty threat, Citizen. . . . Sacré tonnerre! if that woman escapes now, by all the devils in hell I swear that I'll wield the guillotine myself and cut off the head of every able-bodied man or woman in Boulogne, with my own hands."

As he said this his face assumed such an expression of inhuman cruelty, such a desire to kill, such a savage lust for blood, that instinctively Chauvelin shuddered and shrank away from his colleague. All through his career there is no doubt that this man, who was of gentle birth, of gentle breeding, and who had once been called M. le Marquis de Chauvelin, must have suffered in his susceptibilities and in his pride when in contact with the revolutionaries with whom he had chosen to cast his lot. He could not have thrown off all his old ideas of refinement quite so easily, as to feel happy in the presence of such men as Collot d'Herbois, or Marat in his day—men who had become brute beasts, more ferocious far than any wild animal, more scientifically cruel than any feline prowler in jungle or desert.

One look in Collot's distorted face was sufficient at this moment to convince Chauvelin that it were useless for him to view the proclamation against the citizens of Boulogne merely as an idle threat, even if he had wished to do so. That Marguerite would not, under the circumstances, attempt to escape, that Sir Percy Blakeney himself would be forced to give up all thoughts of rescuing her, was a foregone conclusion in Chauvelin's mind, but if this high-born English gentleman had not happened to be the selfless hero that he was, if Marguerite Blakeney were cast in a different, a rougher mould—if, in short, the Scarlet Pimpernel in the face of the proclamation did succeed in dragging his wife out of the clutches of the Terrorists, then it was equally certain that Collot d'Herbois would carry out his rabid and cruel reprisals to the full. And if in the course of the wholesale butchery of the able-bodied and wage-earning inhabitants of Boulogne, the headsman should sink worn out, then would this ferocious sucker of blood put his own hand to the guillotine, with the same joy and lust which he had felt when he ordered one hundred and thirty-eight women of Nantes to be stripped naked by the soldiery before they were flung helter-skelter into the river.

A touch of strength and determination! Aye! Citizen Collot d'Herbois had plenty of that. Was it he, or Carrière who at Arras commanded mothers to stand by while their children were being guillotined? And surely it was Maignet, Collot's friend and colleague, who at Bedouin, because the Red Flag of the Republic had been mysteriously torn down over night, burnt the entire little village down to the last hovel and guillotined every one of the three hundred and fifty inhabitants.

And Chauvelin knew all that. Nay, more! he was himself a member of that so-called government which had countenanced these butcheries, by giving unlimited powers to men like Collot, like Maignet and Carrière. He was at one with them in their republican ideas and he believed in the regeneration and the purification of France, through the medium of the guillotine, but he propounded his theories and carried out his most blood-thirsty schemes with physically clean hands and in an immaculately cut coat.

Even now when Collot d'Herbois lounged before him, with mud-bespattered legs stretched out before him, with dubious linen at neck and wrists, and an odour of rank tobacco and stale, cheap wine pervading his whole personality, the more fastidious man of the world, who had consorted with the dandies of London and Brighton, winced at the enforced proximity.

But it was the joint characteristic of all these men who had turned France into a vast butchery and charnel-house, that they all feared and hated one another, even more whole-heartedly than they hated the aristocrats and so-called traitors whom they sent to the guillotine. Citizen Lebon is said to have dipped his sword into the blood which flowed from the guillotine, whilst exclaiming: "Comme je l'aime ce sang coulé de traitre!" but he and Collot and Danton and Robespierre, all of them in fact, would have regarded with more delight still the blood of any one of their colleagues.

At this very moment Collot d'Herbois and Chauvelin would with utmost satisfaction have denounced, one the other, to the tender mercies of the Public Prosecutor. Collot made no secret of his hatred for Chauvelin, and the latter disguised it but thinly under the veneer of contemptuous indifference.

"As for that dammed Englishman," added Collot now, after a slight pause, and with another savage oath, "if 'tis my good fortune to lay hands on him, I'd shoot him then and there like a mad dog, and rid France once and forever of this accursed spy."

"And think you, Citizen Collot," rejoined Chauvelin with a shrug of the shoulders, "that France would be rid of all English adventurers by the summary death of this one man?"

"He is the ringleader, at any rate . . ."

"And has at least nineteen disciples to continue his traditions of conspiracy and intrigue. None perhaps so ingenuous as himself, none with the same daring and good luck perhaps, but still a number of ardent fools only too ready to follow in the footsteps of their chief. Then there's the halo of martyrdom around the murdered hero, the enthusiasm created by his noble death . . . Nay! nay, Citizen, you have not lived among these English people, you do not understand them, or you would not talk of sending their popular hero to an honoured grave."

But Collot d'Herbois only shook his powerful frame like some big, sulky dog, and spat upon the floor to express his contempt of this wild talk which seemed to have no real tangible purpose.

"You have not caught your Scarlet Pimpernel yet, Citizen," he said with a snort.

"No, but I will, after sundown to-morrow."

"How do you know?"

"I have ordered the Angelus to be rung at one of the closed churches, and he agreed to fight a duel with me on the southern ramparts at that hour and on that day," said Chauvelin simply.

"You take him for a fool?" sneered Collot.

"No, only for a foolhardy adventurer."

"You imagine that with his wife as hostage in our hands, and the whole city of Boulogne on the lookout for him for the sake of the amnesty, that the man would be fool enough to walk on those ramparts at a given hour, for the express purpose of getting himself caught by you and your men?"

"I am quite sure that if we do not lay hands on him before that given hour, that he will be on the ramparts at the Angelus to-morrow," said Chauvelin emphatically.

Collot shrugged his broad shoulders.

"Is the man mad?" he asked with an incredulous laugh.

"Yes, I think so," rejoined the other with a smile.

"And having caught your hare," queried Collot, "how do you propose to cook him?"

"Twelve picked men will be on the ramparts ready to seize him the moment he appears."

"And to shoot him at sight, I hope."

"Only as a last resource, for the Englishman is powerful and may cause our half-famished men a good deal of trouble. But I want him alive, if possible . . ."

"Why? a dead lion is safer than a live one any day."

"Oh! we'll kill him right enough, Citizen. I pray you have no fear. I hold a weapon ready for that meddlesome Scarlet Pimpernel, which will be a thousand times more deadly and more effectual than a chance shot, or even the guillotine."

"What weapon is that, Citizen Chauvelin?"

Chauvelin leaned forward across the table and rested his chin in his hands; instinctively Collot too leaned towards him, and both men peered furtively round them as if wondering if prying ears happened to be lurking round. It was Chauvelin's pale eyes which now gleamed with hatred and with an insatiable lust for revenge at least as powerful as Collot's lust for blood; the unsteady light of the tallow candles threw grotesque shadows across his brows, and his mouth was set in such rigid lines of implacable cruelty that the brutish sot beside him gazed on him amazed, vaguely scenting here a depth of feeling which was beyond his power to comprehend. He repeated his question under his breath:

"What weapon do you mean to use against that accursed spy, Citizen Chauvelin?"

"Dishonour and ridicule!" replied the other quietly.

"Bah!"

"In exchange for his life and that of his wife."

"As the woman told you just now . . . he will refuse."

"We shall see, Citizen."

"You are mad to think such things, Citizen, and ill serve the Republic by sparing her bitterest foe."

A long, sarcastic laugh broke from Chauvelin's parted lips.

"Spare him?—spare the Scarlet Pimpernel! . . ." he ejaculated. "Nay, Citizen, you need have no fear of that. But believe me, I have schemes in my head by which the man whom we all hate will be more truly destroyed than your guillotine could ever accomplish: schemes, whereby the hero who is now worshipped in England as a demi-god will suddenly become an object of loathing and of contempt. . . . Ah! I see you understand me now . . . I wish to so cover him with ridicule that the very name of the small wayside flower will become a term of derision and of scorn. Only then shall we be rid of these pestilential English spies, only then will the entire League of the Scarlet Pimpernel become a thing of the past when its whilom leader, now thought akin to a god, will have found refuge in a suicide's grave, from the withering contempt of the entire world."

Chauvelin had spoken low, hardly above a whisper, and the echo of his last words died away in the great, squalid room like a long-drawn-out sigh. There was dead silence for a while save for the murmur in the wind outside and from the floor above the measured tread of the sentinel guarding the precious hostage in No. 6.

Both men were staring straight in front of them. Collot d'Herbois incredulous, half-contemptuous, did not altogether approve of these schemes which seemed to him wild and un-canny: he liked the direct simplicity of a summary trial, of the guillotine, or of his own well stage-managed "Noyades." He did not feel that any ridicule or dishonour would necessarily para-lyze a man in his efforts at intrigue, and would have liked to set Chauvelin's authority aside, to behead the woman upstairs and then to take his chances of capturing the man later on.

But the orders of the Committee of Public Safety had been peremptory: he was to be Chauvelin's help—not his master, and to obey him in all things. He did not dare to take any initiative in the matter, for in that case, if he failed, the reprisals against him would indeed be terrible.

He was fairly satisfied now that Chauvelin had accepted his suggestion of summarily sending to the guillotine one member of every family resident in Boulogne, if Marguerite succeeded in effecting an escape, and, of a truth, Chauvelin had hailed the fiendish suggestion with delight. The old abbé with his nephew and niece were undoubtedly not sufficient deterrents against the daring schemes of the Scarlet Pimpernel, who, as a matter of fact, could spirit them out of Boulogne just as easily as he would his own wife.

Collot's plan tied Marguerite to her own prison cell more completely than any other measure could have done, more so indeed than the originator thereof knew or believed. . . . A man like this d'Herbois—born in the gutter, imbued with every

brutish tradition, which generations of jail-birds had be-
queathed to him,—would not perhaps fully realize the fact that
neither Sir Percy nor Marguerite Blakeney would ever save
themselves at the expense of others. He had merely made the
suggestion, because he felt that Chauvelin's plans were compli-
cated and obscure, and above all insufficient, and that perhaps
after all the English adventurer and his wife would succeed in
once more outwitting him, when there would remain the grand
and bloody compensation of a wholesale butchery in Boulogne.

But Chauvelin was quite satisfied. He knew that under present circumstances neither Sir Percy nor Marguerite would make
any attempt to escape. The ex-ambassador had lived in England:
he understood the class to which these two belonged, and was
quite convinced that no attempt would be made on either side
to get Lady Blakeney away whilst the present ferocious order
against the bread-winner of every family in the town held good.

Aye! the measures were sound enough. Chauvelin was easy in
his mind about that. In another twenty-four hours he would
hold the man completely in his power who had so boldly outwitted him last year; to-night he would sleep in peace: an entire
city was guarding the precious hostage.

"We'll go to bed now, Citizen," he said to Collot, who, tired
and sulky, was moodily fingering the papers on the table. The
scraping sound which he made thereby grated on Chauvelin's
overstrung nerves. He wanted to be alone, and the sleepy
brute's presence here jarred on his own solemn mood.

To his satisfaction, Collot grunted a surly assent. Very
leisurely he rose from his chair, stretched out his loose limbs,
shook himself like a shaggy cur, and without uttering another
word he gave his colleague a curt nod, and slowly lounged out
of the room.

CHAPTER XXV

The Unexpected

Chauvelin heaved a deep sigh of satisfaction when Collot d'Herbois finally left him to himself. He listened for awhile until the heavy footsteps died away in the distance, then leaning back in his chair, he gave himself over to the delights of the present situation.

Marguerite in his power. Sir Percy Blakeney compelled to treat for her rescue if he did not wish to see her die a miserable death.

"Aye! my elusive hero," he muttered to himself, "methinks that we shall be able to cry quits at last."

Outside everything had become still. Even the wind in the trees out there on the ramparts had ceased their melancholy moaning. The man was alone with his thoughts. He felt secure and at peace, sure of victory, content to await the events of the next twenty-four hours. The other side of the door the guard which he had picked out from amongst the more feeble and ill-fed garrison of the little city for attendance on his own person were ranged ready to respond to his call.

"Dishonour and ridicule! Derision and scorn!" he murmured, gloating over the very sound of these words, which expressed all that he hoped to accomplish, "utter abjection, then perhaps a suicide's grave . . ."

He loved the silence around him, for he could murmur these words and hear them echoing against the bare stone walls like the whisperings of all the spirits of hate which were waiting to lend him their aid.

How long he had remained thus absorbed in his meditations, he could not afterwards have said; a minute or two perhaps at most, whilst he leaned back in his chair with eyes closed, savouring the sweets of his own thoughts, when suddenly the silence was interrupted by a loud and pleasant laugh and a drawly voice speaking in merry accents:

"The lud live you, Monsieur Chaubertin, and pray how do you propose to accomplish all these pleasant things?"

In a moment Chauvelin was on his feet and with eyes dilated, lips parted in awed bewilderment, he was gazing towards the open window, where astride upon the sill, one leg inside the room, the other out, and with the moon shining full on his suit of delicate-coloured cloth, his wide caped coat and elegant chapeau-bras, sat the imperturbable Sir Percy.

"I heard you muttering such pleasant words, Monsieur," continued Blakeney calmly, "that the temptation seized me to join in the conversation. A man talking to himself is ever in a sorry plight . . . he is either a madman or a fool . . ."

He laughed his own quaint and inane laugh and added apologetically:

"Far be it from me, sir, to apply either epithet to you . . . demmed bad form calling another fellow names . . . just when he does not quite feel himself, eh? . . . You don't feel quite yourself, I fancy just now . . . eh, Monsieur Chaubertin . . . er . . . beg pardon, Chauvelin . . ."

He sat there quite comfortably, one slender hand resting on the gracefully-fashioned hilt of his sword—the sword of Lorenzo Cenci,—the other holding up the gold-rimmed eyeglass through which he was regarding his avowed enemy; he was dressed as for a ball, and his perpetually amiable smile lurked round the corners of his firm lips.

Chauvelin had undoubtedly for the moment lost his presence of mind. He did not even think of calling to his picked guard, so completely taken aback was he by this unforeseen move on the part of Sir Percy. Yet, obviously, he should have been ready for this eventuality. Had he not caused the town-crier to loudly proclaim throughout the city that if *one* female prisoner escaped

from Fort Gayole the entire able-bodied population of
Boulogne would suffer?

The moment Sir Percy entered the gates of the town, he
could not help but hear the proclamation, and hear at the same
time that this one female prisoner who was so precious a charge,
was the wife of the English spy: the Scarlet Pimpernel.

Moreover, was it not a fact that whenever or wherever the
Scarlet Pimpernel was least expected there and then would he
surely appear? Having once realized that it was his wife who was
incarcerated in Fort Gayole, was it not natural that he would go
and prowl around the prison, and along the avenue on the sum-
mit of the southern ramparts, which was accessible to every
passer-by? No doubt he had lain in hiding among the trees, had
perhaps caught snatches of Chauvelin's recent talk with Collot.

Aye! it was all so natural, so simple! Strange that it should
have been so unexpected!

Furious at himself for his momentary stupor, he now made a
vigorous effort to face his impudent enemy with the same sang-
froid of which the latter had so inexhaustible a fund.

He walked quietly towards the window, compelling his nerves
to perfect calm and his mood to indifference. The situation had
ceased to astonish him; already his keen mind had seen its possibilities, its grimness and its humour, and he was quite prepared to enjoy these to the full.

Sir Percy now was dusting the sleeve of his coat with a lace-
edged handkerchief, but just as Chauvelin was about to come
near him, he stretched out one leg, turning the point of a dainty
boot towards the ex-ambassador.

"Would you like to take hold of me by the leg, Monsieur
Chaubertin?" he said gaily. "'Tis more effectual than a shoulder,
and your picked guard of six stalwart fellows can have the other
leg. . . . Nay! I pray you, sir, do not look at me like that. . . . I vow
that it is myself and not my ghost. . . . But if you still doubt me,
I pray you call the guard . . . ere I fly out again towards that fitful moon . . ."

"Nay, Sir Percy," said Chauvelin, with a steady voice, "I have
no thought that you will take flight just yet. . . . Methinks you

desire conversation with me, or you had not paid me so unexpected a visit."

"Nay, sir, the air is too oppressive for lengthy conversation . . . I was strolling along these ramparts, thinking of our pleasant encounter at the hour of the Angelus to-morrow . . . when this light attracted me. . . . feared I had lost my way and climbed the window to obtain information."

"As to your way to the nearest prison cell, Sir Percy?" queried Chauvelin drily.

"As to anywhere, where I could sit more comfortably than on this demmed sill. . . . It must be very dusty, and I vow 'tis terribly hard . . ."

"I presume, Sir Percy, that you did my colleague and myself the honour of listening to our conversation?"

"An you desired to talk secrets, Monsieur . . . er . . . Chaubertin . . . you should have shut this window . . . and closed this avenue of trees against the chance passer-by."

"What we said was no secret, Sir Percy. It is all over the town to-night."

"Quite so . . . you were only telling the devil your mind . . . eh?"

"I had also been having conversation with Lady Blakeney. . . . Pray, did you hear any of that, sir?"

But Sir Percy had evidently not heard the question, for he seemed quite absorbed in the task of removing a speck of dust from his immaculate chapeau-bras.

"These hats are all the rage in England just now," he said airily, "but they have had their day, do you not think so, Monsieur? When I return to town, I shall have to devote my whole mind to the invention of a new headgear . . ."

"When will you return to England, Sir Percy?" queried Chauvelin with good-natured sarcasm.

"At the turn of the tide to-morrow eve, Monsieur," replied Blakeney.

"In company with Lady Blakeney?"

"Certainly, sir . . . and yours if you will honour us with your company."

"If you return to England to-morrow, Sir Percy, Lady Blakeney, I fear me, cannot accompany you."

"You astonish me, sir," rejoined Blakeney with an exclamation of genuine and unaffected surprise. "I wonder now what would prevent her?"

"All those whose death would be the result of her flight, if she succeeded in escaping from Boulogne . . ."

But Sir Percy was staring at him, with wide open eyes, expressive of utmost amazement.

"Dear, dear, dear. . . . Lud! but that sounds most unfortunate . . ."

"You have not heard of the measures which I have taken to prevent Lady Blakeney quitting this city without our leave?"

"No, Monsieur Chaubertin . . . no . . . I have heard nothing . . ." rejoined Sir Percy blandly. "I lead a very retired life when I come abroad and . . ."

"Would you wish to hear them now?"

"Quite unnecessary, sir, I assure you . . . and the hour is getting late . . ."

"Sir Percy, are you aware of the fact that unless you listen to what I have to say, your wife will be dragged before the Committee of Public Safety in Paris within the next twenty-four hours?" said Chauvelin firmly.

"What swift horses you must have, sir," quoth Blakeney pleasantly. "Lud! to think of it! . . . I always heard that these demmed French horses would never beat ours across country."

But Chauvelin now would not allow himself to be ruffled by Sir Percy's apparent indifference. Keen reader of emotions as he was, he had not failed to note a distinct change in the drawly voice, a sound of something hard and trenchant in the flippant laugh, ever since Marguerite's name was first mentioned. Blakeney's attitude was apparently as careless, as audacious as before, but Chauvelin's keen eyes had not missed the almost imperceptible tightening of the jaw and the rapid clenching of one hand on the sword hilt even whilst the other toyed in graceful idleness with the filmy Mechlin lace cravat.

Sir Percy's head was well thrown back, and the pale rays of the moon caught the edge of the clear-cut profile, the low massive brow, the drooping lids through which the audacious plotter was lazily regarding the man who held not only his own life, but that of the woman who was infinitely dear to him, in the hollow of his hand.

"I am afraid, Sir Percy," continued Chauvelin drily, "that you are under the impression that bolts and bars will yield to your usual good luck, now that so precious a life is at stake as that of Lady Blakeney."

"I am a greater believer in impressions, Monsieur Chauvelin."

"I told her just now that if she quitted Boulogne ere the Scarlet Pimpernel is in our hands, we should summarily shoot one member of every family in the town—the bread-winner."

"A pleasant conceit, Monsieur . . . and one that does infinite credit to your inventive faculties."

"Lady Blakeney, therefore, we hold safely enough," continued Chauvelin, who no longer heeded the mocking observations of his enemy; "as for the Scarlet Pimpernel . . ."

"You have but to ring a bell, to raise a voice, and he too will be under lock and key within the next two minutes, eh? . . . Passons, Monsieur . . . you are dying to say something further . . . I pray you proceed . . . your engaging countenance is becoming quite interesting in its seriousness."

"What I wish to say to you, Sir Percy, is in the nature of a proposed bargain."

"Indeed? . . . Monsieur, you are full of surprises . . . like a pretty woman. . . . And pray what are the terms of this proposed bargain?"

"Your side of the bargain, Sir Percy, or mine? Which will you hear first?"

"Oh yours, Monsieur . . . yours, I pray you. . . . Have I not said that you are like a pretty woman? . . . Place aux dames, sir! always!"

"My share of the bargain, sir, is simple enough: Lady Blakeney, escorted by yourself and any of your friends who

might be in this city at the time, shall leave Boulogne harbour at
sunset to-morrow, free and unmolested, if you on the other
hand will do your share . . ."

"I don't yet know what my share in this interesting bargain is
to be, sir . . . but for the sake of argument let us suppose that I
do not carry it out. . . . What then? . . ."

"Then, Sir Percy . . . putting aside for the moment the question of the Scarlet Pimpernel altogether . . . then, Lady
Blakeney will be taken to Paris, and will be incarcerated in the
prison of the Temple lately vacated by Marie Antoinette—there
she will be treated in exactly the same way as the ex-queen is
now being treated in the Conciergerie. . . . Do you know what
that means, Sir Percy? . . . It does not mean a summary trial and
a speedy death, with the halo and glory of martyrdom thrown in
. . . it means days, weeks, nay, months, perhaps, of misery and
humiliation . . . it means, that like Marie Antoinette, she will
never be allowed solitude for one single instant of the day or
night . . . it means the constant proximity of soldiers, drunk with
cruelty and with hate . . . the insults, the shame . . ."

"You hound! . . . you dog! . . . you cur! . . . do you not see that
I must strangle you for this! . . ."

The attack had been so sudden and so violent that Chauvelin
had not the time to utter the slightest call for help. But a second
ago, Sir Percy Blakeney had been sitting on the window-sill, outwardly listening with perfect calm to what his enemy had to say;
now he was at the latter's throat, pressing with long and slender
hands the breath out of the Frenchman's body, his usually placid
face distorted into a mask of hate.

"You cur! . . . you cur! . . ." he repeated, "am I to kill you or
will you unsay those words?"

Then suddenly he relaxed his grip. The habits of a lifetime
would not be gainsaid even now. A second ago his face had been
livid with rage and hate, now a quick flush overspread it, as if he
were ashamed of this loss of self-control. He threw the little
Frenchman away from him like he would a beast which had
snarled, and passed his hand across his brow.

"Lud forgive me!" he said quaintly, "I had almost lost my temper."

Chauvelin was not slow in recovering himself. He was plucky and alert, and his hatred for this man was so great that he had actually ceased to fear him. Now he quietly readjusted his cravat, made a vigorous effort to re-conquer his breath, and said firmly as soon as he could contrive to speak at all:

"And if you did strangle me, Sir Percy, you would do yourself no good. The fate which I have mapped out for Lady Blakeney, would then irrevocably be hers, for she is in our power and none of my colleagues are disposed to offer you a means of saving her from it, as I am ready to do."

Blakeney was now standing in the middle of the room, with his hands buried in the pockets of his breeches, his manner and attitude once more calm, debonnair, expressive of lofty self-possession and of absolute indifference. He came quite close to the meagre little figure of his exultant enemy, thereby forcing the latter to look up at him.

"Oh! . . . ah! . . . yes!" he said airily, "I had nigh forgotten . . . you were talking of a bargain . . . my share of it . . . eh? . . . Is it me you want? . . . Do you wish to see me in your Paris prisons? . . . I assure you, sir, that the propinquity of drunken soldiers may disgust me, but it would in no way disturb the equanimity of my temper."

"I am quite sure of that, Sir Percy—and I can but repeat what I had the honour of saying to Lady Blakeney just now—I do not desire the death of so accomplished a gentleman as yourself."

"Strange, Monsieur," retorted Blakeney, with a return of his accustomed flippancy. "Now I do desire your death very strongly indeed—there would be so much less vermin on the face of the earth. . . . But pardon me—I was interrupting you. . . . Will you be so kind as to proceed?"

Chauvelin had not winced at the insult. His enemy's attitude now left him completely indifferent. He had seen that self-possessed man of the world, that dainty and fastidious dandy, in the throes of an overmastering passion. He had very nearly paid with his life for the joy of having roused that supercilious and dormant lion. In fact he was ready to welcome any insults from Sir Percy Blakeney now, since these would be only additional evidences that the Englishman's temper was not yet under control.

"I will try to be brief, Sir Percy," he said, setting himself the task of imitating his antagonist's affected manner. "Will you not sit down? . . . We must try and discuss these matters like two men of the world. . . . As for me, I am always happiest beside a board littered with papers. . . . I am not an athlete, Sir Percy . . . and serve my country with my pen rather than with my fists."

Whilst he spoke he had reached the table and once more took the chair whereon he had been sitting lately, when he dreamed the dreams which were so near realization now. He pointed with a graceful gesture to the other vacant chair, which Blakeney took without a word.

"Ah!" said Chauvelin with a sigh of satisfaction, "I see that we are about to understand one another. . . . I have always felt that it was a pity, Sir Percy, that you and I could not discuss certain matters pleasantly with one another. . . . Now, about this unfortunate incident of Lady Blakeney's incarceration, I would like you to believe that I had no part in the arrangements which have been made for her detention in Paris. My colleagues have arranged it all . . . and I have vainly tried to protest against the rigorous measures which are to be enforced against her in the Temple prison. . . . But these are answering so completely in the case of the ex-queen, they have so completely broken her spirit and her pride, that my colleagues felt that they would prove equally useful in order to bring the Scarlet Pimpernel—through his wife—to an humbler frame of mind."

He paused a moment, distinctly pleased with his peroration, satisfied that his voice had been without a tremor and his face impassive, and wondering what effect this somewhat lengthy preamble had upon Sir Percy, who through it all had remained singularly quiet. Chauvelin was preparing himself for the next effect which he hoped to produce, and was vaguely seeking for the best words with which to fully express his meaning, when he was suddenly startled by a sound as unexpected as it was disconcerting.

It was the sound of a loud and prolonged snore. He pushed the candle aside, which somewhat obstructed his line of vision, and casting a rapid glance at the enemy, with whose life he was toying even as a cat doth with that of a mouse, he saw that the aforesaid mouse was calmly and unmistakably asleep.

An impatient oath escaped Chauvelin's lips, and he brought his fist heavily down on the table, making the metal candlesticks rattle and causing Sir Percy to open one sleepy eye.

"A thousand pardons, sir," said Blakeney with a slight yawn. "I am so demmed fatigued, and your preface was unduly long. . . . Beastly bad form, I know, going to sleep during a sermon . . . but I haven't had a wink of sleep all day. . . . I pray you to excuse me . . ."

"Will you condescend to listen, Sir Percy?" queried Chauvelin peremptorily, "or shall I call the guard and give up all thoughts of treating with you?"

"Just whichever you demmed well prefer, sir," rejoined Blakeney impatiently.

And once more stretching out his long limbs, he buried his hands in the pockets of his breeches and apparently prepared himself for another quiet sleep. Chauvelin looked at him for a moment, vaguely wondering what to do next. He felt strangely irritated at what he firmly believed was mere affectation on Blakeney's part, and although he was burning with impatience to place the terms of the proposed bargain before this man, yet he would have preferred to be interrogated, to deliver his "either–or" with becoming sternness and decision, rather than to take the initiative in this discussion, where he should have been calm and indifferent, whilst his enemy should have been nervous and disturbed.

Sir Percy's attitude had disconcerted him, a touch of the grotesque had been given to what should have been a tense moment, and it was terribly galling to the pride of the ex-diplomatist that with this elusive enemy and in spite of his own preparedness for any eventuality, it was invariably the unforeseen that happened.

After a moment's reflection, however, he decided upon a fresh course of action. He rose and crossed the room, keeping as much as possible an eye upon Sir Percy, but the latter sat placid and dormant and evidently in no hurry to move. Chauvelin having reached the door, opened it noiselessly, and to the sergeant in command of his bodyguard who stood at attention outside, he whispered hurriedly:

"The prisoner from No. 6. . . . Let two of the men bring her hither back to me at once."

CHAPTER XXVI

THE TERMS OF THE BARGAIN

Less than three minutes later, there came to Chauvelin's expectant ears the soft sound made by a woman's skirts against the stone floor. During those three minutes, which had seemed an eternity to his impatience, he had sat silently watching the slumber—affected or real—of his enemy.

Directly he heard the word: "Halt!" outside the door, he jumped to his feet. The next moment Marguerite had entered the room.

Hardly had her foot crossed the threshold than Sir Percy rose, quietly and without haste but evidently fully awake, and turning towards her, made her a low obeisance.

She, poor woman, had of course caught sight of him at once. His presence here, Chauvelin's demand for her reappearance, the soldiers in a small compact group outside the door, all these were unmistakable proofs that the awful cataclysm had at last occurred.

The Scarlet Pimpernel, Percy Blakeney, her husband, was in the hands of the Terrorists of France, and, though face to face with her now, with an open window close to him, and an apparently helpless enemy under his hand, he could not—owing to the fiendish measures taken by Chauvelin—raise a finger to save himself and her.

Mercifully for her, nature—in the face of this appalling tragedy—deprived her of the full measure of her senses. She could move and speak and see, she could hear and in a measure understand what was said, but she was really an automaton or a

191

sleep-walker, moving and speaking mechanically and without due comprehension.

Possibly, if she had then and there fully realized all that the future meant, she would have gone mad with the horror of it all.

"Lady Blakeney," began Chauvelin after he had quickly dismissed the soldiers from the room, "when you and I parted from one another just now, I had no idea that I should so soon have the pleasure of a personal conversation with Sir Percy. . . . There is no occasion yet, believe me, for sorrow or for fear. . . . Another twenty-four hours at most, and you will be on board the 'Day-Dream' outward bound for England. Sir Percy himself might perhaps accompany you; he does not desire that you should journey to Paris, and I may safely say, that in his mind, he has already accepted certain little conditions which I have been forced to impose upon him ere I sign the order for your absolute release."

"Conditions?" she repeated vaguely and stupidly, looking in bewilderment from one to the other.

"You are tired, m'dear," said Sir Percy quietly, "will you not sit down?"

He held the chair gallantly for her. She tried to read his face, but could not catch even a flash from beneath the heavy lids which obstinately veiled his eyes.

"Oh! it is a mere matter of exchanging signatures," continued Chauvelin in response to her inquiring glance and toying with the papers which were scattered on the table. "Here you see is the order to allow Sir Percy Blakeney and his wife, née Marguerite St. Just, to quit the town of Boulogne unmolested."

He held a paper out towards Marguerite, inviting her to look at it. She caught sight of an official-looking document, bearing the motto and seal of the Republic of France, and of her own name and Percy's written thereon in full.

"It is perfectly en règle, I assure you," continued Chauvelin, "and only awaits my signature."

He now took up another paper which looked like a long closely-written letter. Marguerite watched his every movement, for instinct told her that the supreme moment had come. There was a look of almost superhuman cruelty and malice in the little Frenchman's eyes as he fixed them on the impassive figure of Sir Percy, the while with slightly trembling hands he fingered that piece of paper and smoothed out its creases with loving care.

"I am quite prepared to sign the order for your release, Lady Blakeney," he said, keeping his gaze still keenly fixed upon Sir Percy. "When it is signed you will understand that our measures against the citizens of Boulogne will no longer hold good, and that on the contrary, the general amnesty and free pardon will come into force."

"Yes, I understand that," she replied.

"And all that will come to pass, Lady Blakeney, the moment Sir Percy will write me in his own hand a letter, in accordance with the draft which I have prepared, and sign it with his name.

"Shall I read it to you?" he asked.

"If you please."

"You will see how simple it all is. . . . A mere matter of form. . . . I pray you do not look upon it with terror, but only as the prelude to that general amnesty and free pardon, which I feel sure will satisfy the philanthropic heart of the noble Scarlet Pimpernel, since three score at least of the inhabitants of Boulogne will owe their life and freedom to him."

"I am listening, Monsieur," she said calmly.

"As I have already had the honour of explaining, this little document is in the form of a letter addressed personally to me and of course in French," he said finally, and then he looked down on the paper and began to read:

Citizen Chauvelin—

In consideration of a further sum of one million francs and on the understanding that this ridiculous charge brought against me of conspiring against the Republic of France is immediately withdrawn, and I am allowed to return to England unmolested, I am quite prepared to acquaint you with the names and whereabouts of certain persons who under the guise of the League of the Scarlet Pimpernel are even now conspiring to free the woman Marie Antoinette and her son from prison and to place the latter upon the throne of France. You are quite well aware that under the pretence of being the leader of a gang of

English adventurers, who never did the Republic of France and her people any real harm, I have actually been the means of unmasking many a royalist plot before you, and of bringing many persistent conspirators to the guillotine. I am surprised that you should cavil at the price I am asking this time for the very important information with which I am able to furnish you, whilst you have often paid me similar sums for work which was a great deal less difficult to do. In order to serve your government effectually, both in England and in France, I must have a sufficiency of money, to enable me to live in a costly style befitting a gentleman of my rank. Were I to alter my mode of life I could not continue to mix in that same social milieu to which all my friends belong and wherein, as you are well aware, most of the royalist plots are hatched.

Trusting therefore to receive a favourable reply to my just demands within the next twenty-four hours, whereupon the names in question shall be furnished you forthwith,

I have the honour to remain, Citizen,

Your humble and obedient servant,

When he had finished reading, Chauvelin quietly folded the paper up again, and then only did he look at the man and the woman before him.

Marguerite sat very erect, her head thrown back, her face very pale and her hands tightly clutched in her lap. She had not stirred whilst Chauvelin read out the infamous document, with which he desired to brand a brave man with the ineradicable stigma of dishonour and of shame. After she heard the first words, she looked up swiftly and questioningly at her husband, but he stood at some little distance from her, right out of the flickering circle of yellowish light made by the burning tallow-candle. He was as rigid as a statue, standing in his usual attitude with legs apart and hands buried in his breeches pockets.

She could not see his face.

Whatever she may have felt with regard to the letter, as the meaning of it gradually penetrated into her brain, she was, of course, convinced of one thing, and that was that never for a moment would Percy dream of purchasing his life or even hers at such a price. But she would have liked some sign from him, some look by which she could be guided as to her immediate conduct: as, however, he gave neither look nor sign, she preferred to assume an attitude of silent contempt.

But even before Chauvelin had had time to look from one face to the other, a prolonged and merry laugh echoed across the squalid room.

Sir Percy, with head thrown back, was laughing whole-heartedly.

"A magnificent epistle, sir," he said gaily, "Lud love you, where did you wield the pen so gracefully? . . . I vow that if I signed this interesting document no one will believe I could have expressed myself with perfect ease . . . and in French too . . ."

"Nay, Sir Percy," rejoined Chauvelin drily, "I have thought of all that, and lest in the future there should be any doubt as to whether your own hand had or had not penned the whole of this letter, I also make it a condition that you write out every word of it yourself, and sign it here in this very room, in the presence of Lady Blakeney, of myself, of my colleagues and of at least half a dozen other persons whom I will select."

"It is indeed admirably thought out, Monsieur," rejoined Sir Percy, "and what is to become of the charming epistle, may I ask, after I have written and signed it? . . . Pardon my curiosity. . . . I take a natural interest in the matter . . . and truly your ingenuity passes belief . . ."

"Oh! the fate of this letter will be as simple as was the writing thereof. . . . A copy of it will be published in our "Gazette de Paris" as a bait for enterprising English journalists. . . . They will not be backward in getting hold of so much interesting matter. . . . Can you not see the attractive headlines in 'The London Gazette,' Sir Percy? 'The League of the Scarlet Pimpernel unmasked! A gigantic hoax! The origin of the Blakeney millions!' . . . I believe that journalism in England has reached a high standard of excellence . . . and even the 'Gazette de Paris' is greatly read in certain towns of your charming country. . . . His Royal Highness the Prince of Wales, and various other influential gentlemen in London, will, on the other hand, be granted a private view of the original through the kind offices of certain devoted

friends whom we possess in England. . . . I don't think that you
need have any fear, Sir Percy, that your caligraphy will sink into
oblivion. It will be our business to see that it obtains the full
measure of publicity which it deserves . . ."

He paused a moment, then his manner suddenly changed:
the sarcastic tone died out of his voice, and there came back into
his face that look of hatred and cruelty which Blakeney's persiflage had always the power to evoke.

"You may rest assured of one thing, Sir Percy," he said with a
harsh laugh, "that enough mud will be thrown at that erstwhile
glorious Scarlet Pimpernel . . . some of it will be bound to
stick . . ."

"Nay, Monsieur . . . er . . . Chaubertin," quoth Blakeney
lightly, "I have no doubt that you and your colleagues are past
masters in the graceful art of mud-throwing. . . . But pardon me
. . . er . . . I was interrupting you. . . . Continue, Monsieur . . .
continue, I pray. 'Pon my honour, the matter is vastly diverting."

"Nay, sir, after the publication of this diverting epistle,
meseems your honour will cease to be a marketable commodity."

"Undoubtedly, sir," rejoined Sir Percy, apparently quite unruffled, "pardon a slip of the tongue . . . we are so much the
creatures of habit. . . . As you were saying . . . ?"

"I have but little more to say, sir. . . . But lest there should
even now be lurking in your mind a vague hope that, having
written this letter, you could easily in the future deny its au-
thorship, let me tell you this: my measures are well taken, there
will be witnesses to your writing of it. . . . You will sit here in this
room, unfettered, uncoerced in any way, and the money spoken
of in the letter will be handed over to you by my colleague, after
a few suitable words spoken by him, and you will take the money
from him, Sir Percy . . . and the witnesses will see you take it
after having seen you write the letter . . . they will understand
that you are being *paid* by the French government for giving information anent royalist plots in this country and in England . . .
they will understand that your identity as the leader of that so-
called band is not only known to me and to my colleague, but

that it also covers your real character and profession as the paid spy of France."

"Marvellous, I call it . . . demmed marvellous," quoth Sir Percy blandly.

Chauvelin had paused, half-choked by his own emotion, his hatred and prospective revenge. He passed his handkerchief over his forehead, which was streaming with perspiration.

"Warm work, this sort of thing . . . eh . . . Monsieur . . . er . . . Chaubertin? . . ." queried his imperturbable enemy.

Marguerite said nothing; the whole thing was too horrible for words, but she kept her large eyes fixed upon her husband's face . . . waiting for that look, that sign from him which would have eased the agonizing anxiety in her heart, and which never came.

With a great effort now, Chauvelin pulled himself together and, though his voice still trembled, he managed to speak with a certain amount of calm:

"Probably, Sir Percy, you know," he said, "that throughout the whole of France we are inaugurating a series of national fêtes, in honour of the new religion which the people are about to adopt. . . . Demoiselle Désirée Candeille, whom you know, will at these festivals impersonate the Goddess of Reason, the only deity whom we admit now in France. . . . She has been specially chosen for this honour, owing to the services which she has rendered us recently . . . and as Boulogne happens to be the lucky city in which we have succeeded in bringing the Scarlet Pimpernel to justice, the national fête will begin within these city walls, with Demoiselle Candeille as the thrice-honoured goddess."

"And you will be very merry here in Boulogne, I dare swear . . ."

"Aye, merry, sir," said Chauvelin with an involuntary and savage snarl, as he placed a long claw-like finger upon the momentous paper before him, "merry, for we here in Boulogne will see that which will fill the heart of every patriot in France with gladness. . . . Nay! 'twas not the death of the Scarlet Pimpernel we wanted . . . not the noble martyrdom of England's chosen hero . . . but his humiliation and defeat . . . derision and scorn . . .

contumely and contempt. You asked me airily just now, Sir Percy, how I proposed to accomplish this object . . . Well! you know it now—by forcing you . . . aye, *forcing*—to write and sign a letter and to take money from my hands which will brand you forever as a liar and informer, and cover you with the thick and slimy mud of irreclaimable infamy . . ."

"Lud! sir," said Sir Percy pleasantly, "what a wonderful command you have of our language. . . . I wish I could speak French half as well . . ."

Marguerite had risen like an automaton from her chair. She felt that she could no longer sit still, she wanted to scream out at the top of her voice, all the horror she felt for this dastardly plot, which surely must have had its origin in the brain of devils. She could not understand Percy. This was one of those awful moments, which she had been destined to experience once or twice before, when the whole personality of her husband seemed to become shadowy before her, to slip, as it were, past her comprehension, leaving her indescribably lonely and wretched, trusting yet terrified.

She thought that long ere this he would have flung back every insult in his opponent's teeth; she did not know what inducements Chauvelin had held out in exchange for the infamous letter, what threats he had used. That her own life and freedom were at stake, was, of course, evident, but she cared nothing for life, and he should know that certainly she would care still less if such a price had to be paid for it.

She longed to tell him all that was in her heart, longed to tell him how little she valued her life, how highly she prized his honour! but how could she, before this fiend who snarled and sneered in his anticipated triumph, and surely, surely Percy knew!

And knowing all that, why did he not speak? Why did he not tear that infamous paper from out that devil's hands and fling it in his face? Yet, though her loving ear caught every intonation of her husband's voice, she could not detect the slightest harshness in his airy laugh; his tone was perfectly natural and he seemed to be, indeed, just as he appeared—vastly amused.

Then she thought that perhaps he would wish her to go now, that he felt desire to be alone with this man, who had outraged him in everything that he held most holy and most dear, his honour and his wife . . . that perhaps, knowing that his own temper was no longer under control, he did not wish her to witness the rough and ready chastisement which he was intending to meet out to this dastardly intriguer.

Yes! that was it no doubt! Herein she could not be mistaken; she knew his fastidious notions of what was due and proper in the presence of a woman, and that even at a moment like this, he would wish the manners of London drawing-rooms to govern his every action.

Therefore she rose to go, and as she did so, once more tried to read the expression in his face . . . to guess what was passing in his mind.

"Nay, Madam," he said, whilst he bowed gracefully before her, "I fear me this lengthy conversation hath somewhat fatigued you. . . . This merry jest 'twixt my engaging friend and myself should not have been prolonged so far into the night. . . . Monsieur, I pray you, will you not give orders that her ladyship be escorted back to her room?"

He was still standing outside the circle of light, and Marguerite instinctively went up to him. For this one second she was oblivious of Chauvelin's presence, she forgot her well-schooled pride, her firm determination to be silent and to be brave: she could not longer restrain the wild beatings of her heart, the agony of her soul, and with sudden impulse she murmured in a voice broken with intense love and subdued, passionate appeal:

"Percy!"

He drew back a step further into the gloom: this made her realize the mistake she had made in allowing her husband's most bitter enemy to get this brief glimpse into her soul. Chauvelin's thin lips curled with satisfaction, the brief glimpse had been sufficient for him, the rapidly whispered name, the broken accent had told him what he had not known hitherto: namely, that between this man and woman there was a bond far more powerful than that which usually existed between husband and wife, and merely made up of chivalry on the one side and trustful reliance on the other.

Marguerite having realized her mistake, ashamed of having betrayed her feelings even for a moment, threw back her proud head and gave her exultant foe a look of defiance and of scorn. He responded with one of pity, not altogether unmixed with deference. There was something almost unearthly and sublime in this beautiful woman's agonizing despair.

He lowered his head and made her a deep obeisance, lest she should see the satisfaction and triumph which shone through his pity.

As usual Sir Percy remained quite imperturbable, and now it was he, who, with characteristic impudence, touched the hand-bell on the table:

"Excuse this intrusion, Monsieur," he said lightly, "her ladyship is overfatigued and would be best in her room."

Marguerite threw him a grateful look. After all she was only a woman and was afraid of breaking down. In her mind there was no issue to the present deadlock save in death. For this she was prepared and had but one great hope that she could lie in her husband's arms just once again before she died. Now, since she could not speak to him, scarcely dared to look into the loved face, she was quite ready to go.

In answer to the bell, the soldier had entered.

"If Lady Blakeney desires to go . . ." said Chauvelin.

She nodded and Chauvelin gave the necessary orders: two soldiers stood at attention ready to escort Marguerite back to her prison cell. As she went towards the door she came to within a couple of steps from where her husband was standing, bowing to her as she passed. She stretched out an icy cold hand towards him, and he, in the most approved London fashion, with the courtly grace of a perfect English gentleman, took the little hand in his and stooping very low kissed the delicate finger-tips.

Then only did she notice that the strong, nervy hand which held hers trembled perceptibly, and that his lips—which for an instant rested on her fingers—were burning hot.

CHAPTER XXVII

THE DECISION

O nce more the two men were alone.

As far as Chauvelin was concerned he felt that everything was not yet settled, and until a moment ago he had been in doubt as to whether Sir Percy would accept the infamous conditions which had been put before him, or allow his pride and temper to get the better of him and throw the deadly insults back into his adversary's teeth.

But now a new secret had been revealed to the astute diplomatist. A name, softly murmured by a broken-hearted woman, had told him a tale of love and passion, which he had not even suspected before.

Since he had made this discovery he knew that the ultimate issue was no longer in doubt. Sir Percy Blakeney, the bold adventurer, ever ready for a gamble where lives were at stake, might have demurred before he subscribed to his own dishonour, in order to save his wife from humiliation and the shame of the terrible fate that had been mapped out for her. But the same man passionately in love with such a woman as Marguerite Blakeney would count the world well lost for her sake.

One sudden fear alone had shot through Chauvelin's heart when he stood face to face with the two people whom he had so deeply and cruelly wronged, and that was that Blakeney, throwing aside all thought of the scores of innocent lives that were at stake, might forget everything, risk everything, dare everything, in order to get his wife away there and then.

For the space of a few seconds Chauvelin had felt that his

own life was in jeopardy, and that the Scarlet Pimpernel would indeed make a desperate effort to save himself and his wife. But the fear was short-lived: Marguerite—as he had well foreseen—would never save herself at the expense of others, and she was tied! tied! tied! That was his triumph and his joy!

When Marguerite finally left the room, Sir Percy made no motion to follow her, but turned once more quietly to his antagonist.

"As you were saying, Monsieur? . . ." he queried lightly.

"Oh! there is nothing more to say, Sir Percy," rejoined Chauvelin; "my conditions are clear to you, are they not? Lady Blakeney's and your own immediate release in exchange for a letter written to me by your own hand, and signed here by you—in this room—in my presence and that of sundry other persons whom I need not name just now. Also certain money passing from my hand to yours. Failing the letter, a long, hideously humiliating sojourn in the Temple prison for your wife, a prolonged trial and the guillotine as a happy release! . . . I would add, the same thing for yourself, only that I will do you the justice to admit that you probably do not care."

"Nay! a grave mistake, Monsieur. . . . I do care . . . vastly care, I assure you . . . and would seriously object to ending my life on your demmed guillotine . . . a nasty, uncomfortable thing, I should say . . . and I am told that an inexperienced barber is deputed to cut one's hair. . . . Brrr! . . . Now, on the other hand, I like the idea of a national fête . . . that pretty wench Candeille, dressed as a goddess . . . the boom of the cannon when your amnesty comes into force. . . . You *will* boom the cannon, will you not, Monsieur? . . . Cannon are demmed noisy, but they are effective sometimes, do you not think so, Monsieur?"

"Very effective certainly, Sir Percy," sneered Chauvelin, "and we will certainly boom the cannon from this very fort, an it so please you. . . ."

"At what hour, Monsieur, is my letter to be ready?"

"Why! at any hour you please, Sir Percy."

"The 'Day-Dream' could weigh anchor at eight o'clock . . . would an hour before that be convenient to yourself?"

"Certainly, Sir Percy . . . if you will honour me by accepting my hospitality in these uncomfortable quarters until seven o'clock to-morrow eve? . . ."

"I thank you, Monsieur . . ."

"Then am I to understand, Sir Percy, that . . ."

A loud and ringing laugh broke from Blakeney's lips.

"That I accept your bargain, man! . . . Zounds! I tell you I accept . . . I'll write the letter, I'll sign it . . . an you have our free passes ready for us in exchange. . . . At seven o'clock to-morrow eve, did you say? . . . Man! do not look so astonished. . . . The letter, the signature, the money . . . all your witnesses . . . have everything ready. . . . I accept, I say. . . . And now, in the name of all the evil spirits in hell, let me have some supper and a bed, for I vow that I am demmed fatigued."

And without more ado Sir Percy once more rang the hand-bell, laughing boisterously the while: then suddenly, with quick transition of mood, his laugh was lost in a gigantic yawn, and throwing his long body onto a chair, he stretched out his legs, buried his hands in his pockets, and the next moment was peacefully asleep.

CHAPTER XXVIII

THE MIDNIGHT WATCH

Boulogne had gone through many phases, in its own languid and sleepy way, whilst the great upheaval of a gigantic revolution shook other cities of France to their very foundations.

At first the little town had held somnolently aloof, and whilst Lyons and Tours conspired and rebelled, whilst Marseilles and Toulon opened their ports to the English and Dunkirk was ready to surrender to the allied forces, she had gazed through half-closed eyes at all the turmoil, and then quietly turned over and gone to sleep again.

Boulogne fished and mended nets, built boats and manufactured boots with placid content, whilst France murdered her king and butchered her citizens.

The initial noise of the great revolution was only wafted on the southerly breezes from Paris to the little seaport towns of Northern France, and lost much of its volume and power in this aerial transit: the fisher folk were too poor to worry about the dethronement of kings: the struggle for daily existence, the perils and hardships of deep-sea fishing engrossed all the faculties they possessed.

As for the burghers and merchants of the town, they were at first content with reading an occasional article in the "Gazette de Paris" or the "Gazette des Tribunaux," brought hither by one or other of the many travellers who crossed the city on their way to the harbour. They were interested in these articles, at times even comfortably horrified at the doings in Paris, the executions and the tumbrils, but on the whole they liked the idea that the

country was in future to be governed by duly chosen representatives of the people, rather than be a prey to the despotism of
kings, and they were really quite pleased to see the tricolour flag
hoisted on the old Beffroi, there where the snow-white standard
of the Bourbons had erstwhile flaunted its golden fleur-de-lis in
the glare of the midday sun.

The worthy burgesses of Boulogne were ready to shout: "Vive
la République!" with the same cheerful and raucous Normandy
accent as they had lately shouted "Dieu protége le Roi!"

The first awakening from this happy torpor came when that
tent was put up on the landing stage in the harbour. Officials,
dressed in shabby uniforms and wearing tricolour cockades and
scarves, were now quartered in the Town Hall, and repaired
daily to that roughly erected tent, accompanied by so many soldiers from the garrison.

There installed, they busied themselves with examining carefully the passports of all those who desired to leave or enter
Boulogne. Fisher-folk who had dwelt in the city—father and son
and grandfather and many generations before that—and had
come and gone in and out of their own boats as they pleased,
were now stopped as they beached their craft and made to give
an account of themselves to these officials from Paris.

It was, of a truth, more than ridiculous, that these strangers
should ask of Jean-Marie who he was, or of Pierre what was his
business, or of Désiré François whither he was going, when
Jean-Marie and Pierre and Désiré François had plied their nets
in the roads outside Boulogne harbour for more years than they
would care to count.

It also caused no small measure of annoyance that fishermen
were ordered to wear tricolour cockades on their caps. They had
no special ill-feeling against tricolour cockades, but they did not
care about them. Jean-Marie flatly refused to have one pinned
on, and being admonished somewhat severely by one of the
Paris officials, he became obstinate about the whole thing and
threw the cockade violently on the ground and spat upon it, not
from any sentiment of anti-republicanism, but just from a feeling of Norman doggedness.

He was arrested, shut up in Fort Gayole, tried as a traitor and publicly guillotined.

The consternation in Boulogne was appalling.

The one little spark had found its way to a barrel of blasting powder and caused a terrible explosion. Within twenty-four hours of Jean-Marie's execution the whole town was in the throes of the Revolution. What the death of King Louis, the arrest of Marie Antoinette, the massacres of September had failed to do, that the arrest and execution of an elderly fisherman accomplished in a trice.

People began to take sides in politics. Some families realized that they came from ancient lineage, and that their ancestors had helped to build up the throne of the Bourbons. Others looked up ancient archives and remembered past oppressions at the hands of the aristocrats.

Thus some burghers of Boulogne became ardent reactionaries, whilst others secretly nursed enthusiastic royalist convictions: some were ready to throw in their lot with the anarchists, to deny the religion of their fathers, to scorn the priests and close the places of worship; others adhered strictly still to the usages and practices of the Church.

Arrests became frequent: the guillotine, erected in the Place de la Sénéchaussée, had plenty of work to do. Soon the cathedral was closed, the priests thrown into prison, whilst scores of families hoped to escape a similar fate by summary flight.

Vague rumours of a band of English adventurers soon reached the little sea-port town. The Scarlet Pimpernel—English spy or hero, as he was alternately called—had helped many a family with pronounced royalist tendencies to escape the fury of the bloodthirsty Terrorists.

Thus gradually the anti-revolutionaries had been weeded out of the city: some by death and imprisonment, others by flight. Boulogne became the hotbed of anarchism: the idlers and loafers, inseparable from any town where there is a garrison and a harbour, practically ruled the city now. Denunciations were the order of the day. Everyone who owned any money, or lived with any comfort was accused of being a traitor and suspected of conspiracy. The fisher folk wandered about the city, surly and discontented: their trade was at a standstill, but there was a trifle to be earned by giving information: information which meant the arrest, ofttimes the death of men, women and even children who had tried to seek safety in flight, and to denounce whom— as they were trying to hire a boat anywhere along the coast— meant a good square meal for a starving family.

Then came the awful cataclysm.

A woman—a stranger—had been arrested and imprisoned in the Fort Gayole and the town-crier publicly proclaimed that if she escaped from jail, one member of every family in the town—rich or poor, republican or royalist, Catholic or freethinker—would be summarily guillotined.

That member, the bread-winner!

"Why, then, with the Duvals it would be young François-Auguste. He keeps his old mother with his boot-making . . ."

"And it would be Marie Lebon, she has her blind father dependent on her net-mending."

"And old Mother Laferrière, whose grandchildren were left penniless . . . she keeps them from starvation by her wash-tub."

"But François-Auguste is a real Republican; he belongs to the Jacobin Club."

"And look at Pierre, who never meets a *calotin* but he must needs spit on him."

"Is there no safety anywhere? . . . are we to be butchered like so many cattle? . . ."

Somebody makes the suggestion:

"It is a threat . . . they would not dare! . . ."

"Would not dare? . . ."

'Tis old André Lemoine who has spoken, and he spits vigorously on the ground. André Lemoine has been a soldier; he was in La Vendée. He was wounded at Tours . . . and he knows!

"Would not dare? . . ." he says in a whisper. "I tell you, friends, that there's nothing the present government would not dare. There was the Plaine Saint Mauve . . . Did you ever hear about that? . . . little children fusilladed by the score . . . little ones, I say, and women with babies at their breasts . . . weren't they in-

nocent? . . . Five hundred innocent people butchered in La
Vendée . . . until the Headsman sank—worn not . . . I could tell
worse than that . . . for I know. . . . There's nothing they would
not dare! . . ."

Consternation was so great that the matter could not even be
discussed.

"We'll go to Gayole and see this woman at any rate."

Angry, sullen crowds assembled in the streets. The proclamation had been read just as the men were leaving the public
houses, preparing to go home for the night.

They brought the news to the women, who, at home, were
setting the soup and bread on the table for their husbands' supper. There was no thought of going to bed or of sleeping that
night. The bread-winner in every family and all those dependent on him for daily sustenance were trembling for their lives.

Resistance to the barbarous order would have been worse
than useless, nor did the thought of it enter the heads of these
humble and ignorant fisher folk, wearied out with the miserable
struggle for existence. There was not sufficient spirit left in this
half-starved population of a small provincial city to suggest open
rebellion. A regiment of soldiers come up from the South were
quartered in the Chateau, and the natives of Boulogne could not
have mustered more than a score of disused blunderbusses between them.

Then they remembered tales which André Lemoine had told,
the fate of Lyons, razed to the ground, of Toulon burnt to ashes,
and they did not dare rebel.

But brothers, fathers, sons trooped out towards Gayole, in
order to have a good look at the frowning pile, which held the
hostage for their safety. It looked dark and gloomy enough, save
for one window which gave on the southern ramparts. This window was wide open and a feeble light flickered from the room
beyond, and as the men stood about, gazing at the walls in sulky
silence, they suddenly caught the sound of a loud laugh proceeding from within, and of a pleasant voice speaking quite gaily
in a language which they did not understand, but which
sounded like English.

Against the heavy oaken gateway, leading to the courtyard of the prison, the proclamation written on stout parchment had been pinned up. Beside it hung a tiny lantern, the dim light of which flickered in the evening breeze, and brought at times into sudden relief the bold writing and heavy signature, which stood out, stern and grim, against the yellowish background of the paper, like black signs of approaching death.

Facing the gateway and the proclamation, the crowd of men took its stand. The moon, from behind them, cast fitful, silvery glances at the weary heads bent in anxiety and watchful expectancy: on old heads and young heads, dark, curly heads and heads grizzled with age, on backs bent with toil, and hands rough and gnarled like seasoned timber.

All night the men stood and watched.

Sentinels from the town guard were stationed at the gates, but these might prove inattentive or insufficient, they had not the same price at stake, so the entire able-bodied population of Boulogne watched the gloomy prison that night, lest anyone escaped by wall or window.

They were guarding the precious hostage whose safety was the stipulation for their own.

There was dead silence among them, and dead silence all around, save for that monotonous tok-tok-tok of the parchment flapping in the breeze. The moon, who all along had been capricious and chary of her light, made a final retreat behind a gathering bank of clouds, and the crowd, the soldiers and the great grim walls were all equally wrapped in gloom.

Only the little lantern on the gateway now made a ruddy patch of light, and tinged that fluttering parchment with the colour of blood. Every now and then an isolated figure would detach itself from out the watching throng, and go up to the heavy, oaken door, in order to gaze at the proclamation. Then the light of the lantern illumined a dark head or a grey one, for a moment or two: black or white locks were stirred gently in the wind, and a sigh of puzzlement and disappointment would be distinctly heard.

At times a group of three or four would stand there for

awhile, not speaking, only sighing and casting eager questioning glances at one another, whilst trying vainly to find some hopeful word, some turn of phrase of meaning that would be less direful, in that grim and ferocious proclamation. Then a rough word from the sentinel, a push from the butt-end of a bayonet would disperse the little group and send the men, sullen and silent, back into the crowd.

Thus they watched for hours whilst the bell of the Beffroi tolled all the hours of that tedious night. A thin rain began to fall in the small hours of the morning, a wetting, soaking drizzle which chilled the weary watchers to the bone.

But they did not care.

"We must not sleep, for the woman might escape."

Some of them squatted down in the muddy road, the luckier ones managed to lean their backs against the slimy walls.

Twice before the hour of midnight they heard that same quaint and merry laugh proceeding from the lighted room, through the open window. Once it sounded very low and very prolonged, as if in response to a delightful joke.

Anon the heavy gateway of Gayole was opened from within, and half a dozen soldiers came walking out of the courtyard. They were dressed in the uniform of the town-guard, but had evidently been picked out of the rank and file, for all six were exceptionally tall and stalwart, and towered above the sentinel, who saluted and presented arms as they marched out of the gate.

In the midst of them walked a slight, dark figure, clad entirely in black, save for the tricolour scarf round his waist.

The crowd of watchers gazed on the little party with suddenly awakened interest.

"Who is it?" whispered some of the men.

"The citizen-governor," suggested one.

"The new public executioner," ventured another.

"No! no!" quoth Pierre Maxime, the doyen of Boulogne fishermen, and a great authority on every matter public or private within the town; "no, no, he is the man who has come down from Paris, the friend of Robespierre. He makes the laws now, the citizen-governor even must obey him. 'Tis he who made the law that if the woman up yonder should escape . . ."

"Hush! . . . sh! . . . sh! . . ." came in frightened accents from the crowd.

"Hush, Pierre Maxime! . . . the Citizen might hear thee," whispered the man who stood closest to the old fisherman; "the Citizen might hear thee, and think that we rebelled. . . ."

"What are these people doing here?' queried Chauvelin as he passed out into the street.

"They are watching the prison, Citizen," replied the sentinel, whom he had thus addressed, "lest the female prisoner should attempt to escape."

With a satisfied smile, Chauvelin turned toward the Town Hall, closely surrounded by his escort. The crowd watched him and the soldiers as they quickly disappeared in the gloom, then they resumed the stolid, wearisome vigil of the night.

The old Beffroi now tolled the midnight hour, the one solitary light in the old Fort was extinguished, and after that the frowning pile remained dark and still.

CHAPTER XXIX

THE NATIONAL FÊTE

"Citizens of Boulogne, awake!"

They had not slept, only some of them had fallen into drowsy somnolence, heavy and nerve-racking, worse indeed than any wakefulness.

Within the houses, the women too had kept the tedious vigil, listening for every sound, dreading every bit of news, which the wind might waft in through the small, open windows.

If one prisoner escaped, every family in Boulogne would be deprived of the bread-winner. Therefore the women wept, and tried to remember those Paters and Aves which the tyranny of liberty, fraternity and equality had ordered them to forget.

Broken rosaries were fetched out from neglected corners, and knees stiff with endless, thankless toil were bent once more in prayer.

"Oh God! Good God! Do not allow that woman to flee!"

"Holy Virgin! Mother of God! Make that she should not escape!"

Some of the women went out in the early dawn to take hot soup and coffee to their men who were watching outside the prison.

"Has anything been seen?"

"Have ye seen the woman?"

"Which room is she in?"

"Why won't they let us see her?"

"Are you sure she hath not already escaped?"

Questions and surmises went round in muffled whispers as

the steaming cans were passed round. No one had a definite answer to give, although Désiré Melun declared that he had, once during the night, caught sight of a woman's face at one of the windows above: but as he could not describe the woman's face, nor locate with any degree of precision the particular window at which she was supposed to have appeared, it was unanimously decided that Désiré must have been dreaming.

"Citizens of Boulogne, awake!"

The cry came first from the Town Hall, and therefore from behind the crowd of men and women, whose faces had been so resolutely set for all these past hours towards the Gayole prison.

They were all awake! but too tired and cramped to move as yet, and to turn in the direction whence arose that cry.

"Citizens of Boulogne, awake!"

It was just the voice of Auguste Moleux, the town-crier of Boulogne, who, bell in hand, was trudging his way along the Rue Daumont, closely followed by two fellows of the municipal guard.

Auguste was in the very midst of the sullen crowd, before the men even troubled about his presence here, but now with many a vigorous "Allons donc!" and "Voyez-moi ça, fais donc place, voyons!" he elbowed his way through the throng.

He was neither tired nor cramped; he served the Republic in comfort and ease, and had slept soundly on his paillasse in the little garret allotted to him in the Town Hall.

The crowd parted in silence, to allow him to pass. Auguste was lean and powerful, the scanty and meagre food, doled out to him by a paternal government, had increased his muscular strength whilst reducing his fat. He had very hard elbows, and soon he managed, by dint of pushing and cursing, to reach the gateway of Gayole.

"Voyons! enlevez-moi ça," he commanded in stentorian tones, pointing to the proclamation.

The fellows of the municipal guard fell to and tore the parchment away from the door whilst the crowd looked on with stupid amazement.

What did it all mean?

Then Auguste Moleux turned and faced the men.

"Mes enfants," he said, "my little cabbages! wake up! the government of the Republic has decreed that to-day is to be a day of gaiety and public rejoicings!"

"Gaiety? . . . Public rejoicings forsooth, when the bread-winner of every family . . ."

"Hush! Hush! Be silent, all of you," quoth Auguste impatiently, "you do not understand! . . . All that is at an end . . . There is no fear that the woman shall escape. . . . You are all to dance and rejoice. . . . The Scarlet Pimpernel has been captured in Boulogne, last night . . ."

"Qui ça the Scarlet Pimpernel?"

"Mais! 'tis that mysterious English adventurer who rescued people from the guillotine!"

"A hero? quoi?"

"No! no! only an English spy, a friend of aristocrats . . . he would have cared nothing for the bread-winners of Boulogne . . ."

"He would not have raised a finger to save them."

"Who knows?" sighed a feminine voice, "perhaps he came to Boulogne to help them."

"And he has been caught anyway," concluded Auguste Moleux sententiously, "and, my little cabbages, remember this, that so great is the pleasure of the all-powerful Committee of Public Safety at his capture, that because he has been caught in Boulogne, therefore Boulogne is to be specially rewarded!"

"Holy Virgin, who'd have thought it?"

"Sh . . . Jeannette, dost not know that there's no Holy Virgin now?"

"And dost know, Auguste, how we are to be rewarded?"

It is a difficult matter for the human mind to turn very quickly from despair to hope, and the fishermen of Boulogne had not yet grasped the fact that they were to make merry and that thoughts of anxiety must be abandoned for those of gaiety.

Auguste Moleux took out a parchment from the capacious pocket of his coat; he put on his most solemn air of officialdom, and pointing with extended forefinger to the parchment, he said:

"A general amnesty to all natives of Boulogne who are under arrest at the present moment: a free pardon to all natives of Boulogne who are under sentence of death: permission to all natives of Boulogne to quit the town with their families, to embark on any vessel they please, in or out of the harbour, and to go whithersoever they choose, without passports, formalities or questions of any kind."

Dead silence followed this announcement. Hope was just beginning to crowd anxiety and sullenness out of the way.

"Then poor André Legrand will be pardoned," whispered a voice suddenly; "he was to have been guillotined to-day."

"And Denise Latour! she was innocent enough, the gentle pigeon."

"And they'll let poor Abbé Foucquet out of prison too."

"And François!"

"And poor Félicité, who is blind!"

"M. l'Abbé would be wise to leave Boulogne with the children."

"He will too: thou canst be sure of that!"

"It is not good to be a priest just now!"

"Bah! calotins are best dead than alive."

But some in the crowd were silent, others whispered eagerly.

"Thinkest thou it would be safer for us to get out of the country whilst we can?" said one of the men in a muffled tone, and clutching nervously at a woman's wrist.

"Aye! aye! it might leak out about that boat we procured for . . ."

"Sh! . . . I was thinking of that . . ."

"We can go to my aunt Lebrun in Belgium . . ."

Others talked in whispers of England or the New Land across the seas: they were those who had something to hide, money received from refugee aristocrats, boats sold to would-be émigrés, information withheld, denunciations shirked: the amnesty would not last long, 'twas best to be safely out of the way.

"In the meanwhile, my cabbages," quoth Auguste sententiously, "are you not grateful to Citizen Robespierre, who has sent this order specially down from Paris?"

"Aye! aye!" assented the crowd cheerfully.

"Hurrah for Citizen Robespierre!"

"Viva la République!"

"And you will enjoy yourselves to-day?"

"That we will!"

"Processions?"

"Aye! with music and dancing."

Out there, far away, beyond the harbour, the grey light of dawn was yielding to the crimson glow of morning. The rain had ceased and heavy slaty clouds parted here and there, displaying glints of delicate turquoise sky, and tiny ethereal vapours in the dim and remote distance of infinity, flecked with touches of rose and gold.

The towers and pinnacles of old Boulogne detached themselves one by one from the misty gloom of night. The old bell of the Beffroi tolled the hour of six. Soon the massive cupola of Notre Dame was clothed in purple hues, and the gilt cross on St. Joseph threw back across the square a blinding ray of gold.

The town sparrows began to twitter, and from far out at sea in the direction of Dunkirk there came the muffled boom of cannon.

"And remember, my pigeons," admonished Auguste Moleux solemnly, "that in this order which Robespierre has sent from Paris, it also says that from to-day onwards le bon Dieu has ceased to be!"

Many faces were turned towards the East just then, for the rising sun, tearing with one gigantic sweep the banks of cloud asunder, now displayed his magnificence in a gorgeous immensity of flaming crimson. The sea, in response, turned to liquid fire beneath the glow, whilst the whole sky was irradiated with the first blush of morning.

Le bon Dieu has ceased to be!

"There is only one religion in France now," explained Auguste Moleux, "the religion of Reason! We are all citizens! We are all free and all able to think for ourselves. Citizen Robespierre has decreed that there is no good God. Le bon Dieu was a tyrant and an aristocrat, and, like all tyrants and aristocrats, He has been deposed. There is no good God, there is no Holy Virgin and no Saints, only Reason, who is a goddess and whom we all honour."

And the townsfolk of Boulogne, with eyes still fixed on the gorgeous East, shouted with sullen obedience:

"Hurrah! for the Goddess of Reason!"

"Hurrah for Robespierre!"

Only the women, trying to escape the town-crier's prying eyes, or the soldiers' stern gaze, hastily crossed themselves behind their husbands' backs, terrified lest le bon Dieu had, after all, not altogether ceased to exist at the bidding of Citizen Robespierre.

Thus the worthy natives of Boulogne, forgetting their anxieties and fears, were ready enough to enjoy the national fête ordained for them by the Committee of Public Safety, in honour of the capture of the Scarlet Pimpernel. They were even willing to accept this new religion which Robespierre had invented: a religion which was only a mockery, with an actress to represent its supreme deity.

Mais, que voulez-vous? Boulogne had long ago ceased to have faith in God: the terrors of the Revolution, which culminated in that agonizing watch of last night, had smothered all thoughts of worship and of prayer.

The Scarlet Pimpernel must indeed be a dangerous spy that his arrest should cause so much joy in Paris!

Even Boulogne had learned by experience that the Committee of Public Safety did not readily give up a prey, once its vulture-like claws had closed upon it. The proportion of condemnations as against acquittals was as a hundred to one.

But because this one man was taken, scores to-day were to be set free!

In the evening at a given hour—seven o'clock had Auguste Moleux, the town-crier, understood—the boom of the cannon would be heard, the gates of the town would be opened, the harbour would become a free port.

The inhabitants of Boulogne were ready to shout:

"Vive the Scarlet Pimpernel!"

Whatever he was—hero or spy—he was undoubtedly the primary cause of all their joy.

By the time Auguste Moleux had cried out the news throughout the town, and pinned the new proclamation of mercy up on every public building, all traces of fatigue and anxiety had vanished. In spite of the fact that wearisome vigils had been kept in every home that night, and that hundreds of men and women had stood about for hours in the vicinity of the Gayole Fort, no sooner was the joyful news known, than all lassitude was forgotten and everyone set to with a right merry will to make the great fête-day a complete success.

There is in every native of Normandy, be he peasant or gentleman, an infinite capacity for enjoyment, and at the same time a marvellous faculty for co-ordinating and systematizing his pleasures.

In a trice the surly crowds had vanished. Instead of these, there were groups of gaily-visaged men pleasantly chattering outside every eating and drinking place in the town. The national holiday had come upon these people quite unawares, so the early part of it had to be spent in thinking out a satisfactory programme for it. Sipping their beer or coffee, or munching their cherries à l'eau-de-vie, the townsfolk of Boulogne, so lately threatened with death, were quietly organizing processions.

There was to be a grand muster on the Place de la Sénéchaussée, then a torchlight and lanthorn-light march, right round the Ramparts, culminating in a gigantic assembly outside the Town Hall, where the Citizen Chauvelin, representing the Committee of Public Safety, would receive an address of welcome from the entire population of Boulogne.

The procession was to be in costume! There were to be Pierrots and Pierrettes, Harlequins and English clowns, aristocrats and goddesses! All day the women and girls were busy contriving travesties of all sorts, and the little tumbledown shops in the Rue de Château and the Rue Frédéric Sauvage—kept chiefly by Jews and English traders—were ransacked for old bits of finery, and for remnants of costumes, worn in the days when Boulogne was still a gay city and Carnivals were held every year.

And then, of course, there would be the Goddess of Reason, in her triumphal car! the apotheosis of the new religion, which was to make everybody happy, rich and free.

Forgotten were the anxieties of the night, the fears of death, the great and glorious Revolution, which for this one day would cease her perpetual demand for the toll of blood.

Nothing was remembered save the pleasures and joys of the moment, and at times the name of that Englishman—spy, hero or adventurer—the cause of all this bounty: the Scarlet Pimpernel.

CHAPTER XXX

The Procession

The grandfathers of the present generation of Boulonnese re-membered the great day of the National Fête, when all Boulogne, for twenty-four hours, went crazy with joy. So many families had fathers, brothers, sons, languishing in prison under some charge of treason, real or imaginary; so many had dear ones for whom already the guillotine loomed ahead, that the feast on this memorable day of September, 1793, was one of never-to-be-forgotten relief and thanksgiving.

The weather all day had been exceptionally fine. After that glorious sunrise, the sky had remained all day clad in its gor-geous mantle of blue and the sun had continued to smile be-nignly on the many varied doings of this gay, little seaport town. When it began to sink slowly towards the West a few little fluffy clouds appeared on the horizon, and from a distance, although the sky remained clear and blue, the sea looked quite dark and slaty against the brilliancy of the firmament.

Gradually, as the splendour of the sunset gave place to the delicate purple and grey tints of evening, the little fluffy clouds merged themselves into denser masses, and these too soon be-came absorbed in the great, billowy banks which the southwest-erly wind was blowing seawards.

By the time that the last grey streak of dusk vanished in the West, the whole sky looked heavy with clouds, and the evening set in, threatening and dark.

But this by no means mitigated the anticipation of pleasure to come. On the contrary, the fast-gathering gloom was hailed with delight, since it would surely help to show off the coloured lights of the lanthorns, and give additional value to the glow of the torches.

Of a truth 'twas a motley throng which began to assemble on the Place de la Sénéchaussée, just as the old bell of the Beffroi tolled the hour of six. Men, women and children in ragged finery, Pierrots with neck frills and floured faces, hideous masks of impossible beasts roughly besmeared in crude colours. There were gaily-coloured dominoes, blue, green, pink and purple, harlequins combining all the colours of the rainbow in one tight-fitting garment, and Columbines with short, tarlatan skirts, beneath which peeped bare feet and ankles. There were judges' perruques, and soldiers' helmets of past generations, tall Normandy caps adorned with hundreds of streaming ribbons, and powdered headgear which recalled the glories of Versailles.

Everything was torn and dirty, the dominoes were in rags, the Pierrot frills, mostly made up of paper, already hung in strips over the wearers' shoulders. But what mattered that?

The crowd pushed and jolted, shouted and laughed, the girls screamed as the men snatched a kiss here and there from willing or unwilling lips, or stole an arm round a gaily accoutred waist. The spirit of Old King Carnival was in the evening air—a spirit just awakened from a long Rip van Winkle-like sleep.

In the centre of the Place stood the guillotine, grim and gaunt with long, thin arms stretched out towards the sky, the last glimmer of waning light striking the triangular knife, there, where it was not rusty with stains of blood.

For weeks now Madame Guillotine had been much occupied plying her gruesome trade; she now stood there in the gloom, passive and immovable, seeming to wait placidly for the end of this holiday, ready to begin her work again on the morrow. She towered above these merrymakers, hoisted up on the platform whereon many an innocent foot had trodden, the tattered basket beside her, into which many an innocent head had rolled.

What cared they to-night for Madame Guillotine and the horrors of which she told? A crowd of Pierrots with floured faces and tattered neck-frills had just swarmed up the wooden steps, shouting and laughing, chasing each other round and round on the platform, until one of them lost his footing and fell into the basket, covering himself with bran and staining his clothes with blood.

"Ah! vogue la galère! We must be merry to-night!"

And all these people who for weeks past had been staring death and the guillotine in the face, had denounced each other with savage callousness in order to save themselves, or hidden for days in dark cellars to escape apprehension, now laughed, and danced and shrieked with gladness in a sudden, hysterical outburst of joy.

Close beside the guillotine stood the triumphal car of the Goddess of Reason, the special feature of this great national fête. It was only a rough market cart, painted by an unpractised hand with bright, crimson paint and adorned with huge clusters of autumn-tinted leaves, and the scarlet berries of mountain ash and rowan, culled from the town gardens, or the country side outside the city walls.

In the cart the goddess reclined on a crimson-draped seat, she, herself, swathed in white, and wearing a gorgeous necklace around her neck. Désirée Candeille, a little pale, a little apprehensive of all this noise, had obeyed the final dictates of her taskmaster. She had been the means of bringing the Scarlet Pimpernel to France and vengeance, she was to be honoured therefore above every other woman in France.

She sat in the car, vaguely thinking over the events of the past few days, whilst watching the throng of rowdy merrymakers seething around her. She thought of the noble-hearted, proud woman whom she had helped to bring from her beautiful English home to sorrow and humiliation in a dank French prison, she thought of the gallant English gentleman with his pleasant voice and courtly, debonnair manners.

Chauvelin had roughly told her, only this morning, that both were now under arrest as English spies, and that their fate no longer concerned her. Later on the governor of the city had come to tell her that Citizen Chauvelin desired her to take part in the procession and the national féte, as the Goddess of

Reason, and that the people of Boulogne were ready to welcome her as such. This had pleased Candeille's vanity, and all day, whilst arranging the finery which she meant to wear for the occasion, she had ceased to think of England and of Lady Blakeney.

But now, when she arrived on the Place de la Sénéchaussée, and mounting her car, found herself on a level with the platform of the guillotine, her memory flew back to England, to the lavish hospitality of Blakeney Manor, Marguerite's gentle voice, the pleasing grace of Sir Percy's manners, and she shuddered a little when that cruel glint of evening light caused the knife of the guillotine to glisten from out the gloom.

But anon her reflections were suddenly interrupted by loud and prolonged shouts of joy. A whole throng of Pierrots had swarmed into the Place from every side, carrying lighted torches and tall staves, on which were hung lanthorns with many-coloured lights.

The procession was ready to start. A stentorian voice shouted out in resonant accents:

"En avant, la grosse caisse!"

A man now, portly and gorgeous in scarlet and blue, detached himself from out the crowd. His head was hidden beneath the monstrous mask of a cardboard lion, roughly painted in brown and yellow, with crimson for the widely open jaws and the corners of the eyes, to make them seem ferocious and bloodshot. His coat was of bright crimson cloth, with cuts and slashings in it, through which bunches of bright blue paper were made to protrude, in imitation of the costume of mediæval times.

He had blue stockings on and bright scarlet slippers, and behind him floated a large strip of scarlet flannel, on which moons and suns and stars of gold had been showered in plenty.

Upon his portly figure in front he was supporting the big drum, which was securely strapped round his shoulders with tarred cordages, the spoil of some fishing vessel.

There was a merciful slit in the jaw of the cardboard lion, through which the portly drummer puffed and spluttered as he shouted lustily:

"En avant!"

And wielding the heavy drumstick with a powerful arm, he brought it crashing down against the side of the mighty instrument.

"Hurrah! Hurrah! en avant les trompettes!"

A fanfare of brass instruments followed, lustily blown by twelve young men in motley coats of green, and tall, peaked hats adorned with feathers.

The drummer had begun to march, closely followed by the trumpeters. Behind them a bevy of Columbines in many-coloured tarlatan skirts and hair flying wildly in the breeze, giggling, pushing, exchanging ribald jokes with the men behind, and getting kissed or slapped for their pains.

Then the triumphal car of the goddess, with Demoiselle Candeille standing straight up in it, a tall gold wand in one hand, the other resting in a mass of scarlet berries. All round the car, helter-skelter, tumbling, pushing, came Pierrots and Pierrettes, carrying lanthorns, and Harlequins bearing the torches.

And after the car the long line of more sober folk, the older fisherman, the women in caps and many-hued skirts, the serious townfolk who had scorned the travesty, yet would not be left out of the procession. They all began to march, to the tune of those noisy brass trumpets which were thundering forth snatches from the newly composed "Marseillaise."

Above the sky became more heavy with clouds. Anon a few drops of rain began to fall, making the torches sizzle and splutter, and scatter grease and tar around and wetting the lightly-covered shoulders of tarlatan-clad Columbines. But no one cared! The glow of so much merrymaking kept the blood warm and the skin dry.

The flour all came off the Pierrots' faces, the blue paper slashings of the drummer-in-chief hung in pulpy lumps against his gorgeous scarlet cloak. The trumpeters' feathers became streaky and bedraggled.

But in the name of that good God who had ceased to exist, who in the world or out of it cared if it rained, or thundered and stormed! This was a national holiday, for an English spy was captured, and all natives of Boulogne were free of the guillotine to-night.

The revellers were making the circuit of the town, with lanthorns fluttering in the wind, and flickering torches held up aloft illumining laughing faces, red with the glow of a drunken joy, young faces that only enjoyed the moment's pleasure, serious ones that withheld a frown at thought of the morrow. The fitful light played on the grotesque masques of beasts and reptiles, on the diamond necklace of a very earthly goddess, on God's glorious spoils from gardens and country-side, on smothered anxiety and repressed cruelty.

The crowd had turned its back on the guillotine, and the trumpets now changed the inspiriting tune of the "Marseillaise" to the ribald vulgarity of the "Ca ira!"

Everyone yelled and shouted. Girls with flowing hair produced broomsticks, and astride on these, broke from the ranks and danced a mad and obscene saraband, a dance of witches in the weird glow of sizzling torches, to the accompaniment of raucous laughter and of coarse jokes.

Thus the procession passed on, a sight to gladden the eyes of those who had desired to smother all thought of the Infinite, of Eternity and of God in the minds of those to whom they had nothing to offer in return. A threat of death yesterday, misery, starvation and squalor! all the hideousness of a destroying anarchy, that had nothing to give save a national fête, a tinsel goddess, some shallow laughter and momentary intoxication, a travesty of clothes and of religion and a dance on the ashes of the past.

And there along the ramparts where the massive walls of the city encircled the frowning prisons of Gayole and the old Château, dark groups were crouching, huddled together in compact masses, which in the gloom seemed to vibrate with fear. Like hunted quarry seeking for shelter, sombre figures flattened themselves in the angles of the dank walls, as the noisy carousers drew nigh. Then as the torches and lanthorns detached themselves from out the evening shadows, hand would clutch hand and hearts would beat with agonized suspense, whilst the dark and shapeless forms would try to appear smaller, flatter, less noticeable than before.

And when the crowd had passed noisily along, leaving behind it a trail of torn finery, of glittering tinsel and of scarlet berries, when the boom of the big drum and the grating noise of the brass trumpets had somewhat died away, wan faces, pale with anxiety, would peer from out the darkness, and nervous hands would grasp with trembling fingers the small bundles of poor belongings tied up hastily in view of flight.

At seven o'clock, so 'twas said, the cannon would boom from the old Beffroi. The guard would throw open the prison gates, and those who had something or somebody to hide, and those who had a great deal to fear, would be free to go whithersoever they chose.

And mothers, sisters, sweethearts stood watching by the gates, for loved ones to-night would be set free, all along of the capture of that English spy, the Scarlet Pimpernel.

CHAPTER XXXI

FINAL DISPOSITIONS

To Chauvelin the day had been one of restless inquietude and nervous apprehension.

Collot d'Herbois harassed him with questions and complaints intermixed with threats but thinly veiled. At his suggestion Gayole had been transformed into a fully-manned, well-garrisoned fortress. Troops were to be seen everywhere, on the stairs and in the passages, the guard-rooms and offices: picked men from the municipal guard, and the company which had been sent down from Paris some time ago.

Chauvelin had not resisted these orders given by his colleague. He knew quite well that Marguerite would make no attempt at escape, but he had long ago given up all hope of persuading a man of the type of Collot d'Herbois that a woman of her temperament would never think of saving her own life at the expense of others, and that Sir Percy Blakeney, in spite of his adoration for his wife, would sooner see her die before him, than allow the lives of innocent men and women to be the price of hers.

Collot was one of those brutish sots—not by any means infrequent among the Terrorists of that time—who, born in the gutter, still loved to wallow in his native element, and who measured all his fellow-creatures by the same standard which he had always found good enough for himself. In this man there was neither the enthusiastic patriotism of a Chauvelin, nor the ardent selflessness of a Danton. He served the revolution and fostered the anarchical spirit of the times only because these brought him a competence and a notoriety, which an orderly and fastidious government would obviously have never offered him.

History shows no more despicable personality than that of Collot d'Herbois, one of the most hideous products of that utopian Revolution, whose grandly conceived theories of a universal levelling of mankind only succeeded in dragging into prominence a number of half-brutish creatures who, revelling in their own abasement, would otherwise have remained content in inglorious obscurity.

Chauvelin tolerated and half feared Collot, knowing full well that if now the Scarlet Pimpernel escaped from his hands, he could expect no mercy from his colleagues.

The scheme by which he hoped to destroy not only the heroic leader but the entire League by bringing opprobrium and ridicule upon them, was wonderfully subtle in its refined cruelty, and Chauvelin, knowing by now something of Sir Percy Blakeney's curiously blended character, was never for a moment in doubt but that he would write the infamous letter, save his wife by sacrificing his honour, and then seek oblivion and peace in suicide.

With so much disgrace, so much mud cast upon their chief, the League of the Scarlet Pimpernel would cease to be. *That* had been Chauvelin's plan all along. For this end he had schemed and thought and planned, from the moment that Robespierre had given him the opportunity of redeeming his failure of last year. He had built up the edifice of his intrigue, bit by bit, from the introduction of his tool, Candeille, to Marguerite at the Richmond gala, to the arrest of Lady Blakeney in Boulogne. All that remained for him to see now, would be the attitude of Sir Percy Blakeney to-night, when, in exchange for the stipulated letter, he would see his wife set free.

All day Chauvelin had wondered how it would all go off. He had stage-managed everything, but he did not know how the chief actor would play his part.

From time to time, when his feeling of restlessness became quite unendurable, the ex-ambassador would wander round

Fort Gayole and on some pretext or other demand to see one or the other of his prisoners. Marguerite, however, observed complete silence in his presence: she acknowledged his greeting with a slight inclination of the head, and in reply to certain perfunctory queries of his—which he put to her in order to justify his appearance—she either nodded or gave curt monosyllabic answers through partially closed lips.

"I trust that everything is arranged for your comfort, Lady Blakeney."

"I thank you, sir."

"You will be rejoining the 'Day-Dream' to-night. Can I send a messenger over to the yacht for you?"

"I thank you. No."

"Sir Percy is well. He is fast asleep, and hath not asked for your ladyship. Shall I let him know that you are well?"

A nod of acquiescence from Marguerite and Chauvelin's string of queries was at an end. He marvelled at her quietude and thought that she should have been as restless as himself.

Later on in the day, and egged on by Collot d'Herbois and by his own fears, he had caused Marguerite to be removed from No. 6.

This change he heralded by another brief visit to her, and his attitude this time was one of deferential apology.

"A matter of expediency, Lady Blakeney," he explained, "and I trust that the change will be for your comfort."

Again the same curt nod of acquiescence on her part, and a brief:

"As you command, Monsieur!"

But when he had gone, she turned with a sudden passionate outburst towards the Abbé Foucquet, her faithful companion through the past long, weary hours. She fell on her knees beside him and sobbed in an agony of grief.

"Oh! if I could only know . . . if I could only see him! . . . for a minute . . . a second! . . . if I could only know! . . ."

She felt as if the awful uncertainty would drive her mad.

If she could only know! If she could only know what he meant to do.

"The good God knows!" said the old man, with his usual simple philosophy, "and perhaps it is all for the best."

The room which Chauvelin had now destined for Marguerite
was one which gave from the larger one, wherein last night he
had had his momentous interview with her and with Sir Percy.

It was small, square and dark, with no window in it: only a
small ventilating hole high up in the wall and heavily grated.
Chauvelin, who desired to prove to her that there was no
wish on his part to add physical discomfort to her mental
tortures, had given orders that the little place should be
made as habitable as possible. A thick, soft carpet had been
laid on the ground; there was an easy chair and a comfort-
able-looking couch with a couple of pillows and a rug upon
it, and oh, marvel! on the round central table, a vase with a
huge bunch of many-coloured dahlias which seemed to
throw a note as if of gladness into this strange and gloomy
little room.

At the furthest corner, too, a construction of iron uprights and
crossway bars had been hastily contrived and fitted with cur-
tains, forming a small recess, behind which was a tidy wash-
stand, fine clean towels and plenty of fresh water. Evidently the
shops of Boulogne had been commandeered in order to render
Marguerite's sojourn here outwardly agreeable.

But as the place was innocent of window, so was it innocent
of doors. The one that gave into the large room had been taken
out of its hinges, leaving only the frame, on each side of which
stood a man from the municipal guard with fixed bayonet.

Chauvelin himself had conducted Marguerite to her new
prison. She followed him—silent and apathetic—with not a
trace of that awful torrent of emotion which had overwhelmed
her but half-an-hour ago when she had fallen on her knees beside the old priest and sobbed her heart out in a passionate fit of
weeping. Even the sight of the soldiers left her outwardly indifferent. As she stepped across the threshold she noticed that the
door itself had been taken away: then she gave another quick
glance at the soldiers, whose presence there would control her
every movement.

The thought of Queen Marie Antoinette in the Conciergerie prison with the daily, hourly humiliation and shame which this constant watch imposed upon her womanly pride and modesty, flashed suddenly across Marguerite's mind, and a deep blush of horror rapidly suffused her pale cheeks, whilst an almost imperceptible shudder shook her delicate frame.

Perhaps, as in a flash, she had at this moment received an inkling of what the nature of that terrible "either–or" might be, with which Chauvelin was trying to force an English gentleman to dishonour. Sir Percy Blakeney's wife had been threatened with Marie Antoinette's fate.

"You see, Madame," said her cruel enemy's unctuous voice close to her ear, "that we have tried our humble best to make your brief sojourn here as agreeable as possible. May I express a hope that you will be quite comfortable in this room, until the time when Sir Percy will be ready to accompany you to the 'Day-Dream.'"

"I thank you, sir," she replied quietly.

"And if there is anything you require, I pray you to call. I shall be in the next room all day and entirely at your service."

A young orderly now entered bearing a small collation—eggs, bread, milk and wine—which he set on the central table. Chauvelin bowed low before Marguerite and withdrew. Anon he ordered the two sentinels to stand the other side of the doorway, against the wall of his own room, and well out of sight of Marguerite, so that, as she moved about her own narrow prison, if she ate or slept, she might have the illusion that she was unwatched.

The sight of the soldiers had had the desired effect on her. Chauvelin had seen her shudder and knew that she understood or that she guessed. He was now satisfied and really had no wish to harass her beyond endurance.

Moreover, there was always the proclamation which threatened the bread-winners of Boulogne with death if Marguerite Blakeney escaped, and which would be in full force until Sir Percy had written, signed and delivered into Chauvelin's hands the letter which was to be the signal for the general amnesty.

Chauvelin had indeed cause to be satisfied with his measures. There was no fear that his prisoners would attempt to escape.

Even Collot d'Herbois had to admit everything was well done. He had read the draft of the proposed letter and was satisfied with its contents. Gradually now into his loutish brain there had filtrated the conviction that Citizen Chauvelin was right, that that accursed Scarlet Pimpernel and his brood of English spies would be more effectually annihilated by all the dishonour and ridicule which such a letter written by the mysterious hero would heap upon them all, than they could ever be through the relentless work of the guillotine. His only anxiety now was whether the Englishman would write that letter.

"Bah! he'll do it," he would say whenever he thought the whole matter over: "Sacré tonnerre! but 'tis an easy means to save his own skin."

"You would sign such a letter without hesitation, eh, Citizen Collot," said Chauvelin, with well-concealed sarcasm, on one occasion when his colleague discussed the all-absorbing topic with him; "you would show no hesitation, if your life were at stake, and you were given the choice between writing that letter and . . . the guillotine?"

"Parbleu!" responded Collot with conviction.

"More especially," continued Chauvelin drily, "if a million francs were promised you as well?"

"Sacré Anglais!" swore Collot angrily, "you don't propose giving him that money, do you?"

"We'll place it ready to his hand, at any rate, so that it should appear as if he had actually taken it."

Collot looked up at his colleague in ungrudging admiration. Chauvelin had indeed left nothing undone, had thought everything out in this strangely conceived scheme for the destruction of the enemy of France.

"But in the name of all the dwellers in hell, Citizen," admonished Collot, "guard that letter well, once it is in your hands."

"I'll do better than that," said Chauvelin, "I will hand it over to you, Citizen Collot, and you shall ride with it to Paris at once."

"To-night!" assented Collot with a shout of triumph, as he brought his grimy fist crashing down on the table, "I'll have a horse ready saddled at this very gate, and an escort of mounted men . . . we'll ride like hell's own furies and not pause to breathe until that letter is in Citizen Robespierre's hands."

"Well thought of, Citizen," said Chauvelin approvingly. "I pray you give the necessary orders, that the horses be ready saddled, and the men booted and spurred, and waiting at the Gayole gate, at seven o'clock this evening."

"I wish the letter were written and safely in our hands by now."

"Nay! the Englishman will have it ready by this evening, never fear. The tide is high at half-past seven, and he will be in haste for his wife to be aboard his yacht, ere the turn, even if he . . ."

He paused, savouring the thoughts which had suddenly flashed across his mind, and a look of intense hatred and cruel satisfaction for a moment chased away the studied impassiveness of his face.

"What do you mean, Citizen?" queried Collot anxiously, "even if he . . . what? . . ."

"Oh! nothing, nothing! I was only trying to make vague guesses as to what the Englishman will do *after* he has written the letter," quoth Chauvelin reflectively.

"Morbleu! he'll return to his own accursed country . . . glad enough to have escaped with his skin. . . . I suppose," added Collot with sudden anxiety, "you have no fear that he will refuse at the last moment to write that letter?"

The two men were sitting in the large room, out of which opened the one which was now occupied by Marguerite. They were talking at the further end of it, close to the window, and though Chauvelin had mostly spoken in a whisper, Collot had ofttimes shouted, and the ex-ambassador was wondering how much Marguerite had heard.

Now at Collot's anxious query he gave a quick furtive glance in the direction of the further room wherein she sat, so silent and so still, that it seemed almost as if she must be sleeping.

"You don't think that the Englishman will refuse to write the letter?" insisted Collot with angry impatience.

"No!" replied Chauvelin quietly.

"But if he does?" persisted the other.

"If he does, I send the woman to Paris to-night and have him hanged as a spy in this prison yard without further formality or trial . . ." replied Chauvelin firmly; "so either way, you see, Citizen," he added in a whisper, "the Scarlet Pimpernel is done for. . . . But I think that he will write the letter."

"Parbleu! so do I! . . ." rejoined Collot with a coarse laugh.

CHAPTER XXXII

The Letter

Later on, when his colleague left him in order to see to the horses and to his escort for to-night, Chauvelin called Sergeant Hébert, his old and trusted familiar, to him and gave him some final orders.

"The Angelus must be rung at the proper hour, friend Hébert," he began with a grim smile.

"The Angelus, Citizen?" quoth the Sergeant, with complete stupefaction, "'tis months now since it has been rung. It was forbidden by a decree of the Convention, and I doubt me if any of our men would know how to set about it."

Chauvelin's eyes were fixed before him in apparent vacancy, while the same grim smile still hovered round his thin lips. Something of that irresponsible spirit of adventure which was the mainspring of all Sir Percy Blakeney's actions, must for the moment have pervaded the mind of his deadly enemy.

Chauvelin had thought out this idea of having the Angelus rung to-night, and was thoroughly pleased with the notion. This was the day when the duel was to have been fought; seven o'clock would have been the very hour, and the sound of the Angelus to have been the signal for combat, and there was something very satisfying in the thought, that that same Angelus should be rung, as a signal that the Scarlet Pimpernel was withered and broken at last.

In answer to Hébert's look of bewilderment Chauvelin said quietly:

"We must have some signal between ourselves and the guard

at the different gates, also with the harbour officials: at a given moment the general amnesty must take effect and the harbour become a free port. I have a fancy that the signal shall be the ringing of the Angelus: the cannons at the gates and the harbour can boom in response; then the prisons can be thrown open and prisoners can either participate in the evening fête or leave the city immediately, as they choose. The Committee of Public Safety has promised the amnesty: it will carry out its promise to the full, and when Citizen Collot d'Herbois arrives in Paris with the joyful news, all natives of Boulogne in the prisons there will participate in the free pardon too."

"I understand all that, Citizen," said Hébert, still somewhat bewildered, "but not the Angelus."

"A fancy, friend Hébert, and I mean to have it."

"But who is to ring it, Citizen?"

"Morbleu! haven't you one calotin left in Boulogne whom you can press into doing this service?"

"Aye! calotins enough! there's the Abbé Foucquet in this very building . . . in No. 6 cell . . ."

"Sacré tonnerre!" ejaculated Chauvelin exultingly, "the very man! I know his dossier well! Once he is free, he will make straightway for England . . . he and his family . . . and will help to spread the glorious news of the dishonour and disgrace of the much-vaunted Scarlet Pimpernel! . . . The very man, friend Hébert! . . . Let him be stationed here . . . to see the letter written . . . to see the money handed over—for we will go through with that farce—and make him understand that the moment I give him the order, he can run over to his old church St. Joseph and ring the Angelus. . . . The old fool will be delighted . . . more especially when he knows that he will thereby be giving the very signal which will set his own sister's children free. . . . You understand? . . ."

"I understand, Citizen."

"And you can make the old calotin understand?"

"I think so, Citizen. . . . You want him in this room. . . . At what time?"

"A quarter before seven."

"Yes. I'll bring him along myself, and stand over him, lest he play any pranks."

"Oh! he'll not trouble you," sneered Chauvelin, "he'll be deeply interested in the proceedings. The woman will be here too, remember," he added with a jerky movement of the hand in the direction of Marguerite's room, "the two might be made to stand together, with four of your fellows round them."

"I understand, Citizen. Are any of us to escort the Citizen Foucquet when he goes to St. Joseph?"

"Aye! two men had best go with him. There will be a crowd in the streets by then . . . How far is it from here to the church?"

"Less than five minutes."

"Good. See to it that the doors are opened and the bell ropes easy of access."

"It shall be seen to, Citizen. How many men will you have inside this room to-night?"

"Let the walls be lined with men whom you can trust. I anticipate neither trouble nor resistance. The whole thing is a simple formality to which the Englishman has already intimated his readiness to submit. If he changes his mind at the last moment there will be no Angelus rung, no booming of the cannons or opening of the prison doors: there will be no amnesty, and no free pardon. The woman will be at once conveyed to Paris, and . . . But he'll not change his mind, friend Hébert," he concluded in suddenly altered tones, and speaking quite lightly, "he'll not change his mind."

The conversation between Chauvelin and his familiar had been carried on in whispers: not that the Terrorist cared whether Marguerite overheard or not, but whispering had become a habit with this man, whose tortuous ways and subtle intrigues did not lend themselves to discussion in a loud voice.

Chauvelin was sitting at the central table, just where he had been last night when Sir Percy Blakeney's sudden advent broke in on his meditations. The table had been cleared of the litter of multitudinous papers which had encumbered it before. On it now there were only a couple of heavy pewter candlesticks, with the tallow candles fixed ready in them, a leather-pad, an ink-well, a sand-box and two or three quill pens: everything disposed, in fact, for the writing and signing of the letter.

Already in imagination, Chauvelin saw his impudent enemy, the bold and daring adventurer, standing there beside that table and putting his name to the consummation of his own infamy. The mental picture thus evoked brought a gleam of cruel satisfaction and of satiated lust into the keen, ferret-like face, and a smile of intense joy lit up the narrow, pale-coloured eyes.

He looked round the room where the great scene would be enacted: two soldiers were standing on guard outside Marguerite's prison, two more at attention near the door which gave on the passage: his own half-dozen picked men were waiting his commands in the corridor. Presently the whole room would be lined with troops, himself and Collot standing with eyes fixed on the principal actor of the drama! Hébert with specially selected troopers standing on guard over Marguerite!

No, no! he had left nothing to chance this time, and down below the horses would be ready saddled, that were to convey Collot and the precious document to Paris.

No! nothing was left to chance, and in either case he was bound to win. Sir Percy Blakeney would either write the letter in order to save his wife, and heap dishonour on himself, or he would shrink from the terrible ordeal at the last moment and let Chauvelin and the Committee of Public Safety work their will with her and him.

"In that case the pillory as a spy and summary hanging for you, my friend," concluded Chauvelin in his mind, "and for your wife . . . Bah, once you are out of the way, even she will cease to matter."

He left Hébert on guard in the room. An irresistible desire seized him to go and have a look at his discomfited enemy, and from the latter's attitude make a shrewd guess as to what he meant to do to-night.

Sir Percy had been given a room on one of the upper floors of the old prison. He had in no way been closely guarded, and the room itself had been made as comfortable as may be. He had

seemed quite happy and contented when he had been conducted hither by Chauvelin, the evening before.

"I hope you quite understand, Sir Percy, that you are my
guest here to-night," Chauvelin had said suavely, "and that you
are free to come and go, just as you please."

"Lud love you, sir," Sir Percy had replied gaily, "but I verily
believe that I am."

"It is only Lady Blakeney whom we have cause to watch until
to-morrow," added Chauvelin with quiet significance. "Is that
not so, Sir Percy?"

But Sir Percy seemed, whenever his wife's name was mentioned, to lapse into irresistible somnolence. He yawned now
with his usual affectation, and asked at what hour gentlemen in
France were wont to breakfast.

Since then Chauvelin had not seen him. He had repeatedly
asked how the English prisoner was faring, and whether he
seemed to be sleeping and eating heartily. The orderly in charge
invariably reported that the Englishman seemed well, but did
not eat much. On the other hand, he had ordered, and lavishly
paid for, measure after measure of brandy and bottle after bottle of wine.

"Hm! how strange these Englishmen are!" mused Chauvelin;
"this so-called hero is nothing but a wine-sodden brute, who
seeks to nerve himself for a trying ordeal by drowning his faculties in brandy . . . Perhaps after all he doesn't care! . . ."

But the wish to have a look at that strangely complex creature—hero, adventurer or mere lucky fool—was irresistible,
and Chauvelin in the latter part of the afternoon went up to the
room which had been allotted to Sir Percy Blakeney.

He never moved now without his escort, and this time also
two of his favourite bodyguard accompanied him to the upper
floor. He knocked at the door, but received no answer, and after
a second or two he bade his men wait in the corridor and, gently turning the latch, walked in.

There was an odour of brandy in the air; on the table two or
three empty bottles of wine and a glass half filled with cognac
testified to the truth of what the orderly had said, whilst

sprawling across the camp bedstead, which obviously was too small for his long limbs, his head thrown back, his mouth open for a vigorous snore, lay the imperturbable Sir Percy fast asleep.

Chauvelin went up to the bedstead and looked down upon the reclining figure of the man who had oft been called the most dangerous enemy of Republican France.

Of a truth, a fine figure of a man, Chauvelin was ready enough to admit that; the long, hard limbs, the wide chest, and slender, white hands, all bespoke the man of birth, breeding and energy: the face too looked strong and clearly-cut in repose, now that the perpetually inane smile did not play round the firm lips, nor the lazy, indolent expression mar the seriousness of the straight brow. For one moment—it was a mere flash— Chauvelin felt almost sorry that so interesting a career should be thus ignominiously brought to a close.

The Terrorist felt that if his own future, his own honour and integrity were about to be so hopelessly crushed, he would have wandered up and down this narrow room like a caged beast, eating out his heart with self-reproach and remorse, and racking his nerves and brain for an issue out of the terrible alternative which meant dishonour or death.

But this man drank and slept.

"Perhaps he doesn't care!"

And as if in answer to Chauvelin's puzzled musings a deep snore escaped the sleeping adventurer's parted lips.

Chauvelin sighed, perplexed and troubled. He looked round the little room, then went up to a small side table which stood against the wall and on which were two or three quill pens and an ink-well, also some loosely scattered sheets of paper. These he turned over with a careless hand and presently came across a closely written page.

——"Citizen Chauvelin:—In consideration of a further sum of one million francs . . ."

It was the beginning of the letter! . . . only a few words so far . . . with several corrections of misspelt words . . . and a line left out here and there which confused the meaning . . . a beginning made by the unsteady hand of that drunken fool . . . an attempt only at present. . . .

But still . . . a beginning.

Close by was the draft of it as written out by Chauvelin, and which Sir Percy had evidently begun to copy.

He had made up his mind then. . . . He meant to subscribe with his own hand to his lasting dishonour . . . and meaning it, he slept!

Chauvelin felt the paper trembling in his hand. He felt strangely agitated and nervous, now that the issue was so near . . . so sure! . . .

"There's no demmed hurry for that, is there . . . er . . . Monsieur Chaubertin? . . ." came from the slowly wakening Sir Percy in somewhat thick, heavy accents, accompanied by a prolonged yawn. "I haven't got the demmed thing quite ready . . ."

Chauvelin had been so startled that the paper dropped from his hand. He stooped to pick it up.

"Nay! why should you be so scared, sir?" continued Sir Percy lazily, "did you think I was drunk? . . . I assure you, sir, on my honour, I am not so drunk as you think I am."

"I have no doubt, Sir Percy," replied Chauvelin ironically, "that you have all your marvellous faculties entirely at your command. . . . I must apologize for disturbing your papers," he added, replacing the half-written page on the table, "I thought perhaps that if the letter was quite ready . . ."

"It will be, sir . . . it will be . . . for I am not drunk, I assure you. . . . and can write with a steady hand . . . and do honour to my signature. . . ."

"When will you have the letter ready, Sir Percy?"

"The 'Day-Dream' must leave the harbour at the turn of the tide," quoth Sir Percy thickly. "It'll be demmed well time by then . . . won't it, sir? . . ."

"About sundown, Sir Percy . . . not later . . ."

"About sundown . . . not later . . ." muttered Blakeney, as he once more stretched his long limbs along the narrow bed.

He gave a loud and hearty yawn.

"I'll not fail you . . ." he murmured, as he closed his eyes, and gave a final struggle to get his head at a comfortable angle, "the letter will be written in my best cali . . . calig. . . . Lud! but I'm not so drunk as you think I am. . . ."

But as if to belie his own oft-repeated assertion, hardly was the last word out of his mouth than his stertorous and even breathing proclaimed the fact that he was once more fast asleep.

With a shrug of the shoulders and a look of unutterable contempt at his broken-down enemy, Chauvelin turned on his heel and went out of the room.

But outside in the corridor he called the orderly to him and gave strict commands that no more wine or brandy was to be served to the Englishman under any circumstances whatever.

"He has two hours in which to sleep off the effects of all that brandy which he has consumed," he mused as he finally went back to his own quarters, "and by that time he will be able to write with a steady hand."

CHAPTER XXXIII

THE ENGLISH SPY

And now at last the shades of evening were drawing in thick and fast. Within the walls of Fort Gayole the last rays of the setting sun had long ago ceased to shed their dying radiance, and through the thick stone embrasures and the dusty panes of glass, the grey light of dusk soon failed to penetrate.

In the large ground-floor room with its window opened upon the wide promenade of the southern ramparts, a silence reigned which was oppressive. The air was heavy with the fumes of the two tallow candles on the table, which smoked persistently.

Against the walls a row of figures in dark blue uniforms with scarlet facings, drab breeches and heavy riding boots, silent and immovable, with fixed bayonets like so many automatons lining the room all round; at some little distance from the central table and out of the immediate circle of light, a small group composed of five soldiers in the same blue and scarlet uniforms. One of these was Sergeant Hébert. In the centre of this group two persons were sitting: a woman and an old man.

The Abbé Foucquet had been brought down from his prison cell a few minutes ago, and told to watch what would go on around him, after which he would be allowed to go to his old church of St. Joseph and ring the Angelus once more before he and his family left Boulogne forever.

The Angelus would be the signal for the opening of all the prison gates in the town. Everyone to-night could come and go as they pleased, and having rung the Angelus, the abbé would

be at liberty to join François and Félicité and their old mother,
his sister, outside the purlieus of the town.

The Abbé Foucquet did not quite understand all this, which
was very rapidly and roughly explained to him. It was such a very
little while ago that he had expected to see the innocent children mounting up those awful steps which lead to the guillotine,
whilst he himself was looking death quite near in the face, that
all this talk of amnesty and of pardon had not quite fully reached
his brain.

But he was quite content that it had all been ordained by le
bon Dieu, and very happy at the thought of ringing the dearly-
loved Angelus in his own old church once again. So when he was
peremptorily pushed into the room and found himself close to
Marguerite, with four or five soldiers standing round them, he
quietly pulled his old rosary from his pocket and began murmuring gentle "Paters" and "Aves" under his breath.

Beside him sat Marguerite, rigid as a statue: her cloak thrown
over her shoulders, so that its hood might hide her face. She
could not now have said how that awful day had passed, how she
had managed to survive the terrible, nerve-racking suspense,
the agonizing doubt as to what was going to happen. But above
all, what she had found most unendurable was the torturing
thought that in this same grim and frowning building her husband was there . . . somewhere . . . how far or how near she
could not say . . . but she knew that she was parted from him and
perhaps would not see him again, not even at the hour of death.

That Percy would never write that infamous letter and *live*,
she knew. That he might write it in order to save her, she feared
was possible, whilst the look of triumph on Chauvelin's face had
aroused her most agonizing terrors.

When she was summarily ordered to go into the next room,
she realized at once that all hope now was more than futile. The
walls lined with troops, the attitude of her enemies, and above
all that table with paper, ink and pens ready as it were for the accomplishment of the hideous and monstrous deed, all made her
very heart numb, as if it were held within the chill embrace of
death.

"If the woman moves, speaks or screams, gag her at once!" said Collot roughly the moment she sat down, and Sergeant Hébert stood over her, gag and cloth in hand, whilst two soldiers placed heavy hands on her shoulders.

But she neither moved nor spoke, not even presently when a loud and cheerful voice came echoing from a distant corridor, and anon the door opened and her husband came in, accompanied by Chauvelin.

The ex-ambassador was very obviously in a state of acute nervous tension; his hands were tightly clasped behind his back, and his movements were curiously irresponsible and jerky. But Sir Percy Blakeney looked a picture of calm unconcern: the lace bow at his throat was tied with scrupulous care, his eyeglass upheld at quite the correct angle, and his delicate-coloured caped coat was thrown back just sufficiently to afford a glimpse of the dainty cloth suit and exquisitely embroidered waistcoat beneath.

He was the perfect presentation of a London dandy, and might have been entering a royal drawing-room in company with an honoured guest. Marguerite's eyes were riveted on him as he came well within the circle of light projected by the candles, but not even with that acute sixth sense of a passionate and loving woman could she detect the slightest tremor in the aristocratic hand which held the gold-rimmed eyeglass, nor the faintest quiver of the firmly moulded lips.

This had occurred just as the bell of the old Beffroi chimed three-quarters after six. Now it was close on seven, and in the centre of the room and with his face and figure well lighted up by the candles, at the table pen in hand sat Sir Percy writing.

At his elbow just behind him stood Chauvelin on the one side and Collot d'Herbois on the other, both watching with fixed and burning eyes the writing of that letter.

Sir Percy seemed in no hurry. He wrote slowly and deliberately, carefully copying the draft of the letter which was propped up in front of him. The spelling of some of the French words seemed to have troubled him at first, for when he began he made many facetious and self-deprecatory remarks anent his

own want of education, and carelessness in youth in acquiring
the gentle art of speaking so elegant a language.

Presently, however, he appeared more at his ease, or perhaps
less inclined to talk, since he only received curt monosyllabic answers to his pleasant sallies. Five minutes had gone by without
any other sound, save the spasmodic creak of Sir Percy's pen
upon the paper, the while Chauvelin and Collot watched every
word he wrote.

But gradually from afar there had arisen in the stillness of
evening a distant, rolling noise like that of surf breaking against
the cliffs. Nearer and louder it grew, and as it increased in volume, so it gained now in diversity. The monotonous, roll-like,
far-off thunder was just as continuous as before, but now shriller
notes broke out from amongst the more remote sounds, a loud
laugh seemed ever and anon to pierce the distance and to rise
above the persistent hubbub, which became the mere accompaniment to these isolated tones.

The merrymakers of Boulogne, having started from the Place
de la Sénéchaussée, were making the round of the town by the
wide avenue which tops the ramparts. They were coming past
the Fort Gayole, shouting, singing, brass trumpets in front, big
drum ahead, drenched, hot, and hoarse, but supremely happy.

Sir Percy looked up for a moment as the noise drew nearer,
then turned to Chauvelin and pointing to the letter, he said:

"I have nearly finished!"

The suspense in the smoke-laden atmosphere of this room
was becoming unendurable, and four hearts at least were beating wildly with overpowering anxiety. Marguerite's eyes were
fixed with tender intensity on the man she so passionately loved.
She did not understand his actions or his motives, but she felt a
wild longing in her, to drink in every line of that loved face, as if
with this last, long look she was bidding an eternal farewell to all
hopes of future earthly happiness.

The old priest had ceased to tell his beads. Feeling in his
kindly heart the echo of the appalling tragedy which was being
enacted before him, he had put out a fatherly, tentative hand

towards Marguerite, and given her icy fingers a comforting pressure.

And in the hearts of Chauvelin and his colleague there was satisfied revenge, eager, exultant triumph and that terrible nerve-tension which immediately precedes the long-expected climax.

But who can say what went on within the heart of that bold adventurer, about to be brought to the lowest depths of humiliation which it is in the power of man to endure? What behind that smooth unruffled brow still bent laboriously over the page of writing?

The crowd was now on the Place Daumont; some of the foremost in the ranks were ascending the stone steps which lead to the southern ramparts. The noise had become incessant: Pierrots and Pierrettes, Harlequins and Columbines had worked themselves up into a veritable intoxication of shouts and laughter.

Now as they all swarmed up the steps and caught sight of the open window almost on a level with the ground, and of the large dimly-lighted room, they gave forth one terrific and voluminous "Hurrah!" for the paternal government up in Paris, who had given them cause for all this joy. Then they recollected how the amnesty, the pardon, the national fête, this brilliant procession had come about, and somebody in the crowd shouted:

"Allons! let us have a look at that English spy! . . ."

"Let us see the Scarlet Pimpernel!"

"Yes! yes! let us see what he is like!"

They shouted and stamped and swarmed round the open window, swinging their lanthorns and demanding in a loud tone of voice that the English spy be shown to them.

Faces wet with rain and perspiration tried to peep in at the window. Collot gave brief orders to the soldiers to close the shutters at once and to push away the crowd, but the crowd would not be pushed. It would not be gainsaid, and when the soldiers tried to close the window, twenty angry fists broke the panes of glass.

"I can't finish this writing in your lingo, sir, whilst this demmed row is going on," said Sir Percy placidly.

"You have not much more to write, Sir Percy," urged Chauvelin with nervous impatience, "I pray you, finish the matter now, and get you gone from out this city."

"Send that demmed lot away, then," rejoined Sir Percy calmly.

"They won't go. . . . They want to see you . . ."

Sir Percy paused a moment, pen in hand, as if in deep reflection.

"They want to see me," he said with a laugh. "Why, demn it all . . . then, why not let em? . . ."

And with a few rapid strokes of the pen, he quickly finished the letter, adding his signature with a bold flourish, whilst the crowd, pushing, jostling, shouting and cursing the soldiers, still loudly demanded to see the Scarlet Pimpernel.

Chauvelin felt as if his heart would veritably burst with the wildness of its beating.

Then Sir Percy, with one hand lightly pressed on the letter, pushed his chair away and with his pleasant ringing voice, said once again:

"Well! demn it . . . let 'em see me! . . ."

With that he sprang to his feet and up to his full height, and as he did so he seized the two massive pewter candlesticks, one in each hand, and with powerful arms well outstretched he held them high above his head.

"The letter . . ." murmured Chauvelin in a hoarse whisper.

But even as he was quickly reaching out a hand, which shook with the intensity of his excitement, towards the letter on the table, Blakeney, with one loud and sudden shout, threw the heavy candlesticks onto the floor. They rattled down with a terrific crash, the lights were extinguished, and the whole room was immediately plunged in utter darkness.

The crowd gave a wild yell of fear: they had only caught sight for one instant of that gigantic figure—which, with arms outstretched had seemed supernaturally tall—weirdly illumined by the flickering light of the tallow candles and the next moment disappearing into utter darkness before their very gaze. Overcome with sudden superstitious fear, Pierrots and Pierrettes, drummer and trumpeters turned and fled in every direction.

Within the room all was wild confusion. The soldiers had heard a cry:

"La fenêtre! La fenêtre!"

Who gave it no one knew, no one could afterwards recollect: certain it is that with one accord the majority of the men made a rush for the open window, driven thither partly by the wild instinct of the chase after an escaping enemy, and partly by the same superstitious terror which had caused the crowd to flee. They clambered over the sill and dropped down on to the ramparts below, then started in wild pursuit.

But when the crash came, Chauvelin had given one frantic shout:

"The letter!!! . . . Collot!! . . . A moi. . . . In his hand. . . . The letter! . . ."

There was the sound of a heavy thud, of a terrible scuffle there on the floor in the darkness and then a yell of victory from Collot d'Herbois.

"I have the letter! A Paris!"

"Victory!" echoed Chauvelin, exultant and panting, "victory!! The Angelus, friend Hébert! Take the calotin to ring the Angelus!!!"

It was instinct which caused Collot d'Herbois to find the door; he tore it open, letting in a feeble ray of light from the corridor. He stood in the doorway one moment, his slouchy, ungainly form distinctly outlined against the lighter background beyond, a look of exultant and malicious triumph, of deadly hate and cruelty distinctly imprinted on his face and with upraised hand wildly flourishing the precious document, the brand of dishonour for the enemy of France.

"A Paris!" shouted Chauvelin to him excitedly. "Into Robespierre's hands. . . . The letter! . . ."

Then he fell back panting, exhausted on the nearest chair.

Collot, without looking again behind him, called wildly for the men who were to escort him to Paris. They were picked troopers, stalwart veterans from the old municipal guard. They had not broken their ranks throughout the turmoil, and fell into line in perfect order as they followed Citizen Collot out of the room.

Less than five minutes later there was the noise of stamping and champing of bits in the courtyard below, a shout from Collot, and the sound of a cavalcade galloping at break-neck speed towards the distant Paris gate.

CHAPTER XXXIV

THE ANGELUS

And gradually all noises died away around the old Fort Gayole. The shouts and laughter of the merrymakers, who had quickly recovered from their fright, now came only as the muffled rumble of a distant storm, broken here and there by the shrill note of a girl's loud laughter, or a vigorous fanfare from the brass trumpets.

The room where so much turmoil had taken place, where so many hearts had beaten with torrent-like emotions, where the awesome tragedy of revenge and hate, of love and passion had been consummated, was now silent and at peace.

The soldiers had gone: some in pursuit of the revellers, some with Collot d'Herbois, others with Hébert and the calotin who was to ring the Angelus.

Chauvelin, overcome with the intensity of his exultation and the agony of the suspense which he had endured, sat, vaguely dreaming, hardly conscious, but wholly happy and content. Fearless, too, for his triumph was complete, and he cared not now if he lived or died.

He had lived long enough to see the complete annihilation and dishonour of his enemy.

What had happened to Sir Percy Blakeney now, what to Marguerite, he neither knew nor cared. No doubt the Englishman had picked himself up and got away through the window or the door: he would be anxious to get his wife out of the town as quickly as possible. The Angelus would ring directly,

251

the gates would be opened, the harbour made free to everyone. . . .

And Collot was a league outside Boulogne by now . . . a
league nearer to Paris.

So what mattered the humbled wayside English flower?—the
damaged and withered Scarlet Pimpernel? . . .

A slight noise suddenly caused him to start. He had been
dreaming, no doubt, having fallen into some kind of torpor, akin
to sleep, after the deadly and restless fatigue of the past four
days. He certainly had been unconscious of everything around
him, of time and of place. But now he felt fully awake.

And again he heard that slight noise, as if something or someone was moving in the room.

He tried to peer into the darkness, but could distinguish
nothing. He rose and went to the door. It was still open, and
close behind it against the wall a small oil lamp was fixed which
lit up the corridor.

Chauvelin detached the lamp and came back with it into the
room. Just as he did so there came to his ears the first sound of
the little church bell ringing the Angelus.

He stepped into the room holding the lamp high above his
head; its feeble rays fell full upon the brilliant figure of Sir Percy
Blakeney.

He was smiling pleasantly, bowing slightly towards Chauvelin,
and in his hand he held the sheathed sword, the blade of which
had been fashioned in Toledo for Lorenzo Cenci, and the fellow
of which was lying now—Chauvelin himself knew not where.

"The day and hour, Monsieur, I think," said Sir Percy with
courtly grace, "when you and I are to cross swords together;
those are the southern ramparts, meseems. Will you precede,
sir? and I will follow."

At sight of this man, of his impudence and of his daring,
Chauvelin felt an icy grip on his heart. His cheeks became ashen
white, his thin lips closed with a snap, and the hand which held
the lamp aloft trembled visibly. Sir Percy stood before him, still
smiling and with a graceful gesture pointing towards the ramparts.

From the Church of St. Joseph the gentle, melancholy tones of the Angelus sounding the second Ave Maria came faintly echoing in the evening air.

With a violent effort Chauvelin forced himself to self-control, and tried to shake off the strange feeling of obsession which had overwhelmed him in the presence of this extraordinary man. He walked quite quietly up to the table and placed the lamp upon it. As in a flash recollection had come back to him . . . the past few minutes! . . . the letter! and Collot well on his way to Paris!

Bah! he had nothing to fear now, save perhaps death at the hand of this adventurer turned assassin in his misery and humiliation!

"A truce on this folly, Sir Percy," he said roughly, "as you well know, I had never any intention of fighting you with these poisoned swords of yours and . . ."

"I knew that, M. Chauvelin. . . . But do *you* know that I have the intention of killing you now . . . as you stand . . . like a dog! . . ."

And throwing down the sword with one of those uncontrolled outbursts of almost animal passion, which for one instant revealed the real, inner man, he went up to Chauvelin and towering above him like a great avenging giant, he savoured for one second the joy of looking down on that puny, slender figure which he could crush with sheer brute force, with one blow from his powerful hands.

But Chauvelin at this moment was beyond fear.

"And if you killed me now, Sir Percy," he said quietly and looking the man whom he so hated fully in the eyes, "you could not destroy that letter which my colleague is taking to Paris at this very moment."

As he had anticipated, his words seemed to change Sir Percy's mood in an instant. The passion in the handsome, aristocratic face faded in a trice, the hard lines round the jaw and lips relaxed, the fire of revenge died out from the lazy blue eyes, and the next moment a long, loud, merry laugh raised the dormant echoes of the old fort.

"Nay, Monsieur Chaubertin," said Sir Percy gaily, "but this is marvellous . . . demmed marvellous . . . do you hear that, m'dear? . . . Gadzooks! but 'tis the best joke I have heard this past twelve-months. . . . Monsieur here thinks . . . Lud! but I shall die of laughing. . . . Monsieur here thinks . . . that 'twas that demmed letter which went to Paris . . . and that an English gentleman lay scuffling on the floor and allowed a letter to be filched from him . . ."

"Sir Percy! . . ." gasped Chauvelin, as an awful thought seemed suddenly to flash across his fevered brain.

"Lud, sir, you are astonishing!" said Sir Percy, taking a very much crumpled sheet of paper from the capacious pocket of his elegant caped coat, and holding it close to Chauvelin's horror-stricken gaze. "*This* is the letter which I wrote at that table yonder in order to gain time and in order to fool you. . . . But, by the Lord, you are a bigger demmed fool than ever I took you to be, if you thought it would serve any other purpose save that of my hitting you in the face with it."

And with a quick and violent gesture he struck Chauvelin full in the face with the paper.

"You would like to know, Monsieur Chaubertin, would you not? . . ." he added pleasantly, "what letter it is that your friend, Citizen Collot, is taking in such hot haste to Paris for you. . . . Well! the letter is not long and 'tis written in verse. . . . I wrote it myself upstairs to-day whilst you thought me sodden with brandy and three-parts asleep. But brandy is easily flung out of the window. . . . Did you think I drank it all? . . . Nay! as you remember, I told you that I was not so drunk as you thought? . . . Aye! the letter is writ in English verse, Monsieur, and it reads thus:

> "We seek him here! we seek him there!
> Those Frenchies seek him everywhere!
> Is he in heaven? is he in hell?
> That demmed elusive Pimpernel?

"A neat rhyme, I fancy, Monsieur, and one which will, if rightly translated, greatly please your friend and ruler, Citizen Robespierre. . . . Your colleague Citizen Collot is well on his way to Paris with it by now. . . . No, no, Monsieur . . . as you rightly said just now . . . I really could not kill you . . . God having blessed me with the saving sense of humour . . ."

Even as he spoke the third Ave Maria of the Angelus died away on the morning air. From the harbour and the old Château there came the loud boom of cannon.

The hour of the opening of the gates, of the general amnesty and free harbour was announced throughout Boulogne.

Chauvelin was livid with rage, fear and baffled revenge. He made a sudden rush for the door in a blind desire to call for help, but Sir Percy had toyed long enough with his prey. The hour was speeding on: Hébert and some of the soldiers might return, and it was time to think of safety and of flight. Quick as a hunted panther, he had interposed his tall figure between his enemy and the latter's chance of calling for aid, then, seizing the little man by the shoulders, he pushed him back into that portion of the room where Marguerite and the Abbé Foucquet had been lately sitting.

The gag, with cloth and cord, which had been intended for a woman were lying on the ground close by, just where Hébert had dropped them, when he marched the old Abbé off to the Church.

With quick and dexterous hands, Sir Percy soon reduced Chauvelin to an impotent and silent bundle. The ex-ambassador after four days of harrowing nerve-tension, followed by so awful a climax, was weakened physically and mentally, whilst Blakeney, powerful, athletic and always absolutely unperturbed, was fresh in body and spirit. He had slept calmly all the afternoon, having quietly thought out all his plans, left nothing to chance, and acted methodically and quickly, and invariably with perfect repose.

Having fully assured himself that the cords were well fastened, the gag secure and Chauvelin completely helpless, he took the now inert mass up in his arms and carried it into the adjoining room, where Marguerite for twelve hours had endured a terrible martyrdom.

He laid his enemy's helpless form upon the couch, and for

one moment looked down on it with a strange feeling of pity quite unmixed with contempt. The light from the lamp in the further room struck vaguely upon the prostrate figure of Chauvelin. He seemed to have lost consciousness, for the eyes were closed, only the hands, which were tied securely to his body, had a spasmodic, nervous twitch in them.

With a good-natured shrug of the shoulders the imperturbable Sir Percy turned to go, but just before he did so, he took a scrap of paper from his waistcoat pocket, and slipped it between Chauvelin's trembling fingers. On the paper were scribbled the four lines of verse which in the next four and twenty hours Robespierre himself and his colleagues would read.

Then Blakeney finally went out of the room.

CHAPTER XXXV

MARGUERITE

As he re-entered the large room, she was standing beside the
table, with one dainty hand resting against the back of the
chair, her whole graceful figure bent forward as if in an agony of
ardent expectation.

Never for an instant, in that supreme moment when his precious life was at stake, did she waver in courage or presence of
mind. From the moment that he jumped up and took the candlesticks in his hands, her sixth sense showed her as in a flash
what he meant to do and how he would wish her to act.

When the room was plunged in darkness she stood absolutely
still; when she heard the scuffle on the floor she never trembled,
for her passionate heart had already told her that he never
meant to deliver that infamous letter into his enemies' hands.
Then, when there was the general scramble, when the soldiers
rushed away, when the room became empty and Chauvelin
alone remained, she shrank quietly into the darkest corner of
the room, hardly breathing, only waiting. . . . Waiting for a sign
from him!

She could not see him, but she felt the beloved presence
there, somewhere close to her, and she knew that he would wish
her to wait. . . . She watched him silently . . . ready to help if he
called . . . equally ready to remain still and to wait.

Only when the helpless body of her deadly enemy was well
out of the way did she come from out the darkness, and now she
stood with the full light of the lamp illumining her ruddy golden

hair, the delicate blush on her cheek, the flame of love dancing in her glorious eyes.

Thus he saw her as he re-entered the room, and for one second he paused at the door, for the joy of seeing her there seemed greater than he could bear.

Forgotten was the agony of mind which he had endured, the humiliations and the dangers which still threatened: he only remembered that she loved him and that he worshipped her.

The next moment she lay clasped in his arms. All was still around them, save for the gentle patter-patter of the rain on the trees of the ramparts: and from very far away the echo of laughter and music from the distant revellers.

And then the cry of the sea-mew thrice repeated from just beneath the window.

Blakeney and Marguerite awoke from their brief dream: once more the passionate lover gave place to the man of action.

"'Tis Tony, an I mistake not," he said hurriedly, as with loving fingers still slightly trembling with suppressed passion, he readjusted the hood over her head.

"Lord Tony?" she murmured.

"Aye! with Hastings and one or two others. I told them to be ready for us to-night as soon as the place was quiet."

"You were so sure of success then, Percy?" she asked in wonderment.

"So sure," he replied simply.

Then he led her to the window, and lifted her onto the sill. It was not high from the ground and two pairs of willing arms were there ready to help her down.

Then he, too, followed, and quietly the little party turned to walk towards the gate. The ramparts themselves now looked strangely still and silent: the merrymakers were far away, only one or two passers-by hurried swiftly past here and there, carrying bundles, evidently bent on making use of that welcome permission to leave this dangerous soil.

The little party walked on in silence, Marguerite's small hand resting on her husband's arm. Anon they came upon a group of soldiers who were standing somewhat perfunctorily and irresolutely close by the open gate of the Fort.

"Tiens c'est l'Anglais!" said one.

"Morbleu! he is on his way back to England," commented another lazily.

The gates of Boulogne had been thrown open to everyone when the Angelus was rung and the cannon boomed. The general amnesty had been proclaimed, everyone had the right to come and go as they pleased, the sentinels had been ordered to challenge no one and to let everyone pass.

No one knew that the great and glorious plans for the complete annihilation of the Scarlet Pimpernel and his League had come to naught, that Collot was taking a mighty hoax to Paris, and that the man who had thought out and nearly carried through the most fiendishly cruel plan ever conceived for the destruction of an enemy, lay helpless, bound and gagged, within his own stronghold.

And so the little party, consisting of Sir Percy and Marguerite, Lord Anthony Dewhurst and my Lord Hastings, passed unchallenged through the gates of Boulogne.

Outside the precincts of the town they met my Lord Everingham and Sir Philip Glynde, who had met the Abbé Foucquet outside his little church and escorted him safely out of the city, whilst François and Félicité with their old mother had been under the charge of other members of the League.

"We were all in the procession, dressed up in all sorts of ragged finery, until the last moment," explained Lord Tony to Marguerite as the entire party now quickly made its way to the harbour. "We did not know what was going to happen. . . . All we knew was that we should be wanted about this time—the hour when the duel was to have been fought—and somewhere near here on the southern ramparts . . . and we always have strict orders to mix with the crowd if there happens to be one. When we saw Blakeney raise the candlesticks we guessed what was coming, and we each went to our respective posts. It was all quite simple."

The young man spoke gaily and lightly, but through the easy banter of his tone, there pierced the enthusiasm and pride of the solider in the glory and daring of his chief.

Between the city walls and the harbour there was much bustle and agitation. The English packet-boat would lift anchor at the turn of the tide, and as every one was free to get aboard without leave or passport, there were a very large number of passengers, bound for the land of freedom.

Two boats from the "Day-Dream" were waiting in readiness for Sir Percy and my lady and those whom they would bring with them.

Silently the party embarked, and as the boats pushed off and the sailors from Sir Percy's yacht bent to their oars, the old Abbé Foucquet began gently droning a Pater and Ave to the accompaniment of his beads.

He accepted joy, happiness and safety with the same gentle philosophy as he would have accepted death, but Marguerite's keen and loving ears caught at the end of each "Pater" a gently murmured request to le bon Dieu to bless and protect our English rescuer.

❀   ❀   ❀   ❀   ❀

Only once did Marguerite make allusion to that terrible time which had become the past.

They were wandering together down the chestnut alley in the beautiful garden at Richmond. It was evening, and the air was heavy with the rich odour of wet earth, of belated roses and dying mignonette. She had paused in the alley, and placed a trembling hand upon his arm, whilst raising her eyes filled with tears of tender passion up to his face.

"Percy!" she murmured, "have you forgiven?"

"What, m'dear?"

"That awful evening in Boulogne . . . what that fiend demanded . . . his awful 'either–or' . . . I brought it all upon you . . . it was all my fault."

"Nay, my dear, for that 'tis I should thank you . . ."

"Thank me?"

"Aye," he said, whilst in the fast-gathering dusk she could only just perceive the sudden hardening of his face, the look of wild passion in his eyes, "but for that evening in Boulogne, but for that alternative which that devil placed before me, I might never have known how much you meant to me."

Even the recollection of all the sorrow, the anxiety, the torturing humiliations of that night seemed completely to change him; the voice became trenchant, the hands were tightly clenched. But Marguerite drew nearer to him; her two hands were on his breast; she murmured gently:

"And now? . . ."

He folded her in his arms, with an agony of joy, and said earnestly:

"Now I know."

THE END